To all those who suffered or died during the Civil War, especially to my grandfathers and grandmothers and their dozens of brothers and sisters

Confederate Money

Paul Varnes

Pineapple Press, Inc.
Sarasota, Florida

Inquiries should be addressed to:

Pineapple Press, Inc.
P.O. Box 3889
Sarasota, Florida 34230

www.pineapplepress.com

Library of Congress Cataloging in Publication Data

Varnes, Paul.
    Confederate money / by Paul Varnes.
        p.   cm.
        ISBN 1-56164-271-1 (alk. paper)
    1. United States—History—Civil War, 1861–1865—Fiction. 2. Southern States—Fiction. 3. Young Men—Fiction. I. Title.
PS3622.A75 C66 2003
813'.6—dc21
                                                        2002014659

First Edition
10 9 8 7 6 5 4 3 2 1

Design by Shé Sicks
Printed in the United States of America

Author's Note

Many of the episodes in this novel of the Civil War are based on stories passed along in my family. Great-great-great-grandfather Isaac Varnes Sr. moved his family to Florida in 1823, twenty-two years before Florida became a state. (A military census estimated that less than 14,000 people lived in Florida in 1835.) Isaac Jr. married Louisa Ann Mettair, a Florida native of French descent whose parents, grandparents, great-grandparents, and great-great-grandparents date back to early-eighteenth-century Saint Augustine.

Isaac Sr., his son Isaac Jr., and his grandson Henry are designated Florida Pioneers. Isaac Jr. named his first son after Andrew Jackson, with whom his father had served in the First Seminole Indian War. Isaac Sr., at age fifty-five, fought also in the Second Seminole War, alongside all his sons and all of Louisa's brothers.

Of the three sons of Isaac Jr. and Louisa's who fought in the Civil War, two died in service to their country. Andrew Lewis Varnes died November 30, 1862, in Vicksburg, Mississippi, while he was a prisoner en route to a prisoner exchange. Isaac Varnes III died September 3, 1864, near Atlanta. Though seriously ill at the time, Isaac III was in the first wave of the Confederate charge at Jonesboro when he was killed. Isaac Jr. died in 1864 near Olustee, Florida. Louisa died in Lulu, Florida, in 1878.

Isaac Sr.'s fifth child, Henry, was born in Florida. The Florida Ninth Infantry Regiment, with which he served during the Civil War, was assigned to General Lee's army. Henry served with Lee at Petersburg, Virginia, until August of 1864, when he was sent home due to chronic diarrhea with chronic dyspepsia and a degeneration of his arteries. He married Susanna Melissa Hunter in 1867. Isaac Jr.'s brother, George, also had two sons killed in the war, and another who lost an eye. Mercifully, Isaac Sr. had died in 1857 and did not see the war decimate his grandchildren.

All coming from large families, my eight great-grandparents had more than forty brothers and sisters. Most of these great-great uncles served, and many died, in the war. A number of their fathers and uncles also served in the war. Additionally, a half dozen men who married my great-great aunts served in the war.

Being from different parts of the country, or having different points of view, some of my ancestors served on different sides. Thus, it seems appropriate that the novel's main characters serve both sides.

Florida contributed a larger percentage of its male population of military age to the Confederate military than did any other Confederate state. With forty percent dead and thirty-three percent wounded, Florida also took the heaviest losses of any state. Of the 15,000 from Florida who served the Confederacy, 6,000 died and 5,000 more were wounded.

Almost all of Florida's units had been sent out of state by 1862 to fight in Tennessee, Georgia, and Virginia. Although they took large losses in several battles, Florida units took unusually large losses at Gettysburg. Several thousand men from Florida, black and white, also volunteered in the Union army. Since they enlisted in various Northern states, they were counted there, so there is no good record of the exact number.

While the above numbers seem small, it should be remembered that Florida had a small population. Pensacola, then the largest city in Florida, had only 2,886 people in 1860. Jacksonville, then the second largest city in Florida, had only 2,018. Dade County, the location of the town of Miami, and Monroe County, the county covering the Keys, combined had only 670 people.

Acknowledgments

My great uncle Harvey Varnes deserves special mention. Since my grandfathers and dad died before I was old enough for them to pass on stories, it was Harney's stories of the war that started me on Henry's trail. My memory of those stories are now dimmed a little by time, and some of the episodes in this novel might bear little resemblance to anything he told me. Most, however, are based in fact. Other than those few liberties, the story accurately follows historical events.

A number of organizations and books were helpful in developing the historical and cultural setting for the novel. Organizations include the Cedar Key Historical Society, the Florida Park Service, the Jacksonville Historical Society, the Matheson Historical Society of Gainesville, and the National Park Service. Though many other books were helpful, these deserve special mention: Bert E. Brooks, *"Old Oaks" Civil War in North Florida* (2000); Larry J. Daniel, *Shiloh* (1997); T. C. DeLeon, *Four Years in Rebel Capitals* (1890), reprinted in 1983; Shelby Foote, *The Civil War* (1963). Also, Gary W. Gallagher, *The Confederate War* (1997); John Edwin Johns, *Florida during the Civil War* (1963); Edward E. Leslie, *The Devil Knows How to Ride* (1996); James McCague, *Moguls and Iron Men* (1964); Matt Spruill, *Guide to the Battle of Chickamauga* (1993).

I am indebted to my wife, Dr. Jill Tutton Varnes, for her encouragement, patience, and assistance. Thanks are due to Diane Davis who spent nights and weekends typing the original manuscript. People who read the work in progress and offered suggestions include Lorene Breeden, David Burton, Jennifer Wilson Carlstedt, Dr. Bertha Cato, Dr. Seigfred Fagerberg, Dr. Dovie Gamble, Sybil Haveard, Connie Lucius, Jean Mullen, Dr. Barbara Rienzo, and Julia Rae Varnes.

PART I

Revenge

October 4, 1861

What stirred Henry from a deep sleep was the sound of a large number of people trying to move quietly. His step-pa was already up and had thrown back the canvas that served as a front for the lean-to in which they were sleeping. The old man's quiet movement didn't awaken Henry. Familiar sounds or movements never did.

Outlined by the light from the still burning campfire, Henry's step-pa was standing in front of the lean-to with his rifle in hand. Since there wasn't much the old man couldn't handle, Henry wasn't fully awake until the guns started going off. There were several shots, five of which hit his step-pa. There was no reason to shoot the old man. He was standing without raising his rifle.

Leaping from the lean-to, Henry grabbed his step-pa's rifle and was in full flight to the cover of darkness when something slammed into his left shoulder, knocking him to the ground. There was a flash of light and he was unconscious for three days.

That they were in Cedar Key, Florida, at the time of the Yankee raid was a coincidence. Henry and his step-pa had only gone there to get salt and smoked fish. All the other supplies they needed were available in Archer. The truth be known, they could have gotten salt and smoked fish in Archer too. Their trip was mostly so they could ride the train and let Henry see Cedar Key, a booming town of a hundred people. Although they had seen the train several times, neither had ever ridden one.

Cedar Key, prior to the Yankee raid, was one of the chief suppliers of salt to the Confederate Army. One hundred fifty bushels of salt were produced there every week. Salt being the main way of preserving meat, that small town was a mighty important place. Transporting salt and the supplies brought in by Southern blockade-runners were the main reasons that rail tracks had been laid from Cedar Key to Archer.

Henry's family hadn't always lived in the North Florida palmetto scrub. They had been well off until his natural pa died of consumption in 1851. The farm they lived on before his pa died wasn't paid for and his ma couldn't keep it. They then lived pretty much with anyone who would have them until his ma married the old man in 1857. That was when they grubbed out their five-acre farm and built on it.

Although they didn't have much, Henry's ma saw to it that he was well educated. In 1850, the year Henry became old enough to go to school, not many Florida residents could read. Not many people got to go to school back then. The thirty-seat public school in Gainesville, the only public school in the county, was only open three months a year. Living fifteen miles from the school, Henry didn't get to attend. In spite of never attending a school, Henry was, and still is, the best reader that I've ever met. He can also use words and numbers in the smoothest way I ever saw. Henry's ma kept lots of books around and encouraged him. She sat him down to read, write, and do numbers for two hours every day of the year since he can remember.

October 7, 1861

As I said, Henry didn't wake up for three days. When he finally did, he was in a feather bed. No surprise if you know Henry, there was a woman fanning him and patting his head with a wet rag. The woman, Miss Daisy, was one of the old ones. I thought she was at least fifty the way he described her the first time. Actually, she's a handsome woman, and was only forty. As it turned out, Miss Daisy was the doctor's old maid sister. That was fortunate because otherwise some folks wouldn't have thought it proper for her to care for Henry alone at home, even though he was only seventeen at the time.

She spoke when he had barely cracked his eyes. "Now aren't you the feisty one lying there with your eyes wide open. I've been patting and fanning you for three days and nights, and had just about given up on you. You just lie right there. I'm going to get some chicken soup and I'll be back. A big boy like you could starve to death in three days."

Henry didn't say anything, but he managed to get a cup of chicken soup down before sleeping for another day.

The second time he woke up they were changing the bandage

on his head and shoulder. He had caught one minié ball in his left shoulder and another had permanently parted the hair across the top of his head. He was coherent enough to ask questions that time.

"Pa? What about Pa?"

"I'm sorry," Miss Daisy said. "Somebody recognized your step-pa so we sent for your mother. I've known your mother for some time, and you back when you were small. I expect she'll be here on the next train. We have your pa's stuff in the closet, except for his clothes. We buried him in those."

"But who shot us? What happened?" Henry asked.

"Oh, that's right, you don't know," Miss Daisy said, like she hadn't known he was unconscious all the time. "The Yankees raided here to destroy the salt works."

Henry's ma arrived the day after he became fully alert. The two of them stayed with Miss Daisy for the next several days while he got back on his feet.

There was considerable talk going on about the Yankee raid during those days. From what Henry told me he must have talked more than I heard him talk in the first three months I knew him. Henry's a thinker. He usually doesn't talk much until he's figured something out, except where books are concerned. He'll discuss a book at the drop of a hat, and all day.

What Henry learned from all that talk was that on October 4, a party of thirty Federal sailors came ashore in longboats to destroy the Cedar Key salt-producing operation. Though landing unopposed, they were soon routed by a group of twenty citizens with rifles. The Federal sailors retreated to their ship, which was part of the Federal blockade of Florida. That blockade was in place off the coast of all the Southern states for the entire war.

On October 6, over a hundred Federal sailors returned in four longboats. Finding the salt-producing operation under a white flag, they destroyed the tubs and all the equipment. By destroying the salt works, the Union deprived the Confederacy of a major part of its ability to preserve meat that fed its soldiers and citizens.

The sailors then began burning houses on the key. They also harassed those citizens who hadn't fled before they returned to their ships. The raiders piled brush against the doctor's house and lighted it but Miss Daisy put it out. She scolded them until they left without burning Doctor Isaac's house, saving Henry, who was unconscious inside.

Miss Daisy told Henry that the commanding lieutenant of the raid was from the Federal ship, *Tahomas*. From others, who had overheard various conversations, Henry soon learned the names of several sailors in the raiding party, including their commanding lieutenant's name. Someone also said the *Tahomas* was being moved to blockade duty at Pensacola, Florida, for the next few weeks.

By October 19, Henry had quit having dizzy spells from the minié ball crease on his head, and his left arm had just about quit hurting. He couldn't use the arm very well but the movement was improving. All of his talking and gathering information had been for a purpose. At dinner that night he told Miss Daisy, the doctor, and his ma what it was.

"I'm taking Pa's rifle and mule and going after those Yankees who killed him. I'll be leaving on the train for Archer tomorrow. From there, I'll go to Pensacola and see if the *Tahomas* is there. I can't be sure which ones shot pa and me but I expect to get revenge on someone. Ma, I think you ought to go visit Aunt May for a couple of months. I'm not sure how long this will take."

Everyone stared at him, speechless, until the doctor said, "Henry, you shouldn't join the army. You've shown that you're one of the best at reading and math that I've ever met. You need to keep developing your mind."

Henry's ma broke in. "We don't have anything to do with that war. You can't just run off and get mixed up in it. You just can't go."

Henry said, "Ma, I'm going tomorrow. I've got enough money to get a ticket to Archer. I'm sorry to have to leave you, but I know you can take care of yourself. You've done it for more years than I've been around. There's no point in talking about me not going."

At that point in the conversation Miss Daisy got her voice back and said, "You're still hurt. Besides, you ought to stay here with us. Doctor Isaac and I have talked. You could study medicine with him."

Doctor Isaac added, "The medical colleges in the South have all been closed because of the war, but you can still study with me to become a physician. That's how it was done in the past. I mostly learned that way."

Henry said, "I'm not going to join the army. I'm going to take revenge for Pa and some for me, an eye for an eye. You can't possibly know how proud I am of the offer to study to be a doctor. If the offer's still open after this is taken care of, I'll jump right on it. I love you all, but I have to do this. It would be good if you could make suggestions that would help me on the way."

Telling those women he loved them, Henry had just gained their support. But then he always did have a knack for getting along with women. They couldn't do enough after that and set in to telling him all the things he needed to carry with him, mostly food.

Doctor Isaac went to his room and came out with an almost new rifle, a powder horn, a single shot dueling pistol, and a possibles bag containing all the supplies for the rifle and pistol. The rifle was a percussion cap, .45 caliber Thompson Hawken. The pistol was a .44 caliber, which allowed the same size ball to be used in both. A larger caliber ball is used in a pistol to force it in the grooves and increase accuracy.

Handing them to Henry, he said, "I'd like you to take these."

They spent most of the rest of the evening talking about Henry's departure. The women tried a couple of times to talk him out of going but he politely put them off. While they planned, Doctor Isaac left for a short time and returned with a map of

Florida. He and Henry spent most of an hour tracing it. With all the talk that was going on, Henry didn't get to sleep until midnight.

Henry's ma got him up at daylight, even though the train wouldn't leave until 3:00 P.M. After talking all morning, they followed Henry to the train.

At the station Doctor Isaac produced a ten-dollar gold piece. Holding it out to Henry, he said, "Here, you'll need some things along the way."

"No, sir," Henry said. "What with your rifle and my mule, I'll make out. I appreciate the offer though."

If he could have found a job, it would have taken Henry four months to save ten dollars in gold. Workers at the salt works, before it was wrecked, made a dollar a day in Confederate paper money. At the time, a Confederate dollar was worth ninety cents in gold or silver. Those were the highest paying jobs around. Farm laborers earned only twenty-five cents a day. Though the doctor insisted, Henry wouldn't take the money.

When the time came to pay for the train, Henry reached in his pocket for the fare. He only had two twenty-five cent pieces, but his hand came out of his pocket with them and a ten-dollar gold piece. There wasn't but one way it could have gotten in his pocket—Miss Daisy had just been hugging him. Miss Daisy was looking so proud of herself that Henry put the ten dollars back in his pocket, took her in his arms, and kissed her. His ma told us later that it was the talk of Cedar Key for the next few days.

Anyway, Henry got on the train with his baggage, which consisted of one large bag of fried chicken and biscuits, and his sleeping roll. Of course he had the rifle, pistol, and possibles bag. He also had a parting gift from Doctor Isaac, a book of readings for the medical profession.

Six stops, four hours, and thirty-two miles later, Henry arrived in Archer. From there he set out on foot for home, which was several miles north of Archer. One mile north of Archer, while skirting a plantation to avoid disturbing the dogs, he got the fright of his life when a voice spoke from the darkness.

"That you Henry?"

Recognizing the voice instantly, his goose bumps started settling back in his body and Henry said, "Jesus, Jacob, you almost scared me to death. I didn't see you standing there in the dark."

"That's one of the few advantages of being black," Jacob said.

Henry and Jacob, a young slave living on the plantation, had become fast friends after Henry's family settled their little place nearby. They frequently hunted and fished together, especially at night or in the winter when their duties were less demanding.

They sat for the better part of an hour while Henry told Jacob what had happened and what he was going to do. Jacob told Henry he would go with him except that he would only get caught and returned, and certainly punished. Wishing each other well, they both went their separate ways. Henry soon arrived home.

The next morning Henry propped open the chicken coop, gathered the eggs, and placed the eggs in a bag to carry with him. After placing a couple of armloads of wood by the fireplace, he put a note on the door telling that the farm wasn't abandoned, but that travelers could take shelter and food if need be. When he left, his mule's burden included weapons, three books, food, cooking utensils, two live hens, twenty eggs, a bed roll and canvas, a water jug, a change of clothes, and forty pounds of shelled corn for the mule and chickens. Smokey, the mule, being heavily laden, Henry planned to walk most of the 350 miles to Pensacola.

Getting a late start the day he left, Henry was mid-afternoon the second day getting to the Suwannee River. Having crossed the Santa Fe River between the points where the Ichetucknee River joins it and it joins the Suwannee, he was southwest of a town called Branford. Though still wide and deep, north of the junction of the Santa Fe and the Suwannee rivers, the Suwannee runs shallower and narrower when it's in its banks, as it was then.

Henry was standing and planning the river crossing when someone hidden behind an oak tree said, "Boy, you stand real still and you'll live a few more minutes."

The only thing that moved was Henry's head and eyeballs. When they moved he was staring into the small end of a twelve-gauge shotgun. The shotgun's owner was a heavyset man with long hair and a black beard.

Two other armed men approached and took Henry's weapons and mule. One was a thin, hawk-faced man with broken and missing teeth. The other was a short, nervous redhead who talked constantly.

"Man, look at all the stuff he's got. What we'uns gonna do with him? I'll bet they's twenty eggs in this here sack. He's got food fur uh army. He's a bigun, ain't he? Can I shoot 'im, Bud? Can I?" Red said.

"Hush," Bud replied. He then said to Henry, "Get your clothes off, boy. Quick now."

After sitting down and taking off his shoes, Henry stood up and took off his shirt. He wasn't moving slow or fast, just kind of medium, giving his mind time to work. Though it was obvious they meant to kill him, or worse, they apparently didn't want to mess up his clothes.

Bud was watching Henry intensely, as was the hawk-faced man. Both were holding their guns on him. Bud had a shotgun, of course, and Hawkface had a rifle. Red was inspecting the mule pack and not pointing his gun at Henry. At the same time he was talking constantly.

Taking the best chance he had, Henry straightened up from pulling his pants legs over his feet and swung them up into the barrel of Bud's shotgun. In the same motion he stepped and dove for the river, which was three feet away after his step. He figured that, while he was moving, Hawkface would have a harder time shooting him with a rifle than Bud would with the shotgun. Bud jerked, causing his gun to go off, which in turn caused the mule to jump. Because of the mule jumping, neither Hawkface nor Red got off a shot.

Though shallower, the Suwannee River is still dark and deep at that point, so once he hit the water Henry had a chance. Swimming under water, he turned downriver and angled for the other bank. The river is over a hundred yards across there, even when it's in its banks. Henry came up a forth of the way across the river. The river had washed him downstream so he was fifty yards away from Bud's group. They shot at him almost every time he came up for a breath. Having only single shot, muzzle-loading weapons, they couldn't get off shots every time. When he surfaced for the fifth time, he was at the other bank of the river. Though by then they'd moved downstream, Bud's group was well over a hundred yards from Henry.

At least that's the way Henry told it to me.

October 22, 1861

The first time I saw Henry he was scrambling up the west bank of the Suwannee River looking like a drowned rat. Running for cover, he jumped behind the same big live oak that I had been sitting against while watching for a deer or hog. We sat for most of a minute looking at each other without speaking. Him being buck naked, I tried to keep looking him in the eyes. If it hadn't been a serious situation, I would have broken out laughing. At the time I didn't realize what an impact a man only one year my senior would have on my life. It was to be even more than that of my pa, who was killed in the war.

Henry said, "They were trying to kill me." Just like I didn't know.

We sat behind that live oak for almost fifteen minutes with them ranting and raving on the other side of the river the whole time. They didn't know I was there and I saw no reason to tell them. Henry told me a little of his story then. After deciding they weren't going to cross the river, he told me more as we hauled it for the house. Given the scars on his shoulder and head, and the situation in which we met, it wasn't hard to believe him.

I gave him my coat to tie around his waist by the sleeves to make a skirt. That's one reason I remember it was pretty cold on October 22, 1861. Though he must have been near freezing, he didn't say a word about it. That's the way Henry always was under extreme conditions.

Leaving Henry in the woods, I went in the house to get him a pair of pants. I told Ma a little of the story before I brought him in. She listened to the story without expression, other than her eyes taking on a twinkle.

Ma took to Henry right off. She started mothering him like an old hen with only one chick. Don't you know the first thing she did was to take the cover from over the food on the table and make him eat? Although he had eaten two hours before, he didn't say a word about it.

Henry had a natural way of getting along with women. I don't know if it was his size, good looks, big shoulders, smooth way with words, or the way he respected them, but the girls, old and young, were sure cow-eyed about him. My oldest sister Lilly was no exception. Ma wasn't either. Ma commented later that if she had been four or five years younger she would have staked a claim. Henry didn't chase after the girls though. Being the last of the kids at home, and being raised alone, I guess he was a little shy at first. Lilly was thunderstruck the minute Henry walked in the door. Wherever she went, and whatever she was doing, she kept looking at him. Though not yet fifteen, she looked seventeen. All the boys for twenty miles around were panting over her like a pack of hot hounds after a fox chase. Lilly was the spitting image of Ma, but was eighteen years younger.

We didn't have a big family. In addition to Lilly, I also had a younger brother and sister, and one who died as a baby. Pa went off to the war when it first started. We already had a letter saying he had been killed.

As he finished a plate of food, Ma gave Henry a piece of pie.

After taking one bite, he said, "That's the best pie I ever stuck a fork in."

Lilly had made those pies and I thought she was going to melt down like butter on a hot biscuit. The strange thing was that Ma took it as a bigger compliment. But then she was the one who taught Lilly to make pies. I'm telling you Henry could do no wrong around women. Not that I'm complaining, over the years I got close to more women by just standing around him than most men do from trying.

Ma insisted on Henry having a second piece of pie, which was a little strange. She always told us kids that one piece of pie or cake was enough. I took advantage of the situation by getting a piece for myself. When no one even noticed me get the pie, I decided I was going to stick to Henry, figuring that as long as there were womenfolk around neither of us would go hungry.

After eating, Henry sat there and told us lots of the story.

Finishing the story, he turned to Ma and said, "I've got to be going and get my mule and things back. It would be helpful if you would let me borrow a butcher knife, or an ax, to use as a weapon. I promise to bring it back."

I could see Ma was going to tell him he couldn't go, but she didn't. Lilly looked horrified when Henry said he was going, but she didn't speak. She hadn't said much since he set foot in the house. She had never before been that quiet in her life, except in church.

Suddenly the expression on Ma's face changed and she said, "You'll take Ben's shotgun." That's me of course, Ben. "Ben, you'll take the rifle and go with him."

Once she made the decision she scurried around and got everything ready. I couldn't believe it then and I can't believe it now. There she was sending her own boy off with a stranger to possibly shoot someone.

When we started out the door Henry put the sauce on the goose's tail. Without saying a word he picked up Ma's hand, kissed the back of it, and walked off. As we vanished into the woods she was still standing in the doorway with her hand out in front of her just like he left it.

What everyone should have been doing was laughing at that overgrown barefoot boy who was wearing my pants that were five inches too short, and my shirt that was so tight he couldn't get even one button buttoned. His shoulders and arms were exceptionally big from using an axe and grubbing hoe. Standing six feet tall and weighing 180 pounds, at almost eighteen years old, Henry was almost as big as his natural pa had been.

After getting out of sight of Ma, we switched weapons. I preferred the shotgun and Henry preferred a rifle. Also, my shotgun hadn't been modified to use percussion caps. It still had to be primed with powder before the flint was struck. Henry had never used one like that. The rifle was also an old one but it had been modified to use percussion caps. Pa had taken the newer rifle to war with him.

Being upstream from Bud's gang, we headed straight for the river. I had a dugout beached there and it would be easier crossing in it. Also, they wouldn't see us cross that far upriver and around a bend.

Once across the river we eased up to where we had last seen Bud's gang, but they were gone. Their tracks led toward Fort White, fifteen miles to the east. Dark was settling in and we were moving pretty fast on their trail when it came to me that they were going to Sam's place. Sam's is a two-room store and bar that Sam also lives in. They were headed straight for it.

I told Henry about Sam's as we walked. There wasn't much

to tell. It was three more miles east of us. A big front room had store-type goods in one end and a bar with four stools across the other. The bar end is closest to the door. The other room serves as a house for Sam. In order to keep the place as busy as possible, Sam is known to keep a woman around when he can.

Henry asked, "Does Sam keep any dogs around the place?"

I said, "There has never been one when I was there. But it's been over a year since I last went there with Pa."

He put me in front to lead and didn't say another word.

When we got to Sam's, Smokey and three horses were tied up at the hitching rail.

Henry said, "You stay here."

Squatting down in the dark, I waited.

He was back in five minutes, and said, "All three of them are here. There's also a big ugly man behind the bar. Red's in the back room with a woman."

"The man behind the bar is Sam," I said.

"You wait here and don't start anything until I say," Henry said.

"Why don't we just get the mule and go?" I asked. I was thinking, Me start something, not likely.

Henry said, "They have my ten dollars and have eaten my chickens. They also have my weapons inside."

Since I could see there would be no reasoning with him, I hunkered down in the dark to wait. I was still wondering why Ma had volunteered me for this.

Back in ten minutes, Henry said, "They're all in the front room now except the woman. We're going in the front door. I'll go in first and take Bud. He's at the far end of the bar. You step in behind me and cover Hawkface and Red, but keep your gun on Red's belly. He's the crazy one."

He paused for a moment, put his hand on my shoulder, and asked, "Can you do this? Can you shoot Red if he moves?"

Feeling his hand on my shoulder, I had a warm feeling and

my confidence was building. It was suddenly like he was a big brother.

I said, "Yes. Ma told me to. I can do what's needed."

Henry bit the percussion cap tight around the nipple of his rifle before he stepped through the door. I thought the cap might explode in his mouth but it didn't. He then walked straight through the door to Bud, who turned as Henry came in. Henry's left hand was on the rifle barrel and his right hand was on the rifle stock. He didn't even have a finger on the trigger.

While seeing all this, I had my eyes focused on Hawkface and Red. My twelve-gauge, on full cock, was pointed at Red's belly as I heard myself say, "If you want to live, don't move." My voice was much stronger and more powerful than any words I had ever heard out of me.

Out of the corner of my eye I saw Bud reach for a pistol that was lying on the bar and Henry bring the butt of his rifle up under Bud's jaw. Everything was a blur to me as Bud fell to the floor like a sack of potatoes. Then Red started talking real fast and reached for a rifle.

As I had been instructed, I pulled the trigger but the gun didn't go off. One problem with old guns that have to be primed with powder is that sometimes the priming powder sputters for a few seconds before the gun goes off. Sometimes it doesn't go off at all. There I was holding a sputtering gun on Red and him getting his rifle. I was praying my shotgun would fire.

At a glance Henry saw what was happening. He pulled down his rifle from having hit Bud in the jaw, and shot Red in the side of the head. Somehow in those moments I remembered Henry biting down on the percussion cap before we came inside. If he hadn't, the cap would have come off the nipple when he hit Bud, and the rifle wouldn't have fired when he shot Red. Henry had planned the whole thing.

I was still holding a twelve-gauge with a sputtering primer. Since Hawkface was also moving into action, I pulled the shotgun around toward him. As luck would have it, the shotgun went off when I lined it up on Hawkface. That ended the altercation except for Sam, who had reached under the bar.

Having picked up the pistol Bud had been reaching for, Henry leveled it on Sam, but spoke to me, "We can do this legal, or we can kill them all and walk out. What do you say, Ben?"

I heard myself say, still in that authoritative voice, "It don't matter to me. Let's let Sam decide."

Sam said, "Boys, I'll do whatever it takes. Let's do it the clean way. There's a shotgun under the bar. I'll feel better if one of you comes around and gets it."

As I went around the bar to get the shotgun, the woman came out of the back room screaming. I thought she was going to have a stroke.

His voice cold enough to freeze hot water, Henry said, "Shut up and sit on that stool,"

She sat, but kept on sniveling.

Henry said to Sam, "Step outside and look at those horses."

When they returned, Sam was saying, "The three of them rode up on those horses. They were leading the mule. The Bar-S brand belongs to a little planter north of here. I don't have any idea about the Flying W. It's not from around here. The slick horse, the unbranded one, could be from anywhere. I've seen those men before but don't know much about them."

After going through Bud's and his friends' pockets, Henry said, "I only find six dollars and forty cents. They had a ten dollar gold piece that belonged to me."

"It's in the drawer. Take it and go," Sam said.

Henry said, "No. You two worked for your pay. These three owe me three dollars and sixty cents, and for the chickens and eggs. Until someone claims them, and proves ownership, I'm taking these men's outfits and weapons as payment. I'm also going to write out the story just as it happened and all four of us are going to sign it."

Sam got pen, ink, and paper and Henry started writing.

Starting with them taking his things at the river, Henry wrote the story three times. The writing took a full hour.

During the writing the woman quit sniveling and began to come on to us. She wanted fifty cents to go in the back room. Henry wasn't having any of it. To tell the truth she began to look good to me, and I started thinking about it, but I didn't have fifty cents.

Henry took some things from the pack on the mule and showed them to Sam. Sam believed the story after seeing the books with Henry's name in them and the clothes, which fit him.

We left one paper with Sam, along with instructions that he was to fetch the sheriff before cleaning up the place and was to give the sheriff the paper. Henry also explained to Sam that he better do it right or, when we came back through the area, we would stuff his body in a gator hole.

Ma was awake and reading the Bible when we came riding in near midnight. Lilly was also awake. Having eyes only for Henry, I don't think Lilly was aware of me walking in the door.

I told the story, but didn't tell about the woman. Though it was in the paper Henry had written, and Ma would know, Lilly didn't need to know at the time. Ma then said a prayer. She didn't beat it to death. She just said a few words of thanks for us being safe. We all held hands while Ma said the words. Lilly held on to Henry's hands a few seconds longer than to mine. Ma pretended not to notice. I didn't care what either of them did, Henry was my man and I was already planning on going to Pensacola.

We heard later that Bud died from infection in his jaw a few days after the set-to. His jaw was so broken up, and he was so addled, that he never said another word after Henry hit him with the rifle butt. It was also said that the sheriff was satisfied with what Sam and the woman told him. He never even came to talk to us.

A second copy of Henry's paper was left with Ma, along with the Bar-S mare and the extra guns we didn't need. No one ever claimed the guns or the horses. Ma inquired and found out that Bud had actually traded legal for the Bar-S mare. Lilly's still riding that mare. No record was ever found of the other horses.

Ma talked Henry into staying and resting for several days before we left for Pensacola. I don't know what he was resting from. He looked rested enough to me by late the next morning when we both finally got up.

Lilly persuaded Henry to teach her something about riding every day while we were still at the house. Though they were never gone for more than a couple of hours on any day, Lilly quickly became a very confident rider. Henry and I also talked about the stuff in Henry's medical book every day. He was proud of that book.

For those few days I mostly sat in front of the house and cleaned our weapons and saddles, and waited for the right time to announce that I was going to Pensacola. I also started reading that medical book of Henry's. Being a slower reader than Henry, I had to read twice as long as him and had to ask him how to say some words. It turned out that some of the words were just the names of joints, parts, or muscles of animals or people. They're all about the same. Having cut up lots of hogs and deer, I knew those parts. Anatomy was simple once you knew how to say the words. Ma encouraged me to sit and read.

One thing of note happened that made all of them feel I would be safe going off with Henry. Ma had a hen that hatched off some chicks. A big red hawk soon started hanging around and stealing one of those chicks every day or two. As most women do, Ma keeps a snuff can full of arsenic for just such an occasion. When one of the chicks died, she stuffed some arsenic up its rectum and laid it on a horse pen post. Within an hour the hawk swooped in and snatched that chick off the post. Having reloaded his .45 caliber Hawken, which I had just cleaned, Henry was standing at the corner of the house and saw the hawk. Not knowing Ma had poisoned the chick to kill the hawk, he threw up and shot the hawk going away at sixty yards. He killed it dead as a stump. Even though I had to clean the rifle again, I was smiling about that shot.

October 28, 1861

After getting out of bed and eating early, we hung around for what seemed like hours before leaving that morning for Pensacola. Ma and the kids went out and looked for eggs in the various places that hens would hide their nests while Lilly and Henry washed the dishes. I think Ma was just leaving Lilly and Henry alone. I saddled the horses and got the mule loaded. When we were leaving Lilly walked over to the left side of Henry's horse and said something to him that I couldn't quite make out. Reaching down with his left arm, Henry lifted her against him and kissed her. He was as strong as a mule.

I expected at any minute that Ma was going to tell me I couldn't go but she never did. Touching our heels to our horses, we loped off until screened by the woods. We then slowed to a steady walk toward Pensacola. As we rode, I began to understand why they hadn't made a fuss about me going. I was the insurance that Henry would come back. Lilly had set her bonnet for him.

Two days before reaching Tallahassee we were joined by six women and nine children who were also on their way to Tallahassee. Their men off to war, and concerned about Federal forces raiding the coast, the women were seeking a safe inland haven to sit out the war. They thought the war would be over in a few weeks and they could go back home. Thinking their plight temporary, the women were lighthearted and fun to be around. Since they were not carrying much in the way of food, we wound up feeding them for a couple of days. Those were the first refugees we encountered. I frequently thought of them later when seeing other refugees who were not so lighthearted.

Another thing of note happened as we skirted Tallahassee to avoid encountering the Confederate troops garrisoned there. The night after parting company with the group of women, we ran into a drummer and camped overnight with him. The drummer had an old medical bag in his wagon.

Henry didn't say anything about the bag that night but the next morning he said to the drummer, "I've got a friend in Cedar Key that's a physician. Do you mind if I look at the bag?"

Of course the drummer didn't mind and Henry looked in it. There were all kinds of instruments in the bag. There was also a half-pint bottle of laudanum and a small bottle of chloroform concealed under a false bottom.

"How long have you had this bag?" Henry asked.

"Several weeks," the drummer said.

"How much did it set you back?"

"Three dollars."

"Confederate paper I hope. It's not worth more than two dollars in silver or Florida paper money."

The drummer laughed and said, "It was Confederate paper."

Henry said, "I've only got two dollars and forty cents in silver coin, but I can't leave us broke. I'll give you two silver dollars for the bag and contents."

There aren't many buyers for old medical bags so the drummer said, "Make it the two dollars and forty in silver and it's a deal."

Henry said, "I can't do it. That would leave us flat broke. I'll make it two dollars and twenty-five cents, and that's it."

That's when we really got into the physician business. I guess

Henry momentarily forgot about the other four dollars in his pocket.

A Confederate paper dollar was worth ninety cents in silver or Florida paper money at the time. As is well known now, Confederate money was printed with nothing to back it up but the good will of the Confederate government. It was to be redeemed two years after the Confederate states signed a treaty of peace with the United States of America. The Federal government declared a dollar per barrel tax on beer to help finance the war for the North. The Confederate government borrowed from the Southern states and printed money to finance their side. Though we couldn't have known it at the time, there was never a real plan for how to pay the states back, or how to finance the redeeming of the Confederate paper money.

When Florida seceded from the Union, the Florida government confiscated all Federal land in Florida. The state then printed Florida paper money against the value of the public lands. Land, at that time, was valued at ten cents to one dollar and twenty-five cents an acre, depending on where it was located. Because it had the value of land to back it up, Florida paper money was just as valuable as silver. It held its value through much of the war. Confederate paper money, with nothing to back it up, didn't. Actually, all eleven Southern states printed their own money. They planned to make it good in various ways.

Three days after purchasing the medical bag we came to an isolated farmhouse north of Blountstown. It was just a house in the woods. There wasn't much of a farm there. Having talked frequently about home cooking, we decided to ride in and beg, or buy, some home-cooked food. Two barking dogs met us eighty yards from the house. The bluetick coonhounds looked harmless enough. As we approached the house with the blueticks yapping around us, a woman in her late twenties stepped out the front door with a shotgun across her arm. Even at forty yards I could see the hammer was back. A small boy of ten or twelve stepped out behind her with a squirrel rifle across his arm. Pulling his horse up, Henry raised his right hand. I followed suit. Henry spoke, but couldn't be heard over the dogs so the boy came forward and quieted them.

"We're a physician and his assistant on our way to Pensacola. We're looking for a warm meal and friendly greeting along the way," Henry said.

"Coon, tie those dogs. Are you a real physician?" the woman asked.

Without saying anything, Henry lifted his bag. The initials on it were H.W. That was when he temporarily took the name Henry Watson. I had learned to keep my mouth shut, as hard as it might be to believe, and was whoever he introduced me as. He said it might prevent complications down the road.

The woman, Ella Mae, got Henry's mare's bridle and tied her up in front of the house.

"I've got a sick child, please help me with her," she was saying, tears in her eyes. "She's not sick right now, but she gets down with tonsillitis every couple of weeks. It's getting more frequent and is worse every time. She'll probably choke to death next time. I don't know a doctor and don't have any money. Please help us."

Henry replied, "A little hope is better than no hope at all."

He was talking to me but she didn't know it.

Taking his medical bag, Henry walked in just like a doctor on call. The girl, Mary, looked well enough at the moment.

Summoning me to his side, Henry said, "Benjamin, look down her throat."

He knew my name was just plain Ben, but I looked. There wasn't any infection, and her forehead was cool.

"We're going to try to help you out. You have to help us out by being brave. Why, you have the same beautiful blue eyes as your mother," Henry said to the girl.

He was already looking in her eyes and ears, and passing out the smooth talk. I could almost smell the chicken frying.

Strangely enough, Henry really looked like a doctor.

"Stand outside and face the sunlight so we can see what we're doing," Henry told the girl.

I turned to him and whispered, "Are you crazy? We can't take her tonsils out."

"Sure we can. It tells about it in the book. I've had mine out. I was awake and watched most of it. Also, they need to come out now while they aren't infected. They can't be taken out while they're swollen." he said.

After starting a small fire, Henry put a small, slender, flat instrument in it until the instrument was red hot on one end. Still talking to Mary all the time, he gave her a couple of drops of laudanum and talked her in to letting him blindfold her, all laid out on her back. He then washed his hands and scissors. Putting Ella Mae and Coon by Mary's sides to hold her hands and comfort her and me at her head to keep it steady, Henry gave her a whiff of chloroform. He then put a roll of leather in one side of her mouth to keep it open. While holding her tongue out, he started fishing down her throat with a loop on the end of some thread. When he had her tonsils snared, he reached down her throat with his scissors, whacked them off and pulled them out with the thread. Of course there was some blood until he cauterized the wound.

"She can't drink anything hot for three days. Not even soup. Milk, strained fruit juice, cold sugar water, or honey dissolved in cold water will be okay," Henry said.

"We don't have any of that," Ella Mae said. "We only have some bullas jelly and some cane syrup."

"That'll be fine dissolved in water," he said. "Do you have a neighbor with a cow?"

"Yes," she said. "Bout three miles from here."

Turning to Coon, Henry said, "Here's five cents. Take my mare and get some fresh milk. Don't run the horse."

"I'll go with him," I said, thinking to keep him from running the horse.

Handing me a dollar, Henry said, "If there's a place to get them, bring some supplies. I don't think there's much to eat here."

While we were gone I found out their ages. Though he looked to be ten, Coon was fourteen. Mary, who looked older than Coon, wouldn't be twelve until late December. Their mother was barely twenty-eight.

Arriving back at the house we found Mary asleep. She had been sleeping off and on for the whole time the two of us were gone.

Henry said, "Ben, I think we should stay here for a few days to make sure that Mary gets along okay."

Smitten by Mary and her mother, I replied, "That's fine with me."

Henry and I stayed five days and nights. Mary was up and around and eating scrambled eggs, grits, and chicken soup before we left. The rest of us were eating a lot of stuffed raccoon and fall greens. Coon got his name from his constant coon hunting. Fortunately, I had bought some beans, rice, flour, grits, and salt pork with the dollar. It was a pleasurable and restful five days.

Our luck remained strong. Ella Mae and her husband, who was off at the war, were from a little settlement north of Pensacola. As a result of having lived there, she knew the lay of the land and drew it out for us. Things couldn't have happened better.

November 15, 1861

*L*eaving some of our things at Ella Mae's lightened Smokey's load enough that Coon, who left with us, could ride him. After we told Coon the entire story about what happened to Henry and what we were going to do, Coon had announced that he was going. He thought it would be a great adventure. I was surprised when his ma said he could go. After giving it some thought, I decided that Coon was allowed to go for the same reason that I was allowed to go. He was the reason for us to go back by his house.

As we rode, I spent lots of time thinking about Ella Mae and Mary. I didn't say anything about my thoughts to Coon or Henry. It was real easy not saying anything to Coon. He never did talk very much.

Henry and I continued reading the medical book and discussed it daily. Those discussions kept me reminded of Mary's tonsils. Having read about taking tonsils out, and having seen Henry take out a set, I figured I could do the same if the situation required it. Occasionally, I daydreamed about removing my first set of tonsils from a child of a young woman with the same qualities as Ella Mae. I was to find the medical profession is usually not so glamorous.

We hadn't been riding long when Coon said, "My pa's fighting for the Yankees. We got a letter from him that says there's lots of Southern men doing the same."

This startling piece of information left Henry and me silent until Henry said, "We're going to kill some Yankees. How do you feel about that?"

"Pa's way up north and I don't know any Yankees down here. I don't care," Coon said.

After reflecting on that, Henry said, "I'm going to get revenge for Pa. I don't care either. I'd take revenge on the Confederates if they were the ones."

· Coon said, "Me too."

I didn't say anything, but Coon's pa being in the Federal army sure jolted me. It started me to thinking about Ella Mae and how I felt about her husband fighting for the North. I also asked myself if her husband being in the Yankee army made me feel any different about her. I immediately said no. Even then, the question kept coming back to haunt me as we rode.

When asked if he had a plan for getting revenge, Henry said he had a few, but would first have to get the lay of the land before finalizing one. He was concerned because we didn't know who actually had killed his pa and he wasn't sure if Ella Mae's map was accurate. Ella Mae had last been in the Pensacola area a couple of years before the war began and her information might not still be good. Also, Coon was eleven years old when he last saw Pensacola and his memory might not be exact. Henry also said that he didn't know which men had killed his pa but that we would get revenge on someone wearing Yankee uniforms.

The area we passed through from Blountstown to Milton was the most desolate any of us had ever seen. Though we'd seen no one for days, we still avoided Milton and Pensacola by riding north of those towns before turning south toward the coast. It was a big detour. Pensacola, then the largest city in Florida and the largest we had ever seen, had a population of 2,886 people, even without the Confederate States of America forces there.

Henry bought a bushel of dried in the hull peanuts at a farm near Pensacola but wouldn't let us eat any. Though I kept thinking those peanuts had something to do with his plan, for the life of me I couldn't think of what.

Upon our arrival, we began to familiarize ourselves with the area. As we were observing the coast road and Fort Pickens late on the morning of November 22, a terrible artillery battle started. Fort Pickens, then held by Union forces, is on the west end of Santa Rosa Island. The batteries in Fort Pickens, two gunboats, and several other batteries on the island were firing on CSA positions in Fort McRee, which is on the mainland. The Federal guns couldn't reach Pensacola, ten miles away, but could hit Fort McRee and other CSA positions. Fort McRee was taking a beating and by nightfall its guns became silent. We learned a few days later that, for all that shooting, there were only two killed and six wounded on the Confederate side.

A barrier island, Santa Rosa Island is near sixty miles long but only a couple of miles wide. Skirting the Florida coast from Shalimar, Florida, almost to Alabama, it partially blocks off Pensacola Bay. The CSA sank some old ships and barges in the channels so the Union couldn't get their gunboats into Pensacola Bay or into the channel between the mainland and Santa Rosa Island. The two sides just sat there shooting cannons back and forth at each other, and raided a little.

Along with a couple of gunboats, the Federal position on the west end of the island allowed their forces to blockade Pensacola Bay and prevented the CSA from importing arms and supplies through that port. The Union did the same thing at Cedar Key, Tampa, and all the rest of the ports along the east and west coasts of Florida and the coasts of all other Southern states. The Federal strategy was to blockade the ports, denying the CSA access to foreign trade.

It was apparent that the three of us couldn't cross an expanse of water and attack two thousand well-armed men in a fort. We didn't stand much chance against a gunboat either. I didn't see any way for us to help Henry get revenge.

During the first day there, Henry produced pen and paper and set about writing Coon a letter from his pa in the Seventh Connecticut. Henry changed Coon's name to Ray Watson. If confronted by Federal troops, Coon, posing as Ray Watson, would produce that letter to show his family's loyalty to the North. Henry also wrote Coon a letter from Ray's cousin, Surgeon Henry Watson, which would introduce him to CSA troops. The two letters were to be carried in different pockets and the correct one produced depending on what troops Ray encountered.

Ray was to steal a boat the next morning at dawn and row over to the island. There he would sell the bushel of peanuts at two cents per double handful to the Federal soldiers. If CSA forces stopped him before he shoved off, he was to offer to spy and report back and then actually do so. Because he was supplied with proper papers of introduction, it should work. His chief job on the island was to offer to bring whiskey and some women for some of the Federal soldiers if they had enough money. The price would be one dollar a quart for the whiskey and three dollars from each of six men, three men for each woman. He was to be sure to tell the soldiers that these women were not whores. They were good Northern sympathizers who desperately needed the money to escape to the North. Additionally, Henry wanted to know if the Federal ship *Tahomas* was in the area on blockade duty, or was on the way there. Ray could ask about that by saying his mother's brother, his uncle, was on board. That way there wouldn't have to be someone on board with the last name "Watson." If intercepted by Confederate forces, Ray was also to learn the name of the CSA commanding officer in the area.

With two thousand men on the island, and no women, he should have no trouble finding ready buyers for women and whiskey. Cut off from the mainland, the island fort was supplied only by ships controlled or operated by the Federal Navy. The supply of whiskey and women to its troops would not be a priority of the Federal military. While there was little or no whiskey available on the Union-held part of the island, whiskey could be purchased in Pensacola for twenty-five cents a gallon. There should also be a ready supply of money in the fort. Having been isolated for months while receiving thirteen dollars a month in pay, there was no place for the Yankee soldiers to spend their money.

After being drilled the rest of the day on his new identity and duties, Ray got them down pretty good. Henry forbade me to call

Ray "Coon" so he could get used to the name.

The next day at daylight Ray stole a rowboat and was a hundred yards out toward the island before some CSA troops shouted at him. He waved, but didn't otherwise respond. Everyone could see he was a child so no one shot at him. Upon his arrival at the island we could see Union soldiers gather around him and escort him toward the fort.

At 10:00 A.M. the artillery battle started again. Ignoring the continuing shelling, Ray pushed off at noon for the mainland. A couple of CSA soldiers met him as he beached the boat and escorted him to a command post. The command post was out of sight of the island and not under bombardment. After being questioned for more than an hour, he emerged and walked up the road before doubling back to us.

Having made a judgment about supply and demand, Coon had gone up to three cents a double handful for the peanuts. When word got around among the Union soldiers about his pa being in the Seventh Connecticut, lots of them gave him five or ten cents. He made three dollars and eighty-seven cents on those peanuts.

When questioned by a CSA colonel, Ray gave him a factual report. He also offered to go back and spy some more if the colonel could get him more peanuts, or something else to sell. Of course the colonel wanted him to do it. We hoped, however, to be gone in two more days.

Coon told us that a lieutenant and three other men were to meet him and get the whiskey and women. Not wanting six people involved, the lieutenant had raised the price to compensate. Each man would pay four dollars for the women if they would stay over until the next night. They would also pay a dollar each for the five quarts of whiskey. The lieutenant even gave him a two-dollar advance to buy whiskey with. He also said that no one on the island knew the location of the Federal ship *Tahomas*.

Henry then said, "It might take us the rest of our lives to

catch up with the *Tahomas*. Even then we couldn't be sure who shot my step-pa. We'll have to use an alternate plan and get revenge where we can."

At 11:15 that night when the moon set and we shoved off for the island, I at least knew the backup plan. Heavily armed, and wearing Ella Mae's bonnets, Henry and I were in the boat. Though we were a few minutes late arriving at the island, hearing our boat paddles, the lieutenant and the three others came to the beach to meet us. To prove they were gallant they stepped out in the water to help beach our boat. Even with the stars reflecting off the white sand, the night was dark enough that they got up close without suspicion. We shot them as the boat touched the sand.

Henry did a quick search of the soldiers while Coon and I loaded their guns into the boat. There was over forty dollars in specie on the four of them. We took their money. Henry also took the lieutenant's shirt and left a sign on his chest. Since we could hear others approaching from toward the fort, we then shoved off and pulled hard for the mainland.

Alerted by the earlier shooting and hearing our paddles in the water as we approached, CSA soldiers were waiting for us as we beached the boat back on the mainland. After taking our guns, they led us to the colonel's command post. Though recognized and spoke to by the colonel, Ray kept quiet and Henry did the talking. Henry told them what of the story he wanted them to hear.

The colonel said, "Why did you do it? What's this all about?"

"Sir, it was a matter of honor," Henry replied. "There were two ladies involved who I can't mention."

Revenge was a personal matter that would not be enhanced by the telling of it. Henry also didn't want the real reason known by anyone who could identify us as associated with the raid. The real reason was weighted down on that Federal lieutenant's chest, however. The sign said, "REVENGE FOR THE CEDAR KEY RAID OF OCTOBER 4, 1861."

The whole thing so impressed the colonel that he ordered us released with our goods. He also asked us to go see General Bragg. After hearing the story, the general commended us in writing about our bravery and asked us to join his unit.

Henry declined, saying, "Sir, we have sick womenfolk in Blountstown. We must return immediately and see to their welfare."

General Bragg wrote us a pass that was good for anywhere in Florida. He signed it himself. Being a very good writer, Henry then had an original signature to work from. Henry also asked for the colonel's signature, saying he wanted folks to know they had met. It puffed the colonel up a little, and got Henry another signature.

As for Coon, he apologized for not being able to spy for the colonel as promised.

Arriving back at our camp that morning, we didn't go to bed even though we had been up and active for most of the past twenty-four hours. The horses rested, we pulled stakes and rode north to clear Pensacola Bay before turning east toward home. Henry had taken a compass off the lieutenant and he used it as we rode. Using the compass and the pass, and traveling as straight a line as possible, we could make it to Coon's house in six days of steady riding.

Though the general took the other Yankee weapons, he let Henry keep a .44 caliber Remington army revolver. Once fully loaded, it could be fired six times without reloading. Trying to find the way to wear the revolver so it could be brought on line easiest and quickest, Henry played around with it almost every day after that. I was carrying Doctor Isaac's dueling pistol in my belt.

November 30, 1861

Loaded with newly purchased supplies, we arrived at Coon's house at mid-afternoon. We also brought a bolt of blue cloth and a new bonnet for Ella Mae. The blueticks announced our arrival before they recognized Coon. After they recognized him I thought they would wag their tails off as they ran around his mule.

Ella Mae came sort of half running toward us, not saying a word. Just seeing her, my heart was beating all the way up in my throat. God knows I was taken with that woman.

She then got Henry and me by the hands and walked us to the horse pen as she chattered away. "You all have been gone for so long. What happened? I want to hear all about it. It's really good to have you back. I was so worried I could have died. You need to stay here and don't be running off."

It was shortly before dark and we had finished supper when Henry stood and said, "I'm going to check the horses before going to bed."

Ella Mae got to her feet and said, "You three clean up and wash the dishes. I'll go close the chicken coop."

Though wanting to go with them, I couldn't very well after she said that. I dried while Mary washed the dishes. Mary soon distracted me a little from thinking about Ella Mae. At almost twelve, she had started to develop physically beyond her years. I got a good look when she reached around to scratch between her shoulder blades. When her loose flour sack dress got tight across the front, there was the evidence of her maturity holding her dress out in a couple of places.

Even after getting in my bedroll that night I thought about being left in the house. While fretting about it until I went to sleep, I also fantasized about both Ella Mae and Mary.

Henry and I stayed there for several days. Henry practiced every day with his revolver, not shooting it so much as just getting it out and level in different directions. The two of us also read the medical book daily. We had been through it twice and were starting a third time. Henry had copies of Jane Austen's *Pride and Prejudice* and Charles Dickens' *Great Expectations*. His mother had given him those. Using those books, he soon had Mary and Coon reading regular. Ella Mae seemed to have little interest in reading. Other than cooking and cleaning, caring for the horses, and gathering wood, none of us did any work except for Ella Mae and Mary. They worked at making their blue dresses.

Though I was quite content and wasn't aware of it, Henry had become restless. In fact, I wasn't aware at all until supper one night when he said, "It's time we got on down to your ma's house, Ben. I think we should be there before Christmas."

Trying to think fast, I responded, "There's no hurry. They're fine. But I guess we should go."

With all my fantasies, I didn't know how to get out of going or what else to say.

Ella Mae saved me by saying, "We could all go. We could find a place to live around there somewhere. There's nothing to do here and it's awful lonely in these woods. It would be nice to live close to someone."

The next morning we went to Blountstown. Arriving there at mid-morning, we found that CSA troops were still in charge of the Apalachicola River, except for the blockade at its mouth. If they ever lost control of that big river, the Yankees could have moved troops on it all the way into Georgia. Seeing a dray behind a store as we walked the town, Henry spoke to the owner about it.

"I assume you own the dray behind the store."

"You assume right."

"I'd be interested in buying it."

"I'll take five dollars."

"Confederate paper."

"Silver."

"Three dollars silver."

The owner laughed, "It's worth five."

"Maybe in paper, and when there's a use for it," Henry said. "Right now the Union has the mouth of the river blockaded and there's not much to haul. You can sell it to me or take your chances later."

The owner scratched his head and said, "I'll take four in silver or gold."

"Five in Confederate paper," Henry said, counting out the money. "We'll be back after we look around."

In May of 1861 Confederate paper money was worth five percent less than silver. By October it was worth ten percent less, and by November it was worth fifteen percent less. When Henry bought the dray in December, a Confederate dollar was only worth eighty cents in coin.

Henry stopped a passing captain, showed him our papers from General Bragg, and said, "Sir, we're thinking about going east to Lake City and were wondering about the railroad from Jacksonville. Do you know where it ends coming this way?"

The captain replied, "The tracks haven't got west of Tallahassee. They go up to Quincy and down to St. Marks from Tallahassee. Going east, they go all the way to Jacksonville. In Baldwin, there are also connections to Fernandina and Cedar Key. It doesn't look like Florida's legislature will ever agree to connect Florida's tracks to the Georgia or Alabama tracks."

"Much obliged," Henry said, and we moved on.

Returning for the dray, we hitched up the mule and started home. I then realized that Ella Mae and Mary would be riding on the dray in the future. I was the loser. Neither of them would be sitting behind me on my horse with their arms around me.

We packed that night, and left going east for the Suwannee and home the next morning. After getting ferried across the Apalachicola River, we set as straight a line as we could for Tallahassee. Because of the dray having such a low axle, we had to stick to roads as much as possible. It took four days to get to

Tallahassee. With CSA forces garrisoned there, and the various people moving there from the coast to take refuge, Tallahassee was full of people.

When challenged by CSA troops in Tallahassee, Henry showed our pass from General Bragg. As was the case many times, those soldiers didn't look at our papers. I don't think many of those who stopped us from time to time could read. Henry always told them what was in the paper he was handing them. Most of them just took his word for it. Like those who stopped us at other times, the soldiers in Tallahassee became polite and waved us on. They probably only wanted to look at Ella Mae and Mary anyway.

Henry posted three letters from Tallahassee: one to his ma in Archer, one to his Aunt May who lived outside Lulu, and one to Miss Daisy in Cedar Key. Lulu is a settlement ten miles southeast of Lake City, Florida. All three letters said the same thing.

December 14, 1861

Dear Ma,

I hope this finds you in good health. Mine is fine.

My work in Pensacola being finished, Pa can rest easy. Although the Tahomas was not there, four good and able men were found to serve in the place of its crew.

Along with traveling companions, I hope to arrive at Aunt May's house in early January. God willing, I'll make it a point to be there by January 15. I hope to see you there.

If you see Miss Daisy or Doctor Isaac, give them my love and blessing. If they aren't otherwise occupied, they might wish to travel to Aunt May's also.

Your obedient son,
Henry F.

Not much else happened in Tallahassee. There was one dog-fight, which didn't last very long. The blueticks got the best of it. We kept them on the dray after that until we got out of town. Also, Henry turned eighteen in Tallahassee. He was a man grown in body and mind if not in years. After getting a few supplies, we moved on. Even with buying supplies we still had the money we took from those Federal soldiers at the fort.

A couple of hours east of Tallahassee we were challenged by three CSA soldiers without horses. Leveling their guns at us, they commanded us to halt. Actually, their guns were leveled at Henry and me. We were on horseback. Ella Mae, Mary, and Coon were on the dray.

Henry said, "We have a pass from General Bragg."

A sergeant replied, "Never mind a pass, boy. Get down. We need horses for artillery wagons. We're taking the mule and dray too. Get down now."

Things didn't look real good. No one had ever challenged the pass and I couldn't see those three being associated with any artillery unit. Anyway, artillery isn't moved on wagons. Real artillery soldiers would have said it different. They would have said something about caissons, guns, rifles, or mortars. Or they would have named their unit or the brand of their field piece.

During the past weeks I had come to sense when Henry was about to do something. I got the feeling then. To distract their attention from him, I moved my reins to my right hand, raised my left hand, and said, "It's a good pass, Sergeant. General Bragg gave it to us."

I thought that raising my left hand and speaking would dis-tract them from Henry. Also, taking the reins in my right hand put it close to the butt of Doctor Isaac's dueling pistol.

Moving at the same time I spoke, Henry started to dismount by swinging his right leg back and over his horse. The move looked like he was just following orders, but it also placed his horse between him and the soldiers. As he was settling to the ground, and was shielded from view by the horse, Henry drew his pistol and shot over the top of his horse. His first bullet hit the sergeant in the chest and his second bullet took one of the privates out.

When Henry's movement distracted them from me, I pulled the dueling pistol and shot the other private in the chest. At the same instant Coon shot him with his squirrel rifle. The sound of Henry's second shot, my shot, and Coon's shot were so near the same time that it was a couple of seconds before I realized they had also shot. I was wondering why both privates fell until I saw the smoke from Coon and Henry's guns.

Henry said, "Something's not right here but we're not going to stay around to find out what. Coon, get their weapons and get the dray moving. Ben, help me drag them out of the road."

After putting their weapons on the dray, Coon left.

Looping a rope around their legs and over our saddle horns, Henry and I dragged them two hundred yards into the woods. Once shielded from the road by the vegetation around a small pond, we also went through their pockets and packs. Though carrying no papers of any kind, they had three dollars in silver and eight dollars in Confederate paper money, which we took. After putting pine straw over them, Henry used a pine bough to brush out the trail we left while dragging them into the woods.

As I reflected on the situation, I began to think those old boys wanted the horses for riding and also wanted Ella Mae and Mary. But then we'll never know for sure.

An hour before dark Henry stopped us and said, "You all go ahead. I'm going to stay here until dark and see that no one is following us. If there are people following, I'm going to give them cause to chase me for awhile. Ben, give me your horse. Two horses will make a better trail if I have to lead them off. I can also switch back and forth to a fresh horse and keep them from catching me. Don't use a fire when you camp tonight."

I offered to do it but I knew, and Henry knew, he could do

it better. Neither of us said that though.

We waited until full dark to camp that night. Unable to find us in the dark, Henry slept a half-mile from us. He found us a few minutes after first light the next morning. Going without breakfast, other than some cold biscuits and syrup, we pulled out right away. Henry checked our back trail several times that morning but didn't find any pursuit.

Thirty miles out of Tallahassee at noon that day, we crossed the Aucilla River. We were still sixty miles from home. At that point Henry again spoke about covering our back trail.

"Ben, I'm going to take your horse, enough food for a couple of days, and my bed roll and wait on the other side of the river. You don't have to worry about anybody following you. I'll not join you until after it rains enough to wipe out any sign you make from the river to home. When you break camp, don't leave any trash or other sign of the camp; and after having a fire, put the coals in a bucket until you find water, then throw them in the water. You'll just disappear on this side of the Aucilla."

Ella Mae hugged him. Seeing her ma do it, Mary hugged him too. We didn't shake hands. Henry, Coon, and I were beyond that.

The trip was uneventful from there on. Due to a broken wheel, however, it took us four days to make the sixty miles home.

December 21, 1861

We came into view of the house just before dark. Ma and Lilly recognized the mule at a distance, and me after we got close. They said later that I looked two inches taller and ten pounds heavier. It sure made me walk around straight. They came out toward us, walking at first, then Lilly was almost running. As hard as she looked, Henry still wasn't there.

I tried to put both of them at ease by saying, "Henry's safe and on the way. There was something he had to do for us. He'll be on in time."

Lilly took a few steps in the direction from which we had come, so I said, "Lilly, it might be an hour, a day, or a week before he gets here but he's safe and well. I'll tell you all about it."

At that point Ma realized she had ignored my companions. She then did and said all the things that are done when folks come.

Knowing Ma would be put at ease, I said, "Ma, Coon helped with the things we had to do at Pensacola. This is his family. They're traveling with us and will need to stay awhile."

Ma let it go at that until after supper when Coon and I told the whole story. We didn't tell about the three CSA soldiers in front of John and Ivy, my smaller brother and sister. Small children sometimes repeat things without thought. Ella Mae had already told Mary to be careful while talking about those kinds of things. Although Mary was only turning twelve the next day, somehow I almost didn't look at her as a child anymore.

After I finished the story, Ma asked Ella Mae, "How's your husband going to find you after the war?"

Ella Mae said, "I left a couple of notes, and told some folks in Blountstown where I would be. I also posted a letter from Tallahassee, though I don't know if it'll reach him."

That satisfied Ma, but I was pretty sure Ella Mae hadn't spoken to anyone in Blountstown other than to say howdy. I was certain she hadn't posted a letter from Tallahassee. But knowing how the biscuit soaks up the syrup, I didn't let on.

Everybody spent the next day getting settled in. Fortunately, we had brought a good stock of supplies. If we hadn't we would have mostly been eating coon, fish, and greens. There hadn't been much to eat at the house before we arrived, and there was a bunch of us. Thinking I could tell them something new, Lilly and Ma asked several times about Henry that day. It was almost like they wanted me to backtrack and look for him. I finally took Coon, Mary, John, and Ivy fishing to get away from them.

Ma cooked a big cake for Mary's birthday, which was on December 22. There were no presents but Mary wore her new blue dress, which she hadn't had cause to do yet. We all played some games and had a good time. It was while playing those games that I began to notice Ma and Ella Mae were quite different. Ma wasn't any stick-in-the-mud when playing games. She was a real fun person, but she was a ma. Ella Mae was more like one of the kids. It wasn't a pretense. She had been like that all the time. For whatever reason, I just hadn't noticed it before. At that time I began having a little different feeling about things. I still fantasized about being alone with Ella Mae, however.

There was coffee on, and grits and eggs cooking, when I awoke the next morning. It's an amazing thing how Ma can move around and cook without stirring anyone. All of us boys were sleeping on the floor in the room near the fireplace where the cooking was done. There were only two rooms and a loft. The women were sleeping in the other room. Mary, Lilly, and Ivy were in the loft. Since the temperature was thirty-five degrees that morning, it felt good to get up with the fire already going.

Ma soon got everyone up to eat. After we had finished eating, and while the girls were washing the dishes, I asked Ella Mae if she wanted to go with me to check the catfish hooks. It seemed like a lame idea as I asked it in front of Ma, but Ma didn't appear to react in any way.

John said, "I'll go," and started getting his coat on.

Ella Mae said, "No. I think I'll go when it's warmer," which any sane person would have said.

Because of the wind blowing pretty strong, and us getting our hands wet taking the fish off the hooks, John and I almost froze.

Henry came walking in just after we ate at noon that day. He was leading a big lineback dun gelding and our two mares. All three horses were loaded with bags. I was confused. Henry came in from the east, from the side of the house toward the river. He should have been coming from the west. Though the horses were wet, Henry and the bags were dry as an old bone. Going straight to the pole barn, he placed some of the bags in it and handed us the others.

Handing his reins to Coon, Henry said, "Would you and John put the horses up? I'm beat."

He said to the rest of us, "Will you take these bags in the house? Those bags I'm leaving in the barn are not to be touched by anyone."

By that time all of the women had gathered around and were taking their turn hugging Henry and carrying on in general about him being home safe. I was beginning to wish it were me who had stayed behind to watch the back trail.

No one asked about the bags he left in the barn. The ones he gave us to carry to the house were heavy with supplies.

Henry filled us in as he ate. He said he waited until a downpour of rain wiped out our trail. Then, riding northeast, he crossed the Suwannee River above Branford and went all the way to Fort White. After waiting there until certain of not being followed, he bought supplies and headed back west to the house. Henry never did anything halfway. Our trails had just vanished. We hadn't been seen and couldn't be tracked. The one thing he hadn't said anything about was the thing I wanted most to hear about, the dun gelding. That dun was the best-looking horse I had ever seen. There had to be a good story about that horse.

My first question was, "How did you cross the river without you and the bags getting wet?"

He said, "I stripped and swam it. I then took your dugout back and brought everything across in it. After swimming back across, I brought the horses."

It was still only fifty degrees outside and I shivered at the thought.

"What about the dun gelding?" I asked.

Looking at me, he said, "It seems that some CSA deserters are gathering in Taylor County. There are also some in Levy, and in a few other counties. The ones I met were in Taylor County. The dun horse wasn't branded, and was a good one, so after we had settled our differences I picked him out and brought him home."

Thinking it best that not everyone know, I didn't ask any more questions at the time.

So as not to disturb the rest of us, and not to be disturbed, Henry took his bedroll to the barn in the middle of the afternoon to get some sleep. He slept all the way through the night.

The next day being Christmas Eve, the women cooked pies, cakes, greens, beans, bread, fish, venison, and a wild turkey. They cooked enough for two or three days. We boys tended the chores, cut wood, and hung around. Along in the early afternoon Lilly asked Henry if she could ride the dun. They rode for more than an hour.

At first dark Henry said, "Ella Mae, I want you and Ben to go out to the barn. Those bags I put in the back of it need some work, binding and such. It shouldn't take very long. Don't touch the ones under the hay. Everyone else can stay here with me and we'll have coffee, talk, and make sure the kids don't peek."

Since it was Christmas Eve, everyone knew what we were going to do and what the bags contained. Arriving at the barn, however, I found a note on the first bag.

Ben,

The presents are already bound, and the names are attached. You should stay in the barn for a few minutes to make the kids fret a little. Merry Christmas!

Your friend,
Henry F.

Henry Fern was my man. Using the pretext of staying warm, I took advantage of the opportunity to sit close to Ella Mae while we waited the appropriate minutes.

There were presents for everyone in the bags. All the usual trappings were there for the women and kids. And there were oranges. Coon and I got something special. We each got a .36 caliber Remington six shot revolver, complete with holster, belt, and supplies. Remington made a .36 caliber revolver for the Federal Navy. Those Henry gave us were used, but were in prime condition. He said the revolvers came along extra with the dun gelding.

For a few days we lived the good life. Henry and I studied the medical book every day. Henry had everyone else reading something every day, too. He sure is big on reading. His Ma taught him that. Other than the fun things of life, we didn't do much.

The New Year also came in while we were still at the place by the river. Although we were not going to shoot off any guns, everyone said they were going to stay up until the middle of the night to see it come in. Giving it up early, Ma went to bed at 10:00 P.M. The kids fell out one by one after that. By 11:30 Henry, Lilly, Ella Mae, and I were the only ones left awake. We stepped outside at midnight to watch the New Year come in.

A few days later I began to notice that Ma seemed to have an itch she couldn't scratch. I mentioned it to Henry.

"It's Ella Mae," he said. "Your ma doesn't think very much of her. She's pretty sure that you have a case on her and doesn't see any good coming of it."

Of course he was right. I just didn't want to see it at the time.

I said, "What can we do? Maybe we should look for a place for Ella Mae to stay. I know of an old house across the river that nobody lives in."

Henry replied, "That's what has to happen. You ought to bring it up at supper tonight. Don't leave it to your ma."

That night when supper was almost over, I said, "Ella Mae, I think we should start looking for you a house tomorrow."

Everybody got quiet around the table for the better part of a minute.

Ella Mae finally replied, "Yes. I guess I should start tomorrow. Maybe you'll help me."

Seeing the silver lining in that, even though it hadn't been the purpose, I said, "Okay. I know a couple of places."

Ma didn't say anything, which was a clear message that Henry had been right.

As we were leaving the next morning, Ella Mae riding Henry's mare, I said to Ma, "We're going across the river to see a house that's abandoned, and then on to Fort White if we don't find anything usable. We could be gone a couple of days."

Ma just looked at me and nodded. Mary and Coon didn't react at all, or offer to go. I found out a few days later that Ella Mae had told them not to.

After crossing the river we looked at the abandoned house. Though it was as good as her place outside Blountstown, and that's not saying much, Ella Mae wasn't happy with it. We then rode to Fort White. Arriving as dark closed in, we pitched a shelter and spent the night.

Not finding anything usable near Fort White, we headed west toward Branford the next day. At Branford, I went in a store to ask about houses while Ella Mae stayed outside with the horses. When I came out she was laughing and talking with a stranger.

He turned out to be a drummer. She was also holding her bag in which she carried extra clothes.

Ella Mae said, "Ben, I'm going downriver with this man. I want you to ask your ma to keep Mary for awhile. Thanks for your help." And they walked off.

In a daze, I'm not sure how I spent the next couple of hours. But I didn't beg her or shoot him. The last time I saw Ella Mae she was wearing her blue dress while headed downriver on a barge with the drummer.

Delaying a little, I made sure it was dark when I got home. Ma didn't say anything, or even smile, when I told about Ella Mae. I guess she's the smartest ma in the world.

A couple of days later Henry said he wanted to talk to Ma, Lilly, and me out at the barn. He started by saying, "Your ma already knows I have $40,000 in Confederate paper money. I want both of you to know, and to know where it is. It was in one of the bags I left under the hay. I kept out $20,000 and buried the other $20,000 in four jars, $5,000 in each corner of the barn. There's loose hay scattered over the spots."

The next thing that entered my mind was that we couldn't have driven Ella Mae off with a stick if she had known about the money. It came to me later that might have been the reason Henry didn't said anything about the money before she left. He was giving Ella Mae enough time to show her true nature and me time to come to my senses.

Curiosity getting the best of me, I asked, "Where did you get the money?"

He replied, "It came with the dun and the Remington revolvers. It won't be asked about, at least not related to us. Some men in Taylor County who wanted to take my horses had it. Though they can't talk about it anymore, they got it illegal and wouldn't say anything to anyone even if they could. We need to be careful not to cause suspicion by spending too much at one time or place. I'm going to spend my time during the war trying to trade Confederate paper money for specie. The Yankees will win the war, or at best the South will end it in a draw. In either case Confederate paper money won't be worth as much as silver or gold. After seeing what happened at Cedar Key, and what was going on at Pensacola, I don't see how the CSA can win if the war lasts very long."

The value of a Confederate dollar having fallen to seventy-five cents in coin, forty thousand in Confederate money was then worth $30,000 in gold or silver. Still, there was more money than I had ever thought about. This was something we never told Coon until much later. But I'm getting ahead of the story.

January 12, 1862

Following the river upstream, we crossed at Branford. There Henry traded the dray and some Confederate money for a four-seated buggy. From Branford we headed for Henry's Aunt May's house. Lilly, Henry, Coon and I were on horseback. Ma and the kids were riding in the buggy. Only thirty miles as the crow flies, it was over forty miles the way we had to go with the buggy. After camping overnight, we arrived the next afternoon. Doctor Isaac, Miss Daisy, and Henry's ma had arrived two days before.

Aunt May had six children. Her husband, John, and their oldest boy, Bud, had gone to Georgia and enlisted. That was where they lived before moving to Florida. The five kids at home ranged from fifteen years old down to eight.

With four rooms downstairs, two upstairs, an attic, and a big kitchen that was separated from the house, John and May's house was big. They didn't own much property though, only eighty acres, just what the family could tend with some left in timber and pasture. John's family didn't hold with owning slaves. Most of the folks we knew didn't own slaves.

Though theirs was a small place, and they were not wealthy, there was a pantry full of food. Twenty jars of strawberry preserves were among the rows of various kinds of food in jars. Aunt May's strawberry preserves were the best I've ever eaten. She also had sweet potatoes, cured pork shoulders, hams, and sausage. The talking and eating went on all afternoon and most of the night.

At some point, Aunt May asked, "How long can you all stay?"

Henry replied, "I was planning to stay until you ran out of strawberry preserves."

Aunt May flustered around proud as a peacock after that.

The next day Doctor Isaac sat Henry and me down to talk. Everybody was there listening, except for a couple of the women who were out in the kitchen cooking.

"Boys, you did a good job on Mary's tonsils. Have you read the whole book?"

"Yes, sir," I said. "I've read the whole thing three times and Henry reads more than me. We talk about it every day, each of us saying what we think it means."

Doctor Isaac was amazed.

He then started asking Henry and me questions, any of which either of us could answer.

Toward the end of the questioning, he said, "It looks like I've got two people ready to work with a physician. Henry, why don't you come to Cedar Key and intern with me for a couple of years. I can get someone in Gainesville or Archer to take Ben on. Most of the younger doctors are gone to war. It's just terrible."

It didn't take Henry or me long to say yes. Henry also said, "I'll have to stay and help Aunt May with the farm for a couple of weeks. She's still struggling to get the cane ground and syrup made. There are also the strawberries and greens to gather every day and get to the train station. I was going to ask Ben's family to stay a few days and help."

Ma was standing there, proud of me going to be a doctor, and said, "We'll stay as long as needed. I'll go to the kitchen and talk with May about it."

The next morning found us in the field picking strawberries and gathering greens. It was an every-morning job after that. In the afternoons we ground cane and Henry started cooking off a kettle of syrup. The cooking took well into the night. Being the only one other than Aunt May who had cooked syrup before, he did all the syrup cooking. A few of the women stayed up and tended him, bringing cool water and strawberry jam with a biscuit or some other snack. They also helped pour up the syrup when it was ready. Each boiling of cane juice produced ten gallons of syrup.

As cane juice is boiled to cook it down to syrup, foam, called skimmings, is formed on top of the cooking juice. These skimmings include the impurities from the cane juice. Skimmed off constantly during the cooking, the skimmings are put in a barrel that stands under the shelter by the cooking kettle. Since the skimmings stay in the barrel for the entire time that syrup is being cooked, sometimes weeks, it naturally begins to ferment. Some people take advantage of this natural process to make rum.

After Henry had cooked syrup for two weeks, and the barrel was half full, the skimmings were getting ripe. Somehow that night Smokey got out of the pasture and drank his fill of skimmings. He became so falling down drunk that he knocked the barrel over. Before we got up and out the next morning, Aunt May's chickens also got to pecking and eating out of the skimmings, which were all over the ground. When we went out to work, Smokey was on his knees and couldn't get up and the chickens were staggering around. After taking two or three steps, they would have to sit down. When a hen sits down, it's normally a signal to the rooster and he's usually right there to take care of the situation. This time, the rooster was too drunk to take advantage of the situation. It was a great diversion for everyone for a few minutes. Aunt May then shooed the kids off to the strawberry field to begin picking. Since Smokey was useless that day, Coon had to harness one of the horses to pull the cane mill. Surprisingly, egg production picked up for the next couple of days.

On January 19, we got some bad news about Cedar Key. From what we heard the Federal military had again raided Cedar Key on January 16. It was also said that they were moving inland. While ours wasn't fresh news, more news and rumors kept coming every day. Federal forces had taken Cedar Key for sure, had set up camp there, and were making some raids inland. The train was still running but it couldn't get to Cedar Key. Fortunately for them, Doctor Isaac and Miss Daisy were still with us, and it looked like they would be for awhile.

Doctor Isaac said that taking and holding Cedar Key was just another step in closing off supplies to the CSA. The blockade-runners wouldn't have anywhere to land there. The Federal force in place on the ground would also free up some gunboats for something other than blockade duty.

Two things happened then. First, Doctor Isaac asked Aunt May if he and Miss Daisy could stay on and him hang out his shingle. Of course she said yes. The second was that Doctor Isaac said Henry and I should work with him when the cane was finished. As well as studying daily, we were to go on calls with him.

Word soon spread that Doctor Isaac was in business. Because of the war, there wasn't another doctor for miles so he soon became busy. It wasn't long before Henry and I had helped deliver a baby, set broken bones, lanced boils, treated the pinkeye, and tended the sick in general. It wasn't very exciting, but we were learning lots. Also, everyone thought we were heroes and treated us special.

On February 25, Doctor Isaac took Miss Daisy, Henry's ma, and that morning's harvest to the Lake City Station. Since the buggy was full, Henry and I didn't go. We took the kids to a small nearby lake to fish. It was the first time we had done that. Ma stayed home to cook so Aunt May went along with us. Although her going cut down on our shenanigans, it didn't shorten the trip. We arrived back at the house that afternoon just as the buggy did. Doctor Isaac had the mare in a full trot, which we hadn't ever seen him do.

As soon as we were in speaking distance, Doctor Isaac said, "Henry, Ben, Coon, I want you and your mothers to come in for a talk. May, you should come too. I want you kids to go down to the creek and play. Don't come back until you're called."

Without a moment's hesitation they left for the creek, all except Lilly. Henry took her hand and brought her inside. We were all quiet while waiting for Doctor Isaac to speak.

He said, "There was talk at the station about CSA troops hunting three young men who were seen riding two horses and a mule. I couldn't get the straight of why they are being hunted but the description fits you three, and you have been seen about."

Doctor Isaac hadn't mentioned it to them before, and Henry's ma and my ma just about panicked. The Doctor, Henry, and I soon got them quiet enough to talk sense.

After considerable discussion, Henry said, "Some of us had best pull out until things quiet down here. I just can't figure how they got on to us, or for what. We've done enough things, but no one knew. I was the only one involved with the dun and related things. That was clean. It also couldn't be that because Ben and Coon weren't with me."

Doctor Isaac replied, "The three of you shouldn't leave together and you shouldn't take the mule. They're looking for three men, one on a mule."

Being one that's always quick to solve a problem and take action, my ma said, "We'll get you boys' things cleaned and together. Do you think we should talk to someone about the other thing?"

Her comment passed right over my head but Henry understood. "Yes. I'll do that. We'll need Doctor Isaac's help," he said.

The others wanted to know what they were talking about, but Henry said, "There's things that it's best if only a few people know for now. Doctor Isaac, would you walk out to the barn?"

I told the rest of them about everything but the money. Henry told Doctor Isaac the whole story, even the details of how he got the money, guns, and horse. After talking for almost half an hour, Henry called Ma, Lilly, and me.

He said, "Doctor Isaac knows about the Confederate paper money. Agreeing that specie will be more valuable in the long run, he's going to help trade some of the paper for specie, and buy property. I'm pulling stakes and going north until he can check out the rumors. Ben, you should too. I don't know how far I'm going, maybe to Atlanta. I'll be gone for a few months at least. Sooner or later I'll send an address."

Lilly had her face on Henry's arm. She wasn't crying out loud but her body was jerking lightly.

Henry put his arm around her and said, "It'll be fine. I'll just go north for awhile. The war can't last forever."

Thinking of Ella Mae floating off on that barge, I could feel for Lilly. Her hurt was probably just as bad as mine had been. Looking at Ma, I could see that she was struggling with tears too.

Coon pitched a fit to go but Henry talked him out of it.

Henry said, "Coon, we've rode a long trail and we're full partners. If all three of us leave together they'll catch us for sure. It's best if you stay here. Also, if all three of us went, there would be no man here to protect everyone. I'm counting on you to do it."

Henry wasn't trying to put Doctor Isaac down and they both knew it. Coon put up an argument, but none of us ever won an argument after Henry had thought something through.

PART II

The Flight

February 26, 1862

enry and I left at 4:00 A.M., riding north. We cleared the railroad tracks before daylight. Olustee was a couple of miles to our right as we crossed the tracks. After holding north for another hour, we turned northeast, keeping Ocean Pond between us and the Olustee Station. At that point we were twenty-five miles from the tip of Georgia. With the railroad behind us we stood less chance of running into any CSA troops who might be looking for us. Of course all of them wouldn't be looking for us. Communication not being very good, most of them wouldn't know anything about our situation.

Having a pass from General Bragg in the name Watson, we

planned to use that name until leaving Florida. We planned to switch to Williams after that. Henry was to send a letter with an address after we settled down. In the meantime Doctor Isaac would send letters to Henry Williams in Atlanta. We would pick them up if circumstances allowed. Code words for future correspondence were to be hogs and cattle. If the word hog was used, it was safe to return home. If reference was made to cattle, it was not safe to return.

Riding the dun, Henry was leading his mare as a pack animal. I was riding my mare. Each of us was armed with a revolver and a .45 caliber percussion cap muzzleloader. Two shotguns were strapped to the packhorse. We also carried the medical bag, medical reading materials, medical supplies, $25 in specie, and $15,000 in Confederate paper money.

For medical supplies we carried chloroform, salt pork, kerosene, turpentine, cloves, tobacco, goldthread root, Epsom Salts, blackberry root, pumpkinseeds, ginger, and castor oil. We also had a list of known medicinal herbs and their uses. Though neither of us drank, our pack also contained a full quart bottle of corn whiskey. The doctor swore by it as a disinfectant in cleaning medical tools and wounds. The application of alcohol to a raw wound is quite painful, however. We also carried several flannel bellybands for the prevention of umbilical hernia. Attendance at a birthing was one of the most serious duties of a physician. Several bottles of sugar water were also at our disposal. Frequently a patient needs only time before the body heals itself. Sugar water is also a great pacifier for the hypochondriac, or for the child of an overly concerned mother. Though it appeared the development of our medical careers was slowed, Doctor Isaac had made sure we were prepared to practice what medicine we knew.

As night fell, our horses being tired, we camped just south of Moniac, Georgia. Other than a few slaves chipping pine trees, we had not seen a living soul.

Keeping the Okefenokee Swamp, and then Waycross,

Georgia, to our left, we avoided contact with others as we continued north the next few days. On March 8, 1862, I reached my seventeenth birthday on the banks of the Big Satilla River north of Alma, Georgia, but the most memorable event of those few days occurred the following day at a plantation outside Hazelhurst, Georgia, when we observed at the birth of a baby boy by a young slave woman. A black midwife provided the woman's medical assistance. Henry used corn whiskey to disinfect. He also explained the purpose of the whiskey to the midwife. Looked on with suspicion at first, we were later held in high regard by the slaves on the plantation. It was not common for a physician to be in attendance at the birth of a slave's child.

Having slaves in excess of the number required to gain exemption from military service, the male members of the family were still at home. Due to the civility of both the family and the slave population, we stayed on there for a week while providing medical services and resting our horses. During the week we set one broken leg and treated several cases involving diarrhea, earache, and other common illnesses. Since a doctor hadn't been available in the area for some time, there was a rush of patients from the vicinity. We stayed busy all week. Seeing the need, we also treated several of the younger slaves for various forms of worms. Ground pumpkinseed was used initially. That was followed by a garlic treatment over several days. As a courtesy for our concern and assistance, the slaves cared for us far in excess of any directive from their owner.

As our departure drew near, the people from the big house and the slave quarters beseeched us to stay on and hang out our shingle. I think this was because there was no competent medical person within a hard day's ride. Not that we were all that competent. Feeling the need to distance ourselves from possible CSA pursuit, or accidental discovery, we decided to move on.

Asking for no money, but accepting what was offered for our services, we left with a few Confederate paper dollars, two additional quarts of corn whiskey, and enough food and supplies for an additional three weeks. We also had a safe haven at which we could stay at any point in the future. Additionally, Henry asked the owner to write us a letter of introduction that would also recommend us for our medical services.

From his own writing efforts Henry produced a pass from General Bragg that gave us safe passage throughout the sphere of control of the Confederate States of America. It also recommended us as physicians with any military unit we chose to serve. Even after seeing it done, I could not easily distinguish between General Bragg's own handwriting and Henry's effort at forgery.

Flitting to move rapidly and secretly, we bypassed several communities. Passing east of Dublin, Georgia, and on toward Atlanta, we were thinking to lose ourselves momentarily in Atlanta. While in Atlanta we could also learn fresh news of the war. Near Milledgeville, long before approaching Atlanta, we had an opportunity to test the use of our new credentials. Confronted by a patrol of Confederate cavalry, their weapons at the ready, and there being fourteen of them, Henry presented our papers.

Not knowing his words would prove to be a prophecy, Henry said "We are a physician and his assistant on our way to support the action in North Georgia and Tennessee."

Requesting and receiving medicine for a case of diarrhea, the troopers saw us on our way. In parting they expressed envy of us, and a desire to have an opportunity to go participate in the war. Their readiness to accept our papers and story caused us to give up flitting. We rode openly and boldly after that.

We arrived in Atlanta during the middle of the day of March 13. Atlanta, which prior to the war had a population of 9,500, was swollen to 15,000 due to refugees and soldiers. The size of the city took some getting accustomed to. Although stared at by a few, we were not challenged by anyone. Proceeding immediately to the post office, we inquired as to any mail in the name of Henry Williams. There being two letters, Henry opened the one with the oldest date.

Olustee, March 2, 1862

Dear Mr. Williams,
    Hoping this finds you in good health, I take pen in hand to report on our business venture. I have not been able to find suitable or abundant cattle to conclude our business. After continuing the effort, I will report further by future correspondence.

Your partner in business,
I.S.

The second letter provided no more favorable message.

Olustee, March 9, 1862

Dear Mr. Williams,
    Hoping you are well, I must again report that our cattle deal has not been concluded. I am also working on other little matters of one kind or another, and am leaving today for Tallahassee in an effort to conclude our business.

As always,
I. S.

Proceeding immediately, we secured temporary lodging at the edge of town for ourselves, which also had a pen and stable for our animals. Prices being high in Atlanta, the house was costly. We were, however, able to pay the rent in Confederate paper money. Still declining in value, the official rate of exchange then stood at two dollars Confederate paper for one dollar in silver or gold.

As we moved our supplies and weapons into the house,

Henry said, "It would be good if you hung out a sign saying physician's office. While you do that, I'll look to our future comfort. I'll also assess the probability of getting Confederate paper money turned into specie."

Having great faith in Henry's judgment and ability, I replied, "If you'll bring a young lady to cook and clean, and a table and chair for reading and writing, I'll be fine."

Henry said, "When we have patients who have little or no funds, inquire if they can pay with a book or some small item of comparable value. We don't need animals or bulky objects. We might have to leave suddenly."

Within an hour of hanging the shingle I ministered to the first patient. He was a boy of ten who was near temporary blindness from a sty on both eyes. The person accompanying him was a portly, but well dressed, woman of forty years.

She asked, "Where's the physician?"

I said, "About town, ma'am. I expect him to return within two or three hours. If it's about the sties, I've treated many of those both in and outside his presence."

"You look a little young," she said.

"Yes, but the looks don't always tell the ripeness of the melon. However, if you wish to wait for the physician—"

She looked hurried and broke in, "What's the charge?"

I said, "If he's a good patient, one-half dollar, silver. If he's obstinate or impertinent, one dollar." She looked like she had the money, and I didn't like her superior manner.

Lancing the sties in short order, I then wet them with alcohol. I instructed her to wet the sties in the mornings with alcohol, being careful to keep it out of his eyes, and to drop milk in his eyes at night.

The boy did shout one time. His mother promptly thumped him on the head to save the extra half-dollar. Selling her a bottle of sugar water for her complexion, I got the whole dollar anyway.

I was called out an hour later by a boy whose seven-month

pregnant mother was ill. Prescribing complete bed rest and cream of tartar, I promised that the doctor, or I, would call the next day. The payment was one copy of Hamilton's *Lectures on Metaphysics* that had probably seen no use in thirty years.

Upon returning to the house, I found Henry giving work instructions to a white girl of eighteen years named Jolene. She was to be our day servant while we were in Atlanta. I was instant-ly smitten by her charm.

Within days, seeing patients kept me busy full time and Henry part time. He otherwise busied himself trading or selling. He was changing Confederate paper money into specie through whatever scheme he could contrive. Being around the house all the time was not all bad—I was also around Jolene lots.

Henry and I jointly called on a sick woman who had become ill while traveling through Atlanta. Her husband, a captain, proved to be a member of Jefferson Davis' staff who was return-ing east after carrying a message for the president. During the three days Henry continued to treat her for serious diarrhea, from which she recovered, he came to know both of them well.

Due to a shortage of men, and our being physicians, by the end of the first week we were invited to several private socials. News and rumors of the war were rampant at the social gather-ings. We soon had the names of the major units and command-ers to the north of Atlanta. Much to our surprise, having been promoted and sent there with his forces, General Braxton Bragg of our Pensacola encounter was reported to be prominent among the CSA generals north of Atlanta. Using the names of major officials in Atlanta as the authors, Henry wrote us introductions to some of the commanders. He also had a legitimate letter from President Davis' aide.

Me being smaller, and looking younger than Henry, my age was sometimes discreetly inquired about. Henry could easily pass for being in his mid twenties. There seemed to be no concern about his age. Inquiries about me were only a matter of fleeting concern.

At socials, my young appearance sometimes seemed an asset.

During one social, I encountered the mother of my first patient who had consumed a few glasses of wine. In spite of my youthful appearance, she took great pleasure in introducing me to everyone and bragging on how competent I was. I feared that she might solicit me for a late night house call until I was given a reprieve by an intoxicated elderly colonel who deemed her handsome. Needless to say, our life was becoming exciting. We were quickly becoming established in Atlanta.

In a short time we had quite a collection of goblets, and other silver and gold household pieces. Books were also passing through our hands. They were more easily disposed of than were silver and gold pieces. Selling them for from fifty cents to three dollars each, we rarely had more than two or three books beyond our own.

March 28, 1862

From the day's mail, we received a letter.

Tallahassee, March 20, 1862

Dear Mr. Williams,
> *I hope this finds you in good health. Our cattle deal seems to have gone sour. There are more cows around than I can put in place in short order. I suggest you abandon our present business arrangement and proceed to the next best sales location.*

> *Yours in good health,*
> *I. S.*

Henry posted a reply.

Atlanta, March 28, 1862

Dear Uncle Isaac:
    You will no doubt be surprised to hear from me since it has been years. As you know, my father passed away recently and we've been temporarily residing in Atlanta. We've decided to move to Independence, Missouri, and will be traveling there directly.
    My mother's well and sends her love. Give my love to cousin Lilly and her mother. We're looking forward to the hogs being at market.

Henrietta Williams

Returning to the house, Henry apprised me of the situation outside the presence of Jolene.

"It sounds like Doctor Isaac is hearing something about the situation that might be negative. I guess we had better move. The war seems to rage on everywhere. We'll go northwest until we're clear of CSA troops. Or at least to a place where CSA telegraph wires and trains can't reach us. Western Missouri is supposed to be a jumping off point to the Pacific Ocean. We can stay in Independence for awhile and decide further."

"Yes. I guess we must," I replied. "But it's terrible to have to leave Atlanta. We've established ourselves beyond belief in a short time. I've also become quite enamored with Jolene. How long is the trip?"

"It's over seven hundred miles. It'll take over four weeks of steady riding to get there."

"Taking the train would shorten the trip."

"Indeed, or end it all together. Troops will be congregated where there's ready transportation."

"What about the money?"

"We'll take it with us. We started with $25 in specie and $15,000 in Confederate paper, and now have $11,081 in Confederate paper and $2,187 in specie. If the war should end with Federal troops in Atlanta, I fear there will be looting, even of the banks. I think the Confederacy will not be victorious. Should the war go on until there's total collapse, property values will plummet in the South. It'll be best if we buy land or property elsewhere, perhaps around St. Louis or Kansas City. Transportation is the key to the future, and the rivers to transportation."

"Do you think there's a chance the CSA can win?"

"Only with a stroke of genius. Doctor Isaac said that Florida produces only farm goods, cloth, and salt, and the other Southern states little more. The North has superiority on the water, so they control most imports. And the North outnumbers the South more than three to one. Even if there's a massive battlefield victory by a Southern army, Doctor Isaac thinks the best the South can get is a stalemate. In the meantime, our goal is to transfer Confederate paper money into specie or property. Unfortunately, the best opportunities might lie in Atlanta just as we're having to leave."

Packing the valuable items we had acquired, we marked the shipment as farm tools and shipped them to Henry's Aunt May for safekeeping. In order to be welcome when we returned to Atlanta, we also posted a notice on the door before leaving.

Our friend and benefactor, General Braxton Bragg, is in the field to the north. We go to assist him in dulling the enemy's sword of war.
May you live in the best of health.
Henry and Benjamin Williams

Being at the house when she heard of our departure, Jolene was flying to and fro, first helping then hindering. Henry then paid her for the month. She was to deliver messages to our patients. Enamored with her, I would have asked her to go, but it could not be.

By using his compass Henry led us on an almost straight line toward the lower tip of Missouri. After three hours we halted and made camp without a fire. By the light of a candle in the tent, Henry then produced a map and showed me a proposed route.

He said, "I hear there might soon be heavy fighting to the north of Chattanooga. We'll go west-northwest and cross into Tennessee where the Tennessee River touches on Alabama, Tennessee, and Mississippi. From there, we'll go up the far side of the river through Counce, Pittsburgh Landing, and Jackson, Tennessee."

I replied, "That looks like a good route. When running, the straight line is always best. The deer, fox, or coon that circles or trees is the one that gets caught or shot. This route will also allow us to avoid any concentration of troops north of Chattanooga."

At the end of two days we had passed well south of Cedartown, Georgia, and at the end of three days had passed north of Gadsden, Alabama. Stopping hourly to rest our horses, and for an hour at noon for them to graze, we traveled thirty-five miles a day.

We stopped at a modest farm near Hatton, Alabama, toward the end of the fifth day to purchase additional grain for the horses. Since our horses needed the rest, we called off our journey and spent a pleasant afternoon and evening visiting. As is always the case, the people at the farm found a couple of patients who needed minor medical attention.

Late on April 4, as we approached Counce, Tennessee, CSA troops were suddenly everywhere. Without knowing it we had stumbled into the start of the battle at Shiloh Church, called Pittsburgh Landing by the Union.

Early the morning of the April 5, we were challenged by a CSA patrol of seven men.

"Who be you, and where you goin'?" a sergeant asked, while holding his rifle barrel pointed straight at my chest.

"We are a physician and his assistant who are searching for General Braxton Bragg," Henry replied, producing a paper.

Without looking at the paper, the sergeant pointed and said, "He be yonder. About one mile."

Actually, we were surprised. We had thought the general to be north of Chattanooga.

Seeing no alternative but to follow the sergeant's directions, we proceeded. We were again challenged, and that time led to the general. He looked thinner of face and body than he had at Pensacola, though it was hard to tell with his full beard.

A lieutenant, no more than eighteen years old himself, said, "These boys said they were looking for you, General. They have a paper with your name on it."

After looking at us for several seconds, the general said, "I know you men from someplace."

Having reached full growth, I was a full two inches taller and fourteen pounds heavier than when he had previously seen me. I had also started shaving occasionally, but now had a several-days-old beard. Henry looked much the same as before, but was a little taller at six feet and three-fourths of an inch.

"Yes, sir, in Pensacola, Florida," I responded.

"By thunder it was," the general said. "So you two decided to join a unit. There were three of you."

"No, sir," Henry replied. "We were reading and practicing to be physicians at the time you met us, and have followed through on it. Actually, we're on our way to Independence, Missouri. When we heard you were here, we asked to be directed to you."

Turning to the lieutenant, General Bragg said, "These men, along with a fourteen year old, attacked Fort Pickens, killed several Federal soldiers, and brought us the soldier's weapons and a lieutenant's shirt. That revolver he's wearing belonged to one of their officers. Their attack was a matter of honor related to some ladies as I recall. It was the damnedest thing I've ever heard of. If I had ten thousand like them I would take Grant's whole army today."

Turning to me he asked, "Are any ladies involved in your trip to Independence?"

"No, sir," I said.

The general chuckled and said, "You say you men have been practicing medicine?"

"Yes sir," Henry replied. "General kinds of stuff mostly. The only surgery we've done was on boils and sties, and one set of tonsils."

"Well, men," the general said, "you're going to have to stay here. We need you. There's going to be a big battle and we need any kind of physicians we can get. After a few times watching a surgeon, you'll get on to it."

Henry said, "We'll do what we can for you, General, but after it's over we need to head for Missouri. You could write us another pass."

"I'll write you anything you want. We'll have to take your horses and weapons though, other than your revolvers. You can keep them. We have whole regiments in camps of instruction at Corinth without proper weapons."

Turning to the lieutenant, General Bragg said, "Take these men to a field physician and introduce them properly. Send their weapons to Corinth and turn their horses over to the First Florida Cavalry. These two probably know some of those men anyway."

Henry said, "General Bragg, we'll need a warrant for our horses, guns, and gear."

To which the General said, "You write it and I'll sign it.

Adding in the Federal rifles General Bragg had taken at Pensacola, Henry wrote,

This is a receipt for five rifles, two shotguns, and three horses and tack. All are in excellent condition. At the end of the war, reimbursement on

*demand of the bearer of $900 in specie, plus inter-
est at eight percent, is to be made from the
Confederate States of America treasury.*

*Braxton Bragg, Commanding
Army of the Mississippi, 2nd Corps
April 5, 1862*

Taking our signed warrant, saddlebags, medical supplies, and personal things, we were introduced to a physician and his assistant who were positioned near Bragg's advance headquarters. We were advised that there was, in theory, one physician assigned to each regiment and a general field hospital in Corinth where most of the surgery would be done. In reality, however, there were not enough physicians to go around. In spite of the shortage, Henry and I were assigned to another physician. This was almost certainly because of our age and inexperience.

The attack, originally set for April 4, had been reset for April 5, at 8:00 A.M. We happened to get caught up in the advance. But the attack did not occur that day. Heavy rain and a series of miscommunications left the advance stalled as Clark's division arrived on line late in the afternoon. At that time we saw General Beauregard arrive at General Bragg's temporary headquarters. We overheard that several of the other units were also not yet on line. General Albert S. Johnston, the Confederate general commanding the entire battle, then arrived and there was an argument among the generals.

Squatting under oilcloth ponchos for warmth and dryness, we heard some of it. It seemed that Bragg was also blamed for not bringing his units on line promptly. There was some that thought that the battle was already lost because of the thirty-six-hour delay. General Beauregard and Bragg thought that since the element of surprise was lost the entire battle was lost. The Federal forces being only one and a half miles away, we were wondering how there could be a surprise. There had already been several hundred shots fired. We found later that it was some of the boys firing to determine if their rifles would fire after the rain had stopped for a while. General Breckenridge, who joined the group of generals late, thought they should attack, as did General Polk. After listening to the argument for most of an hour, Johnston announced that there would be an attack at dawn.

Henry said, "Doctor Isaac said it would take a stroke of genius for the South to win. I see little genius here."

We were then called away to help tend a man with a cut arm. The bleeding was soon stopped and the wound bandaged. He was then sent toward Corinth.

After dark the generals again gathered to talk. Bragg seemed to have changed his mind. Beauregard then had no support for his opinion that the battle was lost before it started. We got the impression that Bragg and Beauregard thought each other incompetent. Truthfully, we were beginning to doubt the competence of all of them.

Henry said, "The trouble is that there are too many generals. If there were only one general, and the rest were majors and captains, they would jump every time he spoke and would soon have the war won."

As the time for battle approached some of the men made efforts to conceal their fear. Others talked frankly of the fight to come and prayed for the Lord to protect them.

"I'm glad we're not going to be in line with those boys," Henry said.

To which I replied, "I would rather be in Atlanta, even if we got caught. We're within range of rifle and artillery anyway. Who knows which direction this battle or a stray minié ball will take. There seems to be a hundred thousand troops just on the Confederate side. The battle could be all over the place. We might get overrun."

"I don't like being here either, and I don't like how our horses were taken. But we'll do our job as promised and patch up what of these boys we can. After that, one way or another, we're on our way," Henry said.

Awakened at some point during the night to the sound of drums in the distance, I wondered if it was their drums or ours I was hearing. I also wondered about the element of surprise again.

Before daylight, General Johnston and his staff gathered again. Soon, Generals Hardee, Bragg, and Beauregard joined them. The same arguments started as the night before. Johnston didn't say much until 5:30 when there was some scattered rifle fire. He then told everyone the battle had started and that it was too late to change their minds about whether or not to attack.

As General Johnston mounted his thoroughbred, Fireeater, to join the battle, Henry said, "They owe us horses. Given the chance, I'd take that one."

The bulk of the attack was to have started at 6:00 that morning, but by 6:30 we were still hearing only scattered firing. It seemed there would be no surprise. Within minutes the shooting picked up. It was 7:30, however, before the battle was really rolling. Had the Confederate boys got started at 6:00, they might have won it all that day.

By 8:00, we were getting more wounded than we could handle. Our first observation of an amputation was a lower leg. It was so mangled that surgery had to be done immediately. The physician we were with did the cutting. He then took a saw to the bone. The entire operation on the leg took less than twenty minutes. That soldier was one of the lucky ones. He was given ether. Before the end of the battle our supply was gone.

Overwhelmed by the number of wounded, each of us was soon working independently. Our main function was to get the injury patched up well enough that the patient would still be alive when he reached Corinth. We were also to identify those patients whose wounds were so slight that they could return to the battle. We were soon overwhelmed to the point that most of the cases were going straight to Corinth, fifteen miles away, without us having done anything for them. I heard that twenty surgeons worked there. Due to a shortage of ambulance wagons, those who were too wounded to walk soon filled the area around us. Though the battle continued all day, I don't remember very much of it except the crackle and roar of guns and the moans of dying men.

As the sun set, we received word that General Beauregard had called off his attack before dark. The Federal forces then seemed to be escaping across the river. Continuing the attack until after dark might have won the battle for the Confederates even after the late start.

When the fighting stopped for the night we found ourselves close to Shiloh Church. Various units stayed the night there. Bragg's corps camped close to Sherman's former camp that night. Our work hadn't slackened and didn't for several hours. Even though several hundred ambulance loads of wounded had departed for Corinth, with eight to twelve in each wagon, many of the wounded were still with us. After running out of all supplies, we were told that more were on the way from Corinth. The silent dead and the moaning living were all around us as we comforted the wounded from both armies.

There was extensive plundering of the Federal force's previous positions during the night. The sight was like a thousand fireflies as troops roamed around with candles while seeking plunder. Being physicians, we had the ultimate opportunity to loot and plunder from the seriously wounded and the dead, but we didn't. We did requisition two Springfield breach-loading rifles and two hundred cartridges and the uniforms of two dead Federal officers, a captain and a lieutenant, that fit us. Those items were stored against possible future need. With the rifles and our revolvers the general left us, we were then well armed.

Depending on the skill of the person doing the loading, a Springfield breechloader can be loaded and fired three times for every one time a muzzleloader can be loaded and fired. The Springfield also has the same reach and punch of the more-written-about Sharps. Also, a breechloader can be easily loaded from a prone position while a muzzleloader can efficiently be loaded only from a standing position. Many of the Union soldiers were equipped with Springfield breechloaders. Most of the Confederate army was equipped with muzzleloaders.

Before midnight it began to rain; and continued throughout the night. The rain added to our misery and the general confusion. In the dark and rain many men couldn't find their units. They soon quit trying. At some point during this confusion a patrol came in and reported the enemy to be reinforcing, and on our side of the river. Although the rain slackened some time after 3:00 A.M., there was no place to get out of the standing and running water. Given the number of wounded we had to care for, and the miserable weather, it was in the wee hours of the morning when we fell asleep huddled under our ponchos.

As the morning light came, we became aware that the Federal troops had not retreated. They were on the attack. A good opportunity to end the fight to the Confederates' advantage had been lost. Confederate officers tried to organize their forces to continue the fight that second day, but with little success. Cavalry units also searched the rear for stragglers in order to reinforce existing companies and form new companies. Working as though in a daze, we continued caring for the wounded as the battle swirled everywhere.

The battle continued all morning. At times not sure who was attacking whom, we had little time to inquire. I did see Breckenridge plead with Cheatham to get his men into the fight. Cheatham's division then marched by the church to join the battle. Once in the fight, it was said that Cheatham engaged Sherman's forces and drove them from their positions. We had no time to watch or participate.

By noon the Confederates were being driven back all along the line. We were then ordered to withdraw down the Corinth road. The physician we were assigned to, and his orderly, did as

ordered. Henry and I, not wanting to abandon the non-ambula-
tory wounded until wagons came for them, stayed.

By early afternoon Bragg's troops were withdrawn to a position a hundred yards north of the church. There they set up
astride the Pittsburgh-Corinth road, not a hundred yards from
us. After considerable fighting at that position, Bragg's line was
soon about to collapse. Being a hundred yards from the battle,
working in the open, and frequently going forward to assist the
newly wounded, it's a wonder we were not killed many times
over, even if only by a stray round.

In order to allow an orderly disengagement, a rear guard
position was prepared behind us to the south of the church. By
mid-afternoon the new position was complete. It was composed
of a hastily assembled force of two thousand infantry and some
cannons. With help, we managed to move our wounded just
south of them.

Beauregard's line made a final charge an hour later, which in the
end had little effect. A follow up of Beauregard's attack might have
won of battle, even at that late hour, but it was not followed up.

A couple of hours before dark a Confederate withdrawal
occurred. Small units continued to go by us on their way south
until dark. Some of them were lost. We assured them that they
were on the right road, and encouraged them to send back ambulances to pick up the most seriously wounded under our charge.
As far as we knew we were then between the two forces. We were
definitely left alone near the church with many of the non-ambu-
latory wounded. Later we would learn that some units from both
sides stayed all night in their position. They may have been afraid
of becoming lost or running into their enemy in the rain and
dark. Or, in the total confusion that existed, they might not have
received orders.

Knowing our duty, and our desperate situation, we stayed
throughout the night. Many of the wounded died that night,
lying in the mud and continuous rain. In one way the rain was

merciful. It spared us hearing moans that might have come from other locations on the battlefield. Hardly speaking at all and then only in a whisper, we did what little we could to comfort the wounded. They too knew the situation and muffled their moans. Their silent suffering brought tears to my eyes. I feel that Henry also shed tears, though the dark and rain would not allow me to know.

Before first light I said, "Henry, we're left alone here and must leave before dawn. Because we have no medical supplies, I'm sure these men will receive better care from the other side than we can provide."

He didn't reply, but we moved among the living telling them of this. Since it was frequently impossible to tell the dead from the living, I often found myself whispering to the dead. From the packs of the dead we took biscuits and crackers, some they had no doubt previously plundered from the packs of other dead soldiers. Expecting that soon after we left we would come under fire from one side or the other, we then changed the loads in our revolvers and loaded our rifles under our ponchos.

April 8, 1862

oping to avoid a direct confrontation with either side, and ultimately to wind up in Corinth, Henry decided we would move southeast. That direction would bring us to the river. There, we could turn southwest to Corinth. Their fortifications in place at Corinth, that was the destination of the Confederate troops. Gathering our gear, we slipped away as the first hint of light appeared through the dreary morning sky. Our ponchos folded across our belts to allow quiet movement, we flitted from cover to cover.

Within the first hour we saw two small units of CSA infantry. Not wanting to burden ourselves with their slow or indecisive movement, we avoided them. After another half-hour we were fired at by a group of soldiers concealed in a depression. Taking cover behind two trees, and without knowing what army they were from, we returned fire. The exchange of gunfire was furious for several minutes.

During a lull in the firing a voice called out, "Hey Reb."

Neither of us responded.

After a minute had passed the voice called out again, "Hey Reb. We're out of cartridges."

At that time Henry responded, "Come out, one at a time. Walk halfway to us and sit down. Leave your weapons where they are."

The voice answered, "I've got a friend, bad hurt."

"How many of you are there?" Henry asked.

"Five," the voice replied.

"Then those of you who are able come out," Henry said.

We watched as four Federal soldiers emerged, one by one, and took a seat twenty-five yards from us.

"You in the hole, can you speak?" Henry asked.

"Yes," came a reply.

"I'm a physician. I'll come help," Henry said. "If you shoot me, my friends," they couldn't know for sure there were only two of us, "will shoot your friends."

With that, Henry stood and walked toward the depression. He soon called for me to bring my bag. Since I had been issued a bag, we both had bags then.

We took a bullet from the soldier's hip in that depression. Having no antiseptic or disinfectant, we used only nature's water for the latter purpose. Without complaining, or uttering a loud sound, the soldier mercifully passed out as Henry probed for the bullet. Though we ignored them, the other four sat without moving as we worked on their friend.

After finishing the job, Henry called the corporal to us and asked, "Where are you men from?"

"Missouri mostly," replied the corporal. "Over around Kansas City."

Henry said, "We're physicians on our way to Independence. We were conscripted three days ago to help the Confederate troops, and we were near the church throughout the battle and until this morning. We probably worked on two hundred of your wounded."

"Then you're not taking us prisoner?" the corporal asked.

"Certainly not," I replied. "We only fired because you fired."

Henry said, "This man can't walk. The four of you will have to make litters from your rifles and coats and carry him. He also needs his wound washed out with alcohol." As he spoke, he opened his pack and passed out biscuits and crackers.

"I'd suggest you go straight east to the river and flag down a gunboat. East is the shortest way to the river. It's slightly more than a mile from here. There's also less chance of running into any Rebs that way. Your forces control the river," Henry said.

The corporal asked, "Where are you two going?"

"South. Then to Corinth," Henry said. "After that, we'll try to get past your armies and go to Independence."

We sat in silence for a short time, eating our biscuits and

crackers. Then introductions were passed around. The wounded man's name was Marvin Cutter. Having regained consciousness, he was in considerable pain.

The corporal said, "Sir, why don't you go with us? You could get past our armies easily that way."

The "sir" was probably because of us calling ourselves physicians.

Pointing, Henry said, "Ben, walk over by that tree. I need to talk with you."

At the tree he said, "Going with them could be a good idea, or not. Some officer might put in to search us and find our money. I don't know what might happen. Of course the same thing could happen in Corinth. We don't know how they'll react away from the battle. Or we could just make a run for it on foot and on our own. What do you think?"

After thinking for a moment, I said, "You best go ahead and make a decision. If you'll remember, those Rebs just lost the fight because of too many generals making decisions. I'm with you."

Returning to the Federal squad, Henry said, "Because we're not sure what kind of welcome we'll get in Corinth, we are tempted to go with you. But we're also concerned with our reception at your camp. Someone might try to take our weapons and goods."

"They'll have to take ours first," the corporal said.

His companions expressed the same sentiment.

Henry said, "We'll do it then. Ben, let's give them cartridges."

I guess we changed sides that day. Except that we had never been on a side. Carrying a stretcher, and our things, we were at the river in less than an hour, and on a gunboat bound for Pittsburgh Landing in less than two more. We got whiskey from the vessel's captain and cleaned Marvin's wound properly before landing.

Once ashore, we left Marvin in good hands and followed the

other four soldiers. Being from the First Missouri Artillery, they led us to Major General Lew Wallace. General Wallace was commanding the Third Division of the Army of the Tennessee under Major General Ulysses S. Grant. The First Missouri Artillery was assigned to Wallace.

Our reception by Wallace was not the best possible. He was in disfavor with General Grant for supposedly getting lost and for being slow in responding to marching orders during the fighting on April 6. Also, on the seventh he had apparently not been very aggressive in pushing his men forward. General Wallace, occupied with his personal and professional situation, referred us to General Grant. This referral turned out for the best. Without it we might never have seen General Grant. Even with the referral we had to tell the story two times before seeing him. Our audience with the general was supposed to be brief.

He asked, "What can I do for you men?"

Henry said, "Sir, we are two physicians on our way to Independence, Missouri. We were conscripted by the Confederates, and were near Shiloh Church during most of the fighting. We treated the wounded there, both theirs and yours. At daylight this morning we left the church and proceeded to the river. We met the corporal and his men and joined them to make our way here on a gunboat. Our wish, after helping you treat your wounded, is to be on our way to Independence with a pass from you." Henry said nothing of our exchange of gunfire.

The general asked, "What do you know about the current disposition of their troops?"

Henry replied, "Very little, sir."

Our brief audience turned into the better part of an hour, during which the general and his staff interrogated us. After providing factually correct, but little, information, we were sent to assist with the wounded. A colonel then brought us a pass that was signed by General Grant.

They took neither our guns nor supplies. It soon became

clear that the Union army was well armed and supplied. With their loss of soldiers from the two previous days, and their newly captured arms, they had an excess of individual arms. The Confederate forces had several regiments in camps of instruction near Corinth without a single adequate weapon among them. That was a fact we neglected to provide General Grant and his staff. Also, while we had operated with inadequate medical supplies on the Confederate side, the Federal hospital was well supplied. Bandages, quinine, ether, and chloroform were in abundance. All extreme cases were etherized before surgery.

While our two days of practice and training in surgery at Shiloh Church was not long, our experience in that time equipped us suitably to pass the scrutiny of the older and more able men. If the Federal forces were in want of any one thing at that time, it was for medical personnel. We soon earned a twelve-hour rotation at the twenty-four-hour-a-day job of helping the wounded. Our limited ability was probably overlooked because of the thousands who needed attention. We learned later that an estimated 33,000 men, on one side or the other, were injured or killed. Another 7,000 were missing. That estimate had to be a guess. I don't believe anyone knew how many men there were on each side to start with.

While working twelve-hour days over the following week, we filled our bags with medical supplies for the time we would depart. We also spent what little free time we had talking to the men, wounded and not, in order to learn the flow of the rivers and the lay of the land between us and Independence.

Since the need for us was decreasing rapidly, we soon agreed the time was near for us to leave. Thinking someone might detain us at the last minute, we decided to leave unannounced and secretively. Upon discovering that a supply boat, escorted by a gunboat, was leaving at first light on the morning of April 16, for Paducah, Kentucky, we decided to go.

April 16, 1862

rising early, Henry wrote us papers from General Grant ordering us to St. Louis, Missouri. He also wrote a letter to be shared among our new friends. We then shaved our weeks-old beards and dressed in the Federal officers clothing confiscated at Shiloh Church. Upon inspecting each other we agreed that no one would recognize us in those outfits, especially since it was still dark. Leaving our tent so as to arrive at the supply boat ten minutes before it left, we carried all of our property. The crew was preparing to shove off as we stepped aboard.

The captain came rushing over and said, "What's wrong?"

"Nothing," Henry said, as he produced a paper. "We've been ordered to St. Louis by General Grant on the first available transportation. We need to ride with you to Paducah."

"But gentlemen, I have no quarters for passengers," the captain said.

"We need no quarters," Henry replied. "We came prepared to sleep on deck. We also have our own food."

Hesitating only momentarily, the captain turned to the business of clearing the landing. We were soon in the flow of the river. Since no one had seen us leave, our method of departure would not soon be discovered. When our departure was discovered it would be of little consequence. Since everyone knew about our pass from General Grant, our departure would almost certainly not be reported to anyone.

Before the end of the fourth day we reached Paducah. It was a far easier trip than we would have had on horseback. After finding lodging for the night and storing our gear, we walked about and stretched our legs, had supper at a boarding house, and talked to different people for a change. All the while we were alert for another ride downriver.

On the second morning in Paducah we boarded a Federal

Navy vessel and that same day disembarked at Cairo, Illinois.

Having had great success and comfort traveling on the river, we decided to continue in that way. After changing into civilian clothes for the trip up the Mississippi River, we paid for our passage. Since the river was still contested at places by the two sides, a uniform would have made too good a target for a sniper.

Arriving in St. Louis on a steamer, we were sore tempted to remain there. A huge city, St. Louis had a population of 180,000, more than the entire state of Florida. Also, the city was a major shipping point to both the eastern states and the Gulf of Mexico, by train in the one case and barge in the other. Trade on the river was restricted, however, due to the control of the river still being contested in places.

Missouri being a border state, the east of the state, including St. Louis, was still not fully under Federal control. The west half of the state was under less control. At the start of the War, Missouri had two separate state governments. Each governed half of the state, and favored a different side in the War. While there was, then, only one state government in control, the secessionist element was still active; and the military situation there was still in turmoil other than in the garrisoned cities. There were still attacks on some of the garrisoned cities, especially in the western part of the state.

Although it had almost twenty times the population of Atlanta, St. Louis was not on a par with Atlanta in terms of the potential for exchanging Confederate paper money for specie. Even though secessionist sentiment was strong among some of the population, there was not a lot of trust in Confederate money. To make the matter worse, we found that the value of Confederate money had fallen. Its value was then two dollars and ten cents in Confederate paper for one silver dollar. We also discovered that there was considerable black market and smuggling activity in the city. Still, there was great potential in the city and we were hesitant to move on. The character of the city might have even been in our favor with Henry's previous success at trading. Having sent word that we would be in Independence, however, that became the deciding factor as to our final destination. Our mail would be there.

Henry posted a letter to Doctor Isaac telling him to please post copies of all future correspondence to St. Louis and Sedalia. Then, leaving our Federal uniforms stored in our packs, we caught the train for Sedalia. The Pacific Railroad extended some two hundred miles west of St. Louis to Sedalia. The rail's end was there.

We were waiting to depart when Marvin Cutter, walking with a limp and using two canes, boarded the train and set down facing us.

"I'm glad to see the two of you. It was with sorrow that I read your letter and discovered you were gone. I was pleased, however, that you thought of me," he said.

Shaking hands, I said, "When the need for our medical service declined, it was urgent that we proceed to Independence. We boarded a supply boat going downriver."

"We wondered how you left. After your departure I was given two months medical leave for my hip to heal. I'm headed for Kansas City and our farm. We won't be far apart once there. I owe you two my life from your care back at Pittsburgh Landing. Maybe my family can be of service to you in some way."

Henry replied, "It would be an honor to meet your family, but you owe us nothing. Your wound was easy to tend. I'm glad we got a good result."

"Not so," Marvin said. "Many around me died who were less wounded than I. I'm sure that I'm still alive only because of your insistence on washing my wound with alcohol."

"We're glad for the result and pleased to have your company," I said. "After spending some time with your family, maybe you would show us around the area."

Small talk about the war and his family and farm consumed

the better part of an hour. We had barely leaned back in our seats and become silent when a stranger seated nearby spoke.

"Pardon my interruption, gentlemen. I've been listening with interest to your conversation. I gather that the three of you were involved in the battle at Pittsburgh Landing. While I have the privilege of sitting near three of its participants, the whole world is reading with great appetite every morsel written about the battle. May I inquire further about your exploits and those of your units?"

Seeking to avoid publicity, Henry said, "I'm afraid our exploits were limited to tending the wounds of the heroes. There's little we could add to the accounts you've read in the paper."

"He's too modest, sir," Marvin said. "We met through an exchange of gunfire, though mistakenly started, and these two got the better of five of us."

Henry tried to end it then, but the chickens were out of the coop. Others had overheard, and Marvin was more than willing to expound on our adventures. To insure that the story was held within the bounds of reality, we told the whole thing—at least the part after we bumped into the Confederate Army. After the story was told, all three of us were elevated to the status of heroes for the rest of the trip.

Due to the excitement of the moment, introductions had not been made, an oversight corrected by our new acquaintance when the conversation lagged. Our chief inquisitor regarding the details was Lee Greystone. After the stories were over and quiet returned to the car, he further identified himself.

"Gentlemen, I'm on my way to Sedalia to purchase beef and other durable food products for the Federal government. Since the rails are only recently through to Sedalia, it's an untapped area." Speaking to Marvin he added, "You spoke of your family's farm. I'll pay top dollar for beef, sweet potatoes, or any other non-perishable farm products that can be delivered to Sedalia."

Marvin replied, "There might be little enough delivered. By

letter from home I hear that William Quantrill and others supportive of the Southern cause are active in the area. Movement by
a small group for the purpose of supporting either side would
undoubtedly draw opposition from advocates of the other.
Almost certainly it would be armed opposition."

The conversation was continued for some time. Sitting quietly, Henry was the only non-participant.

When all the conversations ended, Henry said to Mr.
Greystone. "Would you be kind enough to talk privately with
Ben and me. We would like to talk to you on a matter of busi-
ness."

Greystone replied, "It would be my honor."

When we were alone, Henry said, "You spoke of top dollar
for beef and Marvin said there would be little enough brought in
due to potential conflict. Ben and I have no cattle but we could
purchase cattle and deliver them. We would have to know what
top dollar meant before undertaking such a venture or it would
be foolish to invest."

It was several seconds before Lee said, "Naturally, I'll have to
negotiate each purchase in the best interest of the government. It
would seem, however, that the government is already in your debt.
Because of your service to the government, and in order to get the
flow of cattle started, I'll pay six dollars in silver for every adult cow,
steer, or bull you can deliver within the next ninety days, or at least
for those that don't appear sickly. We can shake hands on it now,
but only if you agree to keep the terms secret. I expect to buy some
cattle locally for as low as two-fifty in silver at first."

"When bought at the farm, the price of beef does stand at
two dollars and fifty cents a head in silver or gold. By the time we
pay wages, buy horses, pay for cattle, and drive them to Sedalia,
we would lose money with you paying us six dollars. There's also
the risk to life and limb, not to mention the potential loss of the
herd. I'm afraid you'll have to do better than that," Henry said.

After further conversation, Lee increased his offer to ten dollars a head for cattle that we gathered at a distance of twenty or more miles from the railroad. That offer only brought further negotiations.

Finally, Henry said, "We'll deliver cattle to Sedalia for fifteen dollars a head in gold or silver. Otherwise, I'm afraid you'll be riding throughout the countryside trying to avoid secessionists at the same time you gather a herd. For fifteen dollars a head we'll avoid buying local cattle so that you can acquire some local beef inexpensively. "

In the end we shook hands on Henry's offer.

Later, while still on the train, Henry said to Marvin, "Ben and I are going to buy horses in Sedalia and take a slower route to Independence than you'll take on the stage. Is your offer of assistance still good?"

"Of course," Marvin said.

"Then this is my request. I need seven men, with horses and rifles, for fifteen days' work. Each man will be paid twenty dollars in silver upon completion of the job. Since it'll be legal work, I'll expect them to use their rifles if needed. These men need to be supportive of the Federal position. They'll also have to be in Independence twelve days from now. Can you arrange that?"

"I would think so," Marvin replied. "A hard day's farm work earns only thirty cents; and common soldiers are paid only thirteen dollars a month. Can me, my brother, and pa be three of the seven?"

"You can be one, assuming you can ride with your injury." Henry replied. "If your pa has cattle he'll sell, I'll have another proposition for your brother and pa that should be more favorable. If he doesn't have cattle to sell, all three of you are hired."

Marvin said, "I could ride now with pain. We'll be ready when you're ready for us."

Securing two horses, a pack mule, and tack in Sedalia, and the location of several farms to the northwest from the local hostler, we proceeded. At each farm we sought to purchase cattle.

Except for the negotiated price, the same deal was made with each owner. Receiving one-third of the purchase price, the owner would hold the cattle for us for up to forty-five days. If we didn't return within forty-five days to pay the balance and collect the cattle, the owner would keep the cattle and the one-third payment. Our first purchase was for eight steers at $2.60 each. From each owner we discovered the location of another possible purchase to the northwest. Arriving at Independence eight days later, we had binders on 153 head of cattle. The average price paid was $2.55 a head in silver.

Finding no letter under the name of Henry, Ben, or Henrietta Williams in the post office at Independence, we proceeded to the Cutter farm. It turned out that Mr. Cutter owned forty-eight cattle, twenty-one of which he would sell.

Henry told Mr. Cutter our plan to pick up and deliver cattle, and added, "If you wish, you can add your cattle to our herd. I'll pay you two dollars and seventy-five cents a head and hire you for the trip or I'll pay you six dollars a head for them when we reach Sedalia. That's more than twice the going price here. If, however, we lose the herd, it's your loss in the second case. The only requirement is that you have to send one man on the drive for every twelve cattle in the second offer. These have to be men who are willing to use their rifles. Marvin has already agreed to go as one of the hired riders. My goal is to have a group large enough to defend the herd."

Mr. Cutter said, "Toby, my younger son, and I will go. I'll take the second offer"

Henry said, "If you have trusted and close friends to whom you wish to offer this same deal, we'll take them along. They'll also have to provide one rider for each twelve head, or part thereof, and carry their own supplies. Their presence will increase our safety. And I'll pay you fifty cents for every head so gathered that arrives in Sedalia."

When our hired riders arrived three days later we had a herd of 103 cattle gathered and were ready to start the drive. Nine additional rider/owners came with those already assembled cattle. Our seven hired riders, along with Henry and me, made a total of eighteen. That number was far in excess of the number of drovers required to control a herd that should grow to only 250 as we collected our purchased cattle along the trail.

Before leaving Independence, Henry sent a letter by stage to advise Mr. Greystone of our impending arrival in Sedalia by May 26. Following the route required to collect our contracted cattle, we then moved the initial herd out. Due to the large numbers of riders, the herd was easy to control. By noon the second day the initial herd had become so accustomed to travel that only four or five riders would have been required to keep them together.

There was only one incident of note during the trip. Riding out front on the fifth day, Henry and I were confronted by five riders.

Without introduction their leader asked, "Who owns these cattle and where are they bound?"

Answering without introduction, but moving his horse so that his rifle barrel came to bear on the speaker, Henry answered, "I, and several others, own the cattle. They are bound for the mouths of hungry people."

Henry's move did not go unnoticed by the strangers. Nor did the arrival of Marvin and eight armed men to our rear.

Speaking less forcefully, the stranger said, "I fear these cattle go to feed the wrong mouths."

To which Henry replied, "There's no right or wrong where hunger is concerned. I have no concerns about the political nature of those who eat my cattle. It might be best if you don't concern yourself either."

Perhaps it was the numbers on his side and ours that convinced the stranger of the rightness of Henry's argument. Wheeling their horses, they rode off. Though we expected to encounter them again when they were in greater number, we did not.

Acquiring some extra cattle along the way, we arrived in

Sedalia with 263. Our 263 cattle, though far more costly to Greystone, were more than three times what he had arranged to purchase otherwise in the same time. Also, the price of the local cattle he was buying was going up as his purchasing continued and the local supply decreased.

Not one to waste time, Henry assembled everyone the next morning and said, "In two weeks Ben and I will be in Paola, Kansas. We plan to start another drive from there. All seven of you drovers are offered the same pay to join that drive. I'll also need seven additional riders. If some of you owners are interested in being hired, Mr. Cutter will be hiring for that drive."

Mr. Cutter said, "I've already talked to the others. You can count on most of them for another trip. If some decide not to come, at the price you're paying I can get others."

Henry said, "You men know the danger. I tried to decrease it by showing force of numbers on this trip, and will for the next. That might or might not work next time. We'll be taking a different route, however, and aren't likely to encounter the same people. Please say nothing about our next drive. There's no need to invite trouble. I'll see you in Paola."

Leaving immediately, Henry and I rode south. After a full days' ride, toward the end of which we contracted for several cattle, we turned west. Arriving in Paola twelve days later, we had purchased options on 307 cattle at an average price of three dollars a head. Two days later Mr. Cutter arrived with thirteen riders. When introductions were finished, we set out to gather the cattle as we rode toward Sedalia.

At our first time alone, Marvin said to Henry and me, "I asked about the identity of the five men we met on the last trip. The descriptions of two of them are said to fit those of William Quantrill and Cole Younger. Their three companions were not known. It was fortunate that we outnumbered them, otherwise they might have caused serious trouble. Some of us could have ended up dead."

Henry replied, "I recognize the names, but don't know the men. This Quantrill and Younger must be men to be feared the way you speak of them."

Marvin said, "Yes. They're Southern sympathizers who head the largest and most destructive band of Rebel raiders in three states. They haven't been seen together since being in a battle on the Lowe farm on April sixteenth. Four were killed and five captured there. Quantrill and Younger escaped. Since then they've been raiding the farms and stagecoaches, and have been securing fresh mounts by whatever means necessary. No Union man's safe from them in western Missouri except in the garrisoned towns. Sometimes they even attack those."

I didn't say anything. Having seen Henry draw his revolver and fire it against both targets and men, I was thinking there would have been others who were buried that day. I also couldn't help but think of Coon, who practiced daily with his Remington revolver. He would have been a real asset in such a confrontation if he were with us.

Weaving both north and south to pick up the cattle being held for us at various locations, we traveled two hundred miles while making the hundred-mile trip to Sedalia. Securing additional cattle along the way, we arrived with 343 cattle in the herd.

With the $4,000 plus in silver and gold coin we made on that trip, our money had quadrupled due to the two trips. We then had over $10,000 in specie, which was left temporarily in the Sedalia Bank.

At supper that night Lee Greystone said, "I didn't expect you to have the kind of success you've had gathering cattle. Truthfully, I didn't think you had the financial resources or ability to operate at this level. I'm afraid I'm going to have to back out of our agreement that guarantees fifteen dollars for any you bring in. From now on I'll have to negotiate each bunch."

Henry said, "That's okay. We're out of the cattle business anyway. This area has been worked to such an extent that the profit would decline and the risk increase for future efforts. Over the next few months we'll remain in Missouri. We expect to be leaving, however, after all our business is complete. We're going to Independence on personal business. Maybe we can talk again at another time."

The stagecoaches to Independence having been stopped on a number of occasions by armed groups, we rode our horses. Upon arriving in Independence, Henry found a letter waiting at the post office.

Olustee, May 1, 1862

Dear Henry and Ben,

Trusting this finds you in good health, I can report that everyone here is the same. Having raised both cattle and hogs here on the farm, I find equal value in both. I couldn't attempt to advise you as to which you should raise. I'm becoming convinced that you'll be fine raising either. The safest course for the short term might be cattle. I think you could safely deal in cattle any place you choose.

Though everyone sends their love, Lilly wanted hers especially mentioned.

Yours in good health,
I. S.

"This letter was sent before our last letter to him," Henry said. "It sounds like the authorities aren't looking for us very hard, if at all. We're probably free to move around."

"They might not have been after us at all," I said.

"That's a possibility. I don't know how they would know about anything we did. But the safe thing for us is to stay here for awhile. We might come up with a way to increase our funds even though we can't be very successful trading Confederate paper money here. On balance, we've made more money here in the cattle business than we would have by trading all of our Confederate money elsewhere."

Giving credit where it should be, I said, "You mean you might come up with a way to make money. The plan's usually under way before I know what's going on."

"Whatever," Henry said. "We're partners."

We then posted a letter in return.

Sedalia, June 23, 1862

Dear Doctor Isaac,

We've been in the real cattle business here for almost two months. It has proven to be profitable.

Accepting your suggestions on raising cattle, we'll remain in Missouri for awhile. As I wrote earlier, please send copies of all mail to Sedalia and St. Louis. We occasionally have business in both places. Give our love to everyone.

Yours in good health,
Henry and Ben

While in Independence we learned that on June 11, even as we were speaking of him, Quantrill and his reassembled gang had attacked a mail carrier being escorted by twenty-five members of the Missouri State Militia. The attack was carried out between Independence and Pleasant Hill, less than ten miles from the post of the escort's commander. That was only one of many raids being carried out almost daily by one group of raiders or another. Fortunately, we hadn't encountered any of them. We had, however, been only fifteen miles from Quantrill's raid. Had we begun the drive near Kansas City, we would have driven right into them. The resulting fight would have almost certainly cost us those cattle already gathered, and some lives.

On June 24, we received a caller at our room in the boarding house from the lieutenant colonel who was in command of the Union garrison in Independence.

After offering an introduction at the door, he said, "It's said that you two provided medical service to General Grant at the battle at Pittsburgh Landing last April."

I said, "You've heard correctly. After treating hundreds of the wounded, both Union and Confederate, we were given papers providing us safe passage by General Grant."

"So I've heard," he replied. "Due to conflicts with Quantrill and other riffraff sympathetic to the Southern cause, we find ourselves in frequent need of medical services. I was hoping to get you to ride with some of our patrols in pursuit of Quantrill."

Henry said, "You need to understand that we hold no particular political position."

The colonel said, "I was told that you gathered and sold beef to the purchasing agent in Sedalia for our armies."

"That's true," Henry said. "But that was because we were here and the business was here. Were we in Georgia, we would be selling beef to Bragg's commissary. If you or your men have wounds that require attention, we'll attend them without charge beyond our board and medicine costs. We don't plan to ride in the field on behalf of either cause. If you ever have need of our services, you have but to send a message. You might soon find us in St. Louis, and occasionally in Sedalia."

That night, Henry said, "I'm inclined toward going to St. Louis and hanging out a shingle. We could enjoy a comfortable life while we see what business opportunity presents itself, and let some of the war pass."

"Fine. I'm ready to settle down in one place long enough to talk to a girl more than to say howdy and good-bye," I said.

Aware of the frequent raiding by Southern sympathizers

throughout the area, we rode cautiously, avoided all roads on the way back to Sedalia. Our camps were made in concealed areas away from farm or ranch. It was a dangerous time and we were in an area of conflict.

Once back in Sedalia, we again had a conversation with Lee Greystone about the purchase and sale of beef.

Lee said, "The arrival of beef and farm goods has slowed to a trickle since the delivery of your last herd. Why don't you two get back in the cattle business?"

"The farmers and ranchers have increased their prices. Besides that, Quantrill and other Southern sympathizers are alert to such ventures as we carried out. It's far too risky even if you raised the price you were paying us. I'm afraid we'll have to decline the offer," Henry replied.

"I can offer twenty dollars a head in greenbacks. The army needs the food," Lee said.

"We're going to St. Louis and hang out our shingles while some of the war passes. It's our desire to return to Atlanta and reopen our office there. I fear, however, there will be little left of Atlanta after the war. There might be some future time when we'll deal in cattle. But for now, we'll leave it to others, " Henry said.

"Well, I'm going to be here buying. If you change your minds, contact me," Lee said.

July 3, 1862

*W*e arrived in St. Louis four days later. Already a large city, its population was still growing from refugees seeking a safe haven from raiders. In addition to the city's population growth, there was a growing business in trade on the river. The river was the safest and most reliable means of transport when traveling north and south but even that wasn't completely safe. Gangs would frequently force boats to shore to rob the passengers. Like Quantrill and other groups in western Missouri, there were also raiders on a smaller scale in eastern Missouri that made travel unsafe.

Having sold our horses, other than housing for ourselves, we needed only an office. A small but comfortable house was bought for the sum of $630 in specie. All things brought a high price in those days. It would have cost $850 in Federal greenbacks. The owner wouldn't take Confederate paper money, the value of which had then dropped to $2.25 for one dollar in silver.

Since the population of St. Louis had increased without an increase in physicians, we had an abundance of patients. Quinine, chloroform, ether, and other medicines being more available than in areas under CSA control, the practice of medicine was much easier. We settled in to let some time pass. I was soon practicing medicine full time. While practicing medicine half time, Henry spent the other half of his time around the waterfront and other business areas. Though our income from medical services was substantial, he made more on his small dealing than our combined income from the medical practice.

We didn't allow ourselves to become too busy to enjoy the social life of the city. Due to the number of refugees, the proportion of women and children to men was almost as high as it had been in Atlanta. As usual, Henry soon became restless. Stating a need to be out of town, he departed on August 9 for Sedalia to visit Lee Greystone.

Henry was still in Sedalia when a rider brought news on the morning of August 13 that Quantrill and several hundred men had attacked Independence on August 11. When the rider left Independence for Sedalia, the outcome of the battle was not known. Immediately securing a buggy and driver so he could sleep on the way, Henry departed for Independence to fulfill his promise of medical assistance.

After changing horses three times along the way, Henry arrived in Independence late on August 14. He found over a hundred wounded soldiers there, mostly from the Union side. The raiders had carried their less severely wounded with them. Counting the wounded and those not wounded, 150 Union officers and men were still there. Having been captured in the raid, and exchanged for Southern prisoners held by the Union, the colonel and his men were tending their wounded. Those able to walk left on foot the next day for Kansas City. Under the rules of the prisoner exchange program they would be mustered out of the service in Kansas City. Henry then stayed on in Independence for several days and assisted those who were too seriously wounded to walk.

Arriving back in St. Louis on August 31, the outline of our next venture in place, Henry seemed quite content to spend the fall and winter in the city. We quickly settled into a life of medicine, trading, and social engagements.

Over the fall and winter we received two letters from Doctor Isaac. It was apparent from their content that other letters had been mailed that we never received. Information in the two letters clearly showed that the doctor had not been able to determine if we were wanted by the CSA, and if so, why? It appeared that we were not wanted.

During that time our wealth was increasing slowly, but increasing. Henry had invested most of our funds. Quite happy with our life, I never inquired of Henry as to our financial position. I knew that Henry had invested $10,000 in gold and silver for a major interest in a hotel and some riverfront property, which the bank administered.

One day in March, I became fully aware of our wealth, and the results of his trip to Sedalia the prior August when Henry said, "We have $3,000 in specie I'd like to invest in a risky venture. I feel I should discuss this with you before committing. There's considerable risk involved. The plan will also require leaving our office and St. Louis. It'll also involve some personal risk."

I said, "I hate to leave St. Louis. We're comfortable here. But we're going to leave sooner or later so tell me the plan."

"While in Sedalia last August, I had the good fortune of being called to Independence. There I met a hundred and fifty officers and men who were prisoners of war exchanges. They were soon to be mustered out of the army. After interviewing many soldiers, I made a business proposition to twenty-four of them. If they receive a letter from me in time to do so, they are to meet us in Sedalia on April fifteenth. Each man is to bring a horse and weapon for a dangerous trip about which they know nothing except that, if the trip is successful, they will receive one hundred dollars each in Federal greenbacks for less than two months' work. Marvin's pa will also meet us if requested. He'll receive two hundred if the trip is successful."

Unable to restrain myself, I asked, "And what is this dangerous work?"

"It's about cattle," he replied. "I've reached an agreement, through Lee Greystone, with the Union government to pay us thirty-five dollars a head in Federal greenbacks for a herd to be delivered before June tenth. The herd must be delivered to Greystone in Sedalia. Though the value of the greenback fluctuates, and is now thirty percent less valuable than specie, it's still good. After the war it might even be equal to specie."

"Every Southern sympathizer in Missouri will be after us," I said. "I see less than a fifty percent chance of success."

Undaunted, Henry said, "At this time only you, Greystone,

the general commanding the Missouri Militia, the Federal government, and I know about this. Only I know the whole plan. The general knows some of it. Taking eight men each, you, Marvin's pa, and I will go to different locations and start buying cattle. You'll take an area in southeast Kansas, Marvin's pa will take an area in the southwest corner of Missouri, and I'll work between you two. I've drawn up areas on a map. Purchasing what we can, or acquiring them by whatever means is reasonably safe, we'll each attempt to collect a herd of two hundred fifty cattle. You'll bring your cattle together southeast of Fort Scott, Kansas. I'll assemble mine north of Carthage, Missouri, and the third herd will be gathered west of Bolivar, Missouri. The spread of the operation will decrease the chance of total failure. Each of us will have our herd assembled at the designated point, regardless of the number of cattle acquired, by May ninth. The timing of our operation is vital. If we're too early, there won't be enough grass for a large herd of horses and cattle. Delaying might cause us to be raided by Southern cavalry units from Arkansas. They can also move quickly once the grass is tall enough for their horses."

"It's just bold enough to work," I said.

"If the whole thing works we could make twenty thousand dollars. If only one of the three of us gets through with a herd, we can salvage a small profit."

"What happens from our gathering point?"

"We drive our herds to Collins, Missouri, and assemble them into one. Garrison troops from Clinton, Nevada, Springfield, and Sedalia, Missouri, will meet us there, two hundred altogether, and escort us to Sedalia. In either case, fail or succeed, I plan to return to Atlanta and trade the balance of our Confederate paper money into anything we can acquire of value. The gold or silver value of Confederate paper money has depreciated significantly since we left Atlanta. Still, they keep printing it. If we're successful at trading money in Atlanta, we'll return to Florida. We've been gone too long. We might be needed there as the war ends."

Over the next two weeks we closed our practice in St. Louis. We also tried to get all the news we could of the continuing conflict across western Missouri. Nothing had been heard of Quantrill since his unsuccessful raid on the garrison in Lamar, Missouri, on November 5, when the town was set on fire. Quantrill's group also had two of their members killed and several wounded. It was rumored that he and his band had been in Arkansas for the winter and that Quantrill was in Virginia to see President Davis.

While nothing was heard from Quantrill, other smaller groups of raiders robbed and harassed throughout Missouri almost at will. Riverboats were still being fired on and forced to shore so passengers could be robbed, the mail was frequently taken and searched for valuables, stagecoaches were robbed, and various groups raided farms to supply themselves with horses and food. Smaller units of the Missouri militia were also attacked to get their weapons and horses. It was reported that a horse, tack, and rifle would bring seventy-five dollars in Kansas. These could have been bought for less than ten dollars three years earlier.

Twenty of the invited men answered Henry's call to Sedalia. Six also brought one friend each who desperately needed the money and who were supportive of the Union cause. Including Marvin's pa and ourselves, we were twenty-nine.

After riding with the group to a point three miles from town, Henry called a halt, gathered everyone around, and said, "Men the mission we're going on is dangerous. Because this is a trip that supports the Union cause, it's possible we could be fired on. Before I say more, I'm giving each of you a chance to mount and ride off. After I've explained our mission, no one will be allowed to quit or leave us. Anyone who does will be tracked down and shot dead. We'll not be doing anything that doesn't have the support of the Federal government and Missouri militia. If any of you wish to leave now, you can mount up and leave no questions asked."

After most of a minute had passed and no one spoke up or left, Henry added, "I want everyone to be clear about what I just said. Is there anyone who didn't hear, or didn't understand what I said?"

No one said anything. They were all looking Henry straight in the eyes. I was thinking about Sam's bar back east of the Suwannee River, those boys outside Fort Pickens, and those near Tallahassee, and was hoping these men were aware of his veracity.

When no one left, Henry outlined the plan. Producing letters from the Federal government authorizing our venture, he gave copies to Marvin's pa and me. Henry also produced copies of papers from Confederate Cavalry Colonel Warner Lewis, who was known to have been in southwest Missouri in November of '62. The colonel's letter authorized us to gather cattle for Shelby's Confederate troops in Arkansas.

After reading the papers out loud, he said, "We'll use whichever paper we need at the time. The one from Lewis should get you by unless you run into him personally. I understand, however, that he might currently be with Shelby in Arkansas."

We split up at that point, each group riding directly to the area they would start their cattle gathering operation. I had little difficulty gathering my cattle. The only unusual occurrence of any magnitude happened when we had gathered 113 cattle. They were stampeded on purpose one night. After getting all of them back but ten, I set two men to tracking those ten, and the men who were driving them. My men gave up after a few hours and returned. They said they had quit the trail fifteen miles to the south. We arrived at Collins on schedule with 206 cattle.

By the next day at noon Marvin's pa arrived with 263 cattle. They had been confronted by two separate small groups of mounted Southern sympathizers. After being shown the letter from Colonel Lewis, those Southern sympathizers actually provided assistance in gathering cattle for a couple of days.

Henry's group arrived late the same day that Marvin's pa

arrived. His group was driving 217 head of cattle. They also had three more horses than they left with.

When asked about the horses, Henry said, "We had a small encounter and I brought the spare horses along. I also gave a cow to a group of Indians. They had hungry children and might have otherwise caused trouble. Giving them the cow seemed like a good investment. Otherwise, everything went smooth."

Henry never was one to elaborate or exaggerate. One of the three riders who were riding with Henry at the time told more of the story. Riding a couple of miles out front of the herd, they were confronted by seven armed men. One of the seven, probably unaware of the cattle drive and men behind Henry, said, "We're taking your guns and horses."

The rider then described the action that followed the announcement.

"Drawing his revolver before anyone could move, Henry shot two of them dead. When we got into action another of their group was killed and a fourth was wounded. Startled by the swiftness and result of Henry's action, everyone on both sides sat frozen for a moment. I'll swear it's the quickest thing I've ever seen. The others rode for their lives. Henry dug the bullet from the wounded man, put him on his horse, and sent him after his companions."

There was no cavalry escort at Clinton as promised, and we didn't wait for one. Neither seeing nor hearing from the military, we reached Sedalia without further incident. Having made note of the wrong day to meet us, the cavalry detachment arrived in Clinton two days late. Riding hard, they then arrived in Sedalia only hours behind us.

Upon reaching Sedalia we were told that there had been no report of organized Rebel activity in the area through which our operation took place. Later we were to learn that Quantrill was indeed in Virginia. One of his followers was two hundred miles west of us in Kansas, leading a raid near Council Grove, Kansas.

No Southern group of any size was operating where we were. Our good fortune on this venture was just one of a series of favorable circumstances as we ended our stay in Missouri and headed back to Atlanta.

Of the $24,000 in greenbacks coming to us, Henry collected enough to pay off the men. He gave each man a $20 bonus. The balance was received in the form of a warrant on call against the Federal treasury, which would draw interest at eight percent annually until called. In addition to the money from the herd, we still had $1,400 of our $3,000 in specie with which we started the operation.

May 22, 1863

Since our business in Missouri was temporarily finished, we boarded an eastbound train for Louisville, Kentucky. Wearing our blue officer's uniforms, and armed with travel orders to report to General Rosecrans, we went unchallenged. Rosecrans had been assigned command of the Union army that was advancing toward Chattanooga and Atlanta.

Our cargo, contained in two large bags, included quinine and other medical supplies that were in short supply in Confederate-held areas. Due to the blockade, quinine was almost nonexistent in Confederate-held areas of the South. It was the most valuable item we could carry short of gold. To a person with malaria, quinine might be more valuable than gold. Traveling as physicians under orders, our bags should neither be searched nor seized. If they were searched, what more likely items would a physician carry to war? While ours was a cargo that would make us valuable to either side, if not discovered it would make us considerable money and very popular in Atlanta.

In Louisville we learned that General Rosecrans' main logistical headquarters and supply unit was in that city. Since they were shipping Rosecrans supplies from Louisville, trains were running south from there regularly. In spite of the regularity, the Louisville to Nashville railroad was not highly recommended. It was referred to as the railroad to and from hell by some of the officers with whom we spoke. Since half of the residents of the area through which it ran favored each side, every individual had a reason to either expedite or derail the train. Given this information, we secured places on the supply train that was protected from the occasional sniper's fire.

After five days of frequently delayed travel, we arrived in Murfreesboro, Tennessee, where Rosecrans' army was entrenched. There, we inquired about, and were pointed toward, General Rosecrans' quarters. While walking in the opposite direction, we came upon four saddled horses standing without use and unattended. Tying our bags on two, and mounting the other two, we rode south by the railroad track right-of-way toward Tullahoma, Tennessee, some thirty-five miles away. Riding past one Federal unit after another, Henry continually asked about the location of their most forward position.

Finally, Henry repeated his statement for the last time.

"We're looking for your most forward position."

A sergeant answered, "You've found it, sir. We're the advance pickets. There's nothing beyond us but our patrols and Johnny Reb."

"No, Sergeant," Henry said, "there's railroad and trestles beyond you. We have orders from General Rosecrans to blow some."

"No disrespect sir," the sergeant answered, "but that's the most cautious man I know. We're sitting here with over sixty thousand men and should have been in Chattanooga months ago."

"If we don't see you before, we'll see you in Atlanta," Henry said.

Rosecrans had stated that he saw himself riding into Atlanta.

"Good luck," the sergeant said.

"Thanks," Henry said, as we touched our heels to our horses and rode off down the tracks toward Tullahoma. Henry always said the bold way was the best way.

Two miles past the pickets we changed into our civilian clothes, raised a white rag on a rifle barrel, and proceeded toward Tullahoma. Within four more miles we came upon a Rebel cavalry patrol.

While the patrol members were holding their weapons on us, a lieutenant asked, "What's the purpose of the white flag?"

"To keep you boys from shooting us. We've been doing some spying for General Bragg and need to get to Tullahoma and see him. Here's a pass the general gave us at Shiloh," Henry said, as he produced the paper.

"By Jove, I know this man. The mention of Shiloh placed him for me," a corporal said, pointing at me. "He cut a minié ball out of me at the Shiloh Church. It saved my life."

I said, "I'm sorry I don't remember you, Corporal. I must have worked on five hundred men in a few days."

The lieutenant said, "Corporal, take two troopers and escort these men on in. See that they're treated properly."

"Lieutenant," Henry said, "you just as well all go. I can tell you everything you need to know. Rosecrans' advanced picket is six miles north of here. They haven't moved in months and don't plan to move anytime soon. We have more information than a dozen patrols could gather. Why don't you and the corporal arrange to personally escort us to General Bragg? It's a good way to get his eye."

Seeing the wisdom of that statement, and the potential for him personally, the lieutenant immediately turned his patrol south. We had to stop and talk with a colonel along the way but we got our personal escorts into Tullahoma to see General Bragg. The general recognized us that time.

After we explained to him how we had gotten through the Union lines, the general said, "Unbelievable," to everyone within hearing. "These men, with one young helper, raided Fort Pickens in Florida. They killed a score of Federal soldiers there. Later, they set up a hospital at Shiloh Church for me. Now they've ridden through Rosecrans' entire force on confiscated Union horses asking the way to us. If I had five thousand like them, I'd kick Rosecrans' butt in a night attack tonight."

I thought he was kind of stretching things a little. There were only four of them at Fort Pickens, and it was thirty-five miles to Rosecrans' main positions. We couldn't even get there until the next day. Also, counting his reserves and supply lines, Rosecrans commanded 100,000 men.

Henry said, "General, after you get through interrogating us, we would like a train ride to Atlanta. You can keep the horses and rifles but we'll need a warrant for them."

Bragg said, "Men, there's going to be a huge battle here when Rosecrans moves. I'm going to need you two and more like you." Waving his hands toward his troops he added, "These men are going to need you again."

"General, you can take my word on this, Rosecrans has no immediate plan to move against you. Even his enlisted men are grumbling about him being so slow and deliberate. When and if he moves, or you move on him, Ben and I'll be on your first train coming this way. We'll stay the thing out, too. We plan to be in Atlanta for three or four months," Henry replied.

Turning to a colonel, General Bragg said, "Write these men a pass over my name. You can also put them on a train to Atlanta as soon as we're through interrogating them. They'll also need a warrant for six hundred dollars in specie for their horses, tack, and rifles."

"We've still got your pass from Shiloh," Henry said.

"You'll need one with a newer date and my current title on it," General Bragg said.

On May 13, we found ourselves aboard a train arriving in Atlanta after a 140-mile trip that took all day and into the night. Atlanta was packed with people. While there was a large number of garrison soldiers, lots of the people were also refugees. The city was in a state of apprehension never before seen. There was a growing threat even to this safe haven—but Atlanta was one of the safest of safe havens. Everyone was flocking there. Women and children, their husbands, sons, and fathers gone to war, were everywhere. Because of the lateness of the hour and the crowded conditions when we arrived, it was impossible to get quarters. Since there was a continuing rain we persisted in the quest for shelter until we got a tent for the night.

Once settled in, I asked Henry, "Why did you bother to get a warrant for the horses and rifles? It has little or no value."

He replied, "Something's better than nothing. The general was bound to have the horses and rifles anyway."

I said, "What'll we do for housing? We've been told that housing can't be had for love or money."

Henry replied, "Why don't you try to locate Jolene tomorrow while I visit the bank? She might be able to help. You said you were enamored with her. Love might be better than money in this situation."

Quite happy with that assignment, I soon went to sleep.

We stayed in the tent until mid-morning when the rain stopped. Henry then hired a rig and driver in order to keep our supplies with him. His first stop was at the bank. I proceeded on foot in search of Jolene.

Later, Henry reported some of his day to me.

Obtaining an audience with the bank owner, Henry said, "Sir, my partner and I are physicians who have just arrived from St. Louis by way of Tullahoma. We have papers of introduction from General Bragg and are on call to the general when the battle erupts north of Chattanooga. In the meantime we're going to reestablish a practice that we had going last year. We want two things from you. The first is to open an account with a thousand dollars in gold coin. When we withdraw it, it must also be in gold. No paper will be accepted. Secondly, we need adequate accommodations in which to live and practice medicine."

The banker replied, "I can meet your banking needs. Other than if you were sharing with a close relative, I don't believe there's a house to be had in Atlanta."

Standing, Henry said, "My partner and I have at our disposal a rather large supply of scarce medicine, including quinine and chloroform. Hopefully, you or yours will not fall ill in the near future."

Rising also, the banker said, "It's almost noon. Return here at two and let's talk again."

Henry never deposited any money in the bank. It was tucked away in jars ready for our quick departure, or for burial.

While Henry was talking to the banker, I was walking about the city seeking Jolene without success. Rounding the corner of a building I came face to face with an attractive young woman who stopped and stared at me.

After staring for several seconds, she said, "It's you. As sure as I live and breathe it's you."

Being certain that I had seen her before, but not immediately remembering where, I said, "Refresh my mind, ma'am. I can't remember where we last met."

"At Sam's, on the Suwannee," she said.

Though she was dressed quite differently, I recognized her then. Dressed much like the other female residents her age in Atlanta, she was quite striking. Recalling her name from the paper we had all signed describing the incident at Sam's, I spoke to her using her name.

"Of course, Alice. I remember you. Though you were quite attractive to me at the time, in your new attire you're stunning. I was expecting to see anyone but you. I would never have recognized you. What causes you to be in Atlanta?"

She was stunning, but I was mostly just stunned to see her there.

"I was shocked by what happened at Sam's that night. I left Florida and came to Atlanta. I'm married to a captain who's been assigned to General Bragg in Tullahoma," she said. "My other life's behind me now. No one knows about it here."

"That's how it should be," I said. "Henry and I've been studying to be physicians and are seeking quarters in which we can also establish an office. I could purchase lunch and you could search your mind to determine if you know of anything suitable."

We continued our conversation while eating. "I can't for the life of me think of a vacant or available place," she said.

"We'll find something," I said. "We spent last night in a tent and can do the same tonight. It was a miserable night, what with the rain."

Looking down at the table, she said, "Well, I have a small house. It's only two small rooms. I could spend the night with an acquaintance and you two could stay in my house for a couple of nights while you find a place."

"That would be great," I said. "I'll walk you home so I can find the place after I meet Henry."

Upon arriving at her place, she asked me in for a drink of water. "I would offer coffee," she said. "But on a captain's pay, and due to the blockade, it's far too expensive for us. I've been trying to find work but there's too many people in Atlanta for the amount of work."

We sat for most of two hours, sipping water and talking to each other. We must have talked about everything we had in common—Florida, the Suwannee River, and our travels to Atlanta.

Arriving at the tent later, I waited but a few minutes before Henry arrived.

He said, "We've been promised a house after the next day or

so. Also, I've sent a package of medicine and a letter to Doctor Isaac. I mentioned you to Mary."

"We have a house for the next two nights," I said.

I explained as we rode to Alice's house. Henry also stopped the rig long enough to purchase a supply of food, some coffee, and a couple of bottles of corn whiskey for medicinal purposes. We hadn't brought any whiskey on our trip because of the weight of it, and the fact that it was available everywhere.

Once inside the house, Henry said to Alice, "Ben told me about your situation and you have my admiration. His description of your radiance, however, was inadequate. I'm upset about putting you out of your house, even for a day."

"Thank you." Alice said.

"Indeed," Henry said. "We'll be in your house no more than two nights. The banker's making arrangements."

All the while he was placing his sleeping roll in the corner of the living room.

He continued, "We've brought supplies. Maybe you would be good enough to cook for all three of us. Ben said you were looking for work and we've agreed to ask you to work for us. We'll pay a modest sum to start. Someone's needed in the house from mid-morning until after supper Monday through Friday. The job is to clean the house and to cook the noon and evening meals. You would eat with us of course. You will also be assigned other duties around town on some days."

We hadn't discussed employing her, but having no objection I remained silent.

Alice looked like a heavy weight had been removed from her shoulders. Her energy level increased greatly as she set about making coffee and preparing supper.

We had hardly finished eating when Henry excused himself by saying, "I met some old friends today who I'm going to call on. Since I won't be in until eleven or twelve tonight, I'll sleep in the living room so I don't have to disturb you as I come in."

Having said that, he took one of the two bottles of whiskey and a half a pound of coffee, and departed. I didn't hear him come in that night, but he was there fast asleep shortly after daylight when I went out to cook breakfast and make coffee.

By June, the value of Confederate paper money had dropped to six and a half dollars to one dollar in silver and was still dropping. Due to the disparity in value of different types of money and the shortage of housing, we paid $6,000 in Confederate paper for a five-room house. We each then had a room for sleeping and another for an office. The other room was used for cooking and eating. Our patients waited their turn on the porch.

The growing population in the city provided us with more patients than we could provide service. Unfortunately, many of them had little money so we were back in the trading business. Though silver and gold pieces were our favorites, books were more plentiful, and were also of good value. Prices being exorbitant, we also accepted payment enough in food, whiskey, and other supplies that we rarely purchased anything and then only with Confederate paper.

It was on June 12 that Jolene showed up at our door. Alice being away at the time, I showed her into the kitchen for a conversation. When she was seated across the table from me, I inquired about her health and happiness.

She began shaking and, loud enough for Henry and his patient in the adjoining room to hear, blurted out, "After you and Henry left, I married a lieutenant. He was sent off to Chattanooga a week ago. I'm living with Mother again and have no job or money. It's terrible."

In less than a minute Henry came in and poured himself a cup of coffee.

Sitting, he said, "Ben, I've moved my patient to your office and would like for you to examine her. I'll talk with Jolene while you do that."

When I dismissed the patient and returned, Jolene was quite calm.

Henry said, "I've employed Jolene two days each week. On Tuesday and Friday she'll do the cleaning and cooking. Alice can spend those days trying to sell some of the things we've acquired. Also, Alice will purchase things for potential resale that she finds inexpensive. We'll hire Jolene full time if that proves successful."

I noticed, thereafter, that Jolene bestowed most of her favors on Henry, mostly little things like the way our plates were served and our chairs positioned. He paid her no mind in my presence and they were never seen in public together, yet Jolene seemed happy after that.

On June 28, we received a wire from General Bragg's aide. "The enemy has begun moving. Pray have your affairs in order so you can come and assist."

We also received a letter from Florida.

Olustee, Florida, June 12, 1863

Dear Henry and Ben,

Our happiness was without bounds upon hearing of your good health and receiving the supplies you sent.

It finally comes out that the three men being sought were deserters. No one knows of your affair near Tallahassee. There's also no record of any missing soldiers that fits that time or circumstance. Additionally, there's no report on file related to any incident such as you had. They must have been deserters. It's quite clear that you can return to Lulu when you choose. The hogs have all been sold.

Some while back we purchased the hundred-acre farm next door to May's at a price of $1,200 in Confederate paper. Of that amount $700 was for the land and $500 for the buildings. The value of Confederate money has decreased significantly since our purchase. It was money well spent.

Everyone's in good health and still living with May.
Lilly sends her love.

As Always,

I. S.

Laughing, I asked, "And to whom do you think Lilly sends her love?"

Henry smiled and said, "She's your sister. To you I suppose."

I replied, "We've been gone a year and eight months. Lilly's sixteen. She looked sixteen when she was thirteen."

Henry said, "I guess everyone has grown up. Mary will turn fourteen in December."

His comment set my mind to thinking about that loose flour sack dress she was wearing back at Blountstown.

Henry posted a reply to Doctor Isaac before we left the post office.

Atlanta, June 24, 1863

Dear Doctor Isaac,

We were glad to receive your letter regarding the hogs. Unfortunately, we've obligated ourselves to General Bragg for a short time. There will soon be a major battle near Tullahoma. Every possible person will be needed to care for the wounded. Even as I write, the armies move.

We are enclosing this letter in another small shipment of supplies. The supplies were not all sent at one time for fear they would become lost or stolen.

I look forward to seeing Lilly. She must be a striking figure of a woman by now. I pray that she's reading and doing numbers daily under Ma's guidance. Give our love to everyone.

Your obedient servants,
Henry and Ben

The next day another wire arrived. "There's contact all along the line. The enemy advances on a fifty-mile-wide front. Please come immediately."

Asking Jolene to sit with the house and advise patients as to the reason for our departure, we left on the next train. Arriving in Chattanooga that same day, we found that General Bragg was leaving his positions in Tullahoma and building breastworks in Chattanooga. Bragg was outnumbered, 62,000 to 42,000 by deployed troops. Additionally, Rosecrans had 38,000 other troops in his supply line. Bragg was abandoning Tullahoma to keep his flanks from being turned by Rosecrans' wings. Had that happened, Bragg would have almost certainly been defeated.

We stayed on in Chattanooga for a few days even though our services were not needed. In addition to the army's own, there were a number of volunteer nurses and doctors to attend the every need of a relatively small number of wounded, a situation brought about by Bragg's withdrawal to Chattanooga. After a few days we boarded a train and returned to Atlanta.

There was great anxiety by the people of Atlanta. If Chattanooga were captured, only ninety miles of railroad would separate Rosecrans from the city. There were also shortages of some things and the problem was growing. Corn, which had been less than a dollar a bushel two years before, was now bringing eight in Atlanta. Whiskey, which had been bringing twenty cents a gallon, was now $1.60. All other things were equally inflated.

Because Alice then had a mother and four children living with her in her two-room house, and because she was frequently at the office late cleaning up, she was occasionally spending the night at our house. There were more crowded conditions in Atlanta than those in Alice's house, however. In some cases a dozen people lived in two rooms.

Malaria was then a scourge that afflicted soldiers and civilians alike. Dysentery was rampant, brought about by unsanitary conditions in the crowded city. Neither soldier nor civilian morale was high. Times were hard.

Through all of this we were doing well. A seemingly endless supply of quinine, and other medical supplies, made our place the most visited physician's office in the entire area. We had to limit the number of patients we treated and were faced with a moral dilemma. What percent of our efforts should be directed toward the poor and what part toward the wealthy? What charges should we make to insure a profit worthy of our foresight, efforts, and ingenuity while still avoiding trying to drain the last drop of blood from the turnip? At that time, many people were without resources. Adding to the problem for many, Confederate paper money had deteriorated to the point that it took seven and a half dollars in Confederate paper to equal one dollar in silver.

We were offered anything and everything that can be imagined for quinine and other scarce medical supplies. Although large, unfortunately our supply of quinine was not without limit.

In order to insure that only our patients were allowed through the gate, we finally hired a man to stand at it. Armed, he was there from 7:00 A.M. until dark. Though that provided good order during the day, there were still frequent knocks on the door at night.

Working diligently, we saw our fortune grow as the weeks passed. At every opportunity we converted Confederate paper money into specie, or into valuable items in other forms. Our worth in Confederate paper money still remained large. As a result of Confederate paper being the only currency owned by many, and because of its low value, we still received quite a bit of it for our services.

Jolene was soon employed full time so that Alice could work the shops and houses full time. She was both buying and selling items. Alice met no strangers—she was at ease around everyone. Studying reading and numbers with me every night also added to her value. In spite of her success at selling, we were acquiring more things than we disposed of. We soon shipped another box to Aunt May for safekeeping.

Having a large number of patients, I was so busy that I had little free time. Henry, on the other hand, spent only part of his time at the office. His other time was spent at some of the same pursuits in which Alice was engaged.

September 5, 1863

Two months passed after our return from Chattanooga. During that time we heard nothing from General Bragg's aide. Rosecrans was still sitting at Tullahoma. His troops were still spread over a fifty-mile-wide front. His advance units were busily rebuilding the roads and rail lines that Bragg had ordered destroyed to the Tennessee River. Bragg, in the meantime, was fortified in Chattanooga and receiving reinforcements. We expected to receive a wire any day, but only received a letter.

Olustee, August 20, 1863

Dear Mr. Williams,

Hoping to find you in good health, I take pen in hand to write that we received the boxes you sent. All things were enclosed as your inventory described. I fear it might soon become too risky to trust items to shipment. You should probably make other disposition of such items in the future.

We look forward to your returning but also understand that you need to live out your obligation.

Everyone sends their love, especially Lilly. We are all in good health thanks to your packages.

As always,

I. S.

Henry posted a letter in return.

Atlanta, September 5, 1863

Dear Doctor Isaac,

We are well. Due to an inevitable battle, we expect to be summoned back to Chattanooga at any moment.

Please tell Coon to drop whatever he's doing and take the earliest and fastest transportation to Atlanta. If he has a close friend who's a good shot, and not lacking in courage, tell Coon to bring him along. We might need assistance along the way home. His friend will be adequately paid. Tell them to bring nothing but their weapons. Everything will be provided.

If we're not here when Coon arrives, have him ask for Alice. She'll be in charge of the office in our absence. Alice will also have a document for Coon that only he will understand. It's coded with words and phrases from our trip to Pensacola. Should something happen to us, the document will guide him to our buried money.

Our stay here shouldn't be much longer. Some things we'll leave in a safe place here, others we'll bring. Give everyone our love.

Your obedient servants,

Henry and Ben

That night at supper while Henry, Jolene, Alice, and I sat together eating, Henry said, "The first elements of Lieutenant General Longstreet's divisions are in the city. They're on their way to reinforce General Bragg in Chattanooga. Other units are also on the way, or are already there. In terms of deployed troops, it appears that Bragg will soon have an army equal in size to Rosecrans'. Rosecrans is probably close to striking. Since Longstreet is coming here from Virginia, I think there'll be a huge battle at Chattanooga. This could be a deciding point in the war. Ben and I could soon be summoned."

Jolene said, "You don't have to go. You're not in the army."

"I told General Bragg we would," Henry said. "If there's a major battle, and we help, I'll consider our obligation satisfied regardless of the outcome."

"The enemy could soon be in Atlanta," Alice said.

"No," Henry replied. "Bragg might win this battle. I don't think he'll sit still for a siege. Those didn't go well in Vicksburg or other places. He'll want to fight in the open. If defeated, Bragg will almost certainly withdraw ten or fifteen miles and establish another position. Rosecrans is cautious. He'll sit around for months repairing roads and securing his supply lines before he moves toward Atlanta. It could take a year for them to be here unless Rosecrans is replaced by a more aggressive general."

"But Bragg won't necessarily be defeated," I said.

"No," Henry said. "But if Bragg wins, Rosecrans will only withdraw a short distance and regroup. I hear he has a hundred thousand men under his command. Other than his own reserves, there are also other units that could reinforce him. Alice, you and Jolene need to start planning to leave Atlanta. At the very least you need to establish a plan to survive here. Unless wounded, your husbands won't be in Atlanta again until the Yankees force him here. That could be another year or two."

"The South could sue for peace," Jolene said.

"I've heard your mother say that," Henry said. "It wouldn't

be accepted. The Southern officials think they can fight to a draw, but Lincoln won't settle for a draw. He won't stop until he has a complete victory. Look at the situation for a moment. The Union already controls most of Missouri, Kentucky, Tennessee, and Louisiana. They're also fighting, or raiding, in all the other Southern states. The war in the far west has been over since sixty-two. There's no reason for Lincoln to stop without getting what he wants."

"But so many people are dying," Jolene said. "He should think of them."

"I'm sure he does," Henry replied. "His supper probably doesn't sit well some nights. But while that's a concern, it's not a deterrent. The point is that you two need to decide what you're going to do. Ben and I will leave for Florida shortly after we return from Chattanooga. I've sent for a couple of friends to assist here before we leave. They'll then help us move to Florida. One will introduce himself as Coon, or as Ray. In either case I have documents I'm going to leave with Alice for him."

"I don't know what we'll do," Jolene said. "Mother has been selling things to keep us in money. We'll soon be out of everything."

"You'll have to do one of two things," Henry said. "Either increase your income or cut your spending. Hard times must be planned for. Toward the end of the Vicksburg siege it was reported that the price of flour was a thousand dollars a barrel, molasses was twelve dollars a gallon, and other things were equally high. If Atlanta goes under siege the prices will certainly be as high here."

"That's an awful way to talk," Jolene said. "They can't do that here. What would we do?"

"You can prepare now," Henry replied.

"But I don't know how. I don't know what to do," she said.

Henry said, "If I were to stay, I'd convert all my assets into items that'll increase in value after the war—silver, gold, specie, and art pieces mostly. I would invest in things that can be easily concealed and transported, but not in Confederate paper money. The exchange rate of Confederate paper money to silver or gold was today listed as fifteen to one, and the gap is becoming greater monthly."

"That's what you've been doing all along," Alice said.

"Yes. With your help these last few months. But we seem to be taking in almost as much Confederate paper as we're changing out."

On September 8, three days after that conversation, a wire came requesting that we come to the Ringgold train station. We were requested to report by September tenth. I thought it strange that we would be summoned there rather than Chattanooga and said as much to Henry.

He replied, "Bragg learned a lesson from the Vicksburg siege. He plans to fight on the open field."

Jolene and Alice being present, Jolene said, "You just can't go. I don't know what I'll do."

Trying to focus her and give her direction, Henry replied, "You can start by organizing your mother. Tell her to quit selling her valuables and spending the money. Also, don't buy anything else. No more clothes."

Jolene said, "I haven't bought any clothes in weeks. The last I bought were too expensive."

Henry replied, "Right. They are too expensive. You should be selling clothes instead of buying them. They're still valuable now, but if the fighting comes here they'll be worth nothing. Your other valuables will. Sell your expensive clothes for specie now while they're valuable. Put them in a shop on commission and accept only specie in payment. Those coins, and your other valuables, will save you later on. I have some things to tend to so we'll talk more about it this evening."

Later that night I said to Henry, "Jolene seems unusually depressed."

"She's with child," Henry said. "Probably from the last days her husband was here. She talked with me once she suspected.

She's hoping she can work for us until her husband gets back, if he gets back. I can't help but remember those boys at Shiloh Church."

"Could she have become pregnant later?" I asked.

"Probably not," he said. "She said that she missed the second time three weeks ago. Her husband left on the fifth of June."

Carrying our revolvers and a supply of chloroform, we left the morning of September 10. Medicine could be in short supply on the Confederate side. Arriving at Ringgold the same day, we found there had been no casualties. Bragg had left Chattanooga, pulling his force out the day we got our notice to come. He had then deployed his forces from Chickamauga creek to La Fayette, Georgia.

Though the supply point at the Ringgold station was an extremely busy place, we were quickly assigned to a brigade. Being the only two physicians with our brigade, we were expected to move as the unit moved. Three four-wheel ambulances, and two with two wheels, were assigned to us. We were also assigned several litter bearers. It all seemed orderly at the time, probably because we had few wounded to care for over the next few days. At Shiloh, we had just walked in on the battle and didn't know how it was supposed to work. Though it seemed more organized to us, perhaps we were only learning with experience.

It seemed that, given a choice, the army's regular physicians chose to be assigned to the general hospital to which we would funnel patients. It was a good choice on their part. When a battle line is broken, the field physician is frequently in the middle of the battle. Even without that he is right behind the line, tending the fallen men. That the regular physicians should have a choice seemed fair enough. Most of the army's surgeons had attended a medical college, all of which had been closed in the Southern states since the war started. Skilled surgeons were in short supply, especially on the Southern side. Also, in theory, the major surgery would be done in the general hospital. In practice it didn't always work out like that.

As it was developing, this battle looked to be the equal of Shiloh in terms of its magnitude. General Joseph E. Johnston's army had joined Bragg's. General Longstreet's First Corps of the Army of Northern Virginia was in Atlanta, and deploying toward us. It was said that 62,000 men were deployed on the other side.

Elements of our brigade received casualties on September 15, though few in number. A patrol conducting a reconnaissance by fire received those casualties. Though there seemed to be considerable maneuvering by both Generals Bragg and Rosecrans as they sought to better their defenses and find the exact position of their opponent, our unit made little contact for a couple of days after those first casualties.

On the night of September 17, we were alerted that we would be crossing Chickamauga Creek the next morning. Though it was a stressful night, since we were not afflicted by extreme weather conditions everyone got some rest. Even the most fearful finally took their turn sleeping.

Considerable fighting occurred as the crossing of the Chickamauga started on September 18. Our ambulances were soon full and dispatched to the general hospital. The casualties were relatively light that day and by midnight they had pretty much been passed on to the rear and we got a few hours sleep.

Moving forward with the battle at 10:00 A.M. on September 19, we were behind regiments of General Liddell's division. They formed a line facing northward and moved forward in the attack through heavy underbrush. We soon broke through two Union lines. While I worked with the wounded from that heavy fighting, Henry moved forward with the litter bearers to provide assistance to those needing tourniquets and other emergency care as the division advanced. Getting back with me sometime later, Henry reported that Liddell's unit had retired with a right flanking movement and there was no one in front of us. It made the situation no more dangerous. Minié balls and artillery rounds had been striking around me all the time. Being on line with the advance, Henry had been in more danger than I had.

When he returned, Henry was carrying two Spencer repeating rifles and four hundred rounds of ammunition. We had heard of repeating rifles but these were the first we had ever seen. Later, we learned that Colonel John Wilder had a full brigade of mounted infantry armed with them. After seeing how they worked, we wondered how General Bragg's armies had won the day. Sending the last of the wounded to the hospital, we then moved in the direction of Liddell's flanking movement.

Theoretically, we were to follow one unit. When there's considerable movement of units during the battle, however, forward mobile medical units are sometimes still in one place caring for the wounded while the unit might have flanked to another position. As the battle progressed we found ourselves behind different units, and occasionally in front of some. Sometimes there were no other physicians near us and sometimes we had two or three others to help us.

As dark fell the battle continued in spots. Some of those battles continued well after dark. Up most of the night, we took turns sleeping only a couple of hours. Sometime during the night I observed the arrival of Lieutenant-General Longstreet.

The morning of September 20, the battle continued. We saw some of the same kind of confusion previously seen at Shiloh. The chief difference was that there was more advancing and less falling back by the CSA units. There was also better weather. Between the arrival of Longstreet, and the overall confusion of battle, at times there seemed to be confusion as to who was giving orders. There were then too many lieutenant-generals. Some units, after receiving orders from one general, would subsequently receive orders from another. This only added to the already existing confusion that always exists in battle. The fighting was just as fierce as at Shiloh Church.

Late in the day we found ourselves behind one of Longstreet's divisions as they broke the Union line and cut its army in half. Rushing his troops through the enemy's broken line, Longstreet attacked from the flank and rear. Union forces were soon in disarray. In spite of the efforts of some Union officers, most of their troops ran for their life.

Though the battle was over soon after Longstreet's break-through, our work was still beyond comprehension. The field was littered with the wounded and dead from both sides. At one spot I saw a dozen dead soldiers, Confederate and Union, in a space no bigger than a bedroom. Many of the wounded that we cared for were Union soldiers who could not be evacuated by the retreating Union army. To describe the magnitude of our job, it was reported that there were over 16,000 Union casualties from Union forces and 18,000 from the CSA. I fear that both sides gave out a low count to save face.

The next morning the Union forces were gathered in Chattanooga behind their breastwork. Though badly beaten, they had escaped and were safe for the time being. Toward the end of the day we moved back to the general hospital to help with the massive job there.

Our promise kept, and our new Spencer rifles and four hundred rounds of ammunition in hand, five days later Henry and I boarded a train loaded with wounded who were bound for Atlanta.

September 27, 1863

*H*aving arrived a week ahead of us with a companion, Coon was in Atlanta. Coon, one month short of being sixteen, hadn't grown a great deal in the last two years. He still looked like a kid. George, Coon's companion, looked older than his seventeen years. Our meeting was an emotional one for all parties.

Holding me by both forearms Coon said, "We were just about to come looking for you boys."

We talked all evening. Henry and I wanted to hear about the folks and home. Coon, George, Jolene, and Alice wanted to hear about our experiences. Happy, but exhausted, we finally retired for the night. It was the wee hours of the morning before any of us got to sleep.

The next morning when I got up, Henry was drinking coffee while Jolene cooked eggs, sausage, and grits.

Everyone was up and we had been drinking coffee and talking for an hour when a couple of patients showed up. Our guard wasn't at the gate, but somehow the word had gotten around that we were back. I went to see the patients while Alice, George, and Coon left to trade or spend Confederate paper money. That was what they had been doing since arriving. Henry sat for a long time talking to Jolene and watching her move around the kitchen as he drank coffee. She was a little too dependent, but she sure was easy to look at.

Everything was getting back to normal until the third morning when Jolene came to work. Grabbing Henry's arm, she led him straight to his room.

When they came out a few minutes later, he called me to the kitchen table and said, "Jolene's husband came home yesterday. He has an injury to his left arm, so he's on recuperation leave. The arm hurts and she wants me to look at it. I'll be back in an hour or two."

I said, "I'll go."

"No," Henry said. "There's no reason for me not to go."

Arriving at their place, Henry pulled off the bandage and observed that the wound was red. He then scrubbed the wound, washed it with corn whiskey, put some moss on it, and bandaged it. The wound hadn't been washed with anything but clean water. It's a wonder Tyler, Jolene's husband, didn't have gangrene.

Turning to Jolene, Henry said, "I guess you won't be coming to work for awhile."

"Oh yes," She said. "I have to come to work. I'm the only one working. Mother will be with Tyler."

Later when Henry told me the situation, not being certain what Henry and Jolene's relationship was, I asked, "Why don't you let me or an army doctor look after him?"

Henry said again, "There's no reason for me not to look after him."

Though working as hard as we could to trade our Confederate paper money, we were not making much headway. The trouble was that there wasn't enough gold and silver coin in circulation. We also kept accepting Confederate paper when it was the only kind of money a patient had. It's low value against silver caused us to get several Confederate paper dollars every time we treated someone who had to pay with them. That kept our supply of paper money large. Interestingly enough, over the past few months the value of Confederate paper money had stabilized at fifteen dollars to one silver dollar.

As time passed, Tyler healed nicely and was getting the use of his arm back. He soon began showing up at the house every night to walk Jolene home.

On October 20, as all of us but Jolene were sitting at the table after supper for one of our discussions, Henry said, "We need to set a target date and start preparing to leave. Alice hasn't said what she's going to do. She can let us know anytime though. Sometimes Jolene talks without thinking so I don't want her to know we're leaving until we're gone. We'll be carrying valuable things so it's best we leave without anyone knowing. We're going to leave most of our money here. It's hidden well enough, and in five different locations. I was thinking of leaving on November

10, unless something happens that causes us to leave earlier. My chief concern is how to travel. How does that date sound and what do you think?"

"The date's fine. What's wrong with the train?" Coon said. "We rode most of the way on the train and it was okay. There's none that connect with the Florida railroad, though."

"Ninety-five percent of the rail traffic on Confederate trains is now reserved for the military," Henry said. "Also, we'll be carrying some rather bulky luggage. Since we would have to go through Macon and Savannah, and would have to change trains several times, we could be left at a station for four or five days before finding room to ride. We'll also have to take a wagon for sixty miles anyway if we leave the train at its closest point to Lake City."

"Being loaded down would have been a problem coming," Coon said. "How about on horseback?"

"That might be the best way, but would require eight or nine horses to carry all of our things and us. I'll look around but we probably won't find enough horses. The army's taken most of them. I guess the only other way is by wagon. Everyone keep your eyes open for horses or mules we can buy, and for a wagon."

Since all the valuables were being stored in my room, it was kept locked all the time. That allowed us to pack everything without Jolene knowing. Trusting her wasn't the problem. It was that she babbled on occasionally. After bringing in some crate baskets we started packing the things. Everything was wrapped to prevent the items from rattling.

Little progress was made in getting horses. After considerable inquiry, Henry found two that were satisfactory. Though they were expensive, he did manage to pay for them with Confederate paper money.

The night of October 28, when Tyler came by for Jolene, he said, "I have to report back on November tenth."

Henry said, "You're under my care and I won't release you until November twentieth."

Tyler said, "Why? I feel great. But I guess I'm not in a big rush to get back. In fact, I'd rather not go at all because of Jolene being pregnant."

Henry replied, "There are reasons that will become clear soon. I'll wire your commanding officer and advise him. Also, I'll write a letter for you to carry when you report. I guess I could put it off until the thirtieth. Yes. We'll do that. Something big is going to happen at Chattanooga soon and Jolene needs you here."

On November 1, Alice told me she was going to stay in Atlanta. Being married, she needed to stay there. Also she said she didn't want to go to Florida and run into any of her old acquaintances. She was proud of escaping her old life.

The next morning after I told him about Alice, Henry called us to his room and said, "Alice, I'm glad you chose not to go to Florida. I've wanted to ask you something but I wanted you to make that decision first. You've done a great job buying and selling. You've really come a long way. I've been thinking about having someone go to St. Louis to check on the banker's management of our property. We need someone to look over his shoulder and keep him honest. You'll also reach a point in the future that you can manage everything. Ben and I would like for you to do it. Your husband can join you after the war. You can mail him a letter tomorrow morning. We'll have it hand-carried so he can answer before we go."

Alice's jaw almost dropped to her knees. Mine did too. It was the first I'd heard about it.

Alice said, "First, I'm not sure I can do it."

Henry replied, "What I had in mind was you taking a small room in the hotel and studying the situation for awhile—kind of watch what's going on. At the same time you can learn about the books. There are lots of ways a manager can beat you in that business. Ben and I need someone we can trust and who wants to be there a long time."

"But how would I travel with the fighting going on?"

"I'll write you a pass. Ben and I've done it lots. You can be on some kind of mission for a big name person. I'll give you travel and expense money."

"I don't know. It's so far and I don't know anyone."

"You made it to Atlanta. It's not much more than that. Once you pass the Union forces the trains are good. Your husband could get you through his lines. It's just something you haven't done before. You could try it until the war's over. Though Ben or I will probably be there shortly after the war, we'll still need an overseer or manager. I'm sure we'll both be doing something else and won't be around all the time. Why don't you take the day off and talk to someone about it."

"The only people I ever talk to about serious things are you or Ben."

"Why don't you get on a train to Ringgold and see your husband? It takes less than a day each way now that they're in Ringgold. Take the rest of the week off. You'll be paid anyway."

"The trains going north are limited to the military. They won't let me go."

"I'll write you a pass as a nurse. There'll be no problems at all."

Agreeing to go, she caught the train the next morning.

Henry and I were walking down the street the morning of November 7 when a carriage pulled over by us. It was an enclosed, one-horse carriage, pulled by a mighty fine carriage horse. A black driver in his middle twenties was sitting out front. Two white ladies, one of about thirty years and the other in her fifties, were in the carriage.

The older lady stuck her head partially out the window and called out, "Doctor Williams."

Both of us were using that name so we both looked.

"Doctor Williams." She was looking at Henry. "I've been looking for you. I've sent for you twice already but your man won't let my man through the gate. I've got sick grandchildren and need you immediately."

Tipping his hat, Henry said, "Sorry, ma'am, we aren't taking any new patients. We have neither the time nor the medicine."

Now that wasn't totally true. We had enough medicine of various kinds to treat a number of people for a couple of years, but could have used it all up in a month by not restricting the number of patients we took on. Also, knowing we would be faced with the same situation in Florida, we didn't want to run out of medicine.

"Doctor Williams, I'm Janice Whipmore. I have two grandchildren who have malaria. You are needed at the farm immediately," she said.

"I'm afraid you don't understand, ma'am. We aren't taking new patients."

"Doctor Williams," she said, talking louder. "I can pay whatever it takes. Surely you can take care of my grandchildren."

"There are other physicians."

"There are no others with quinine. Doctor Williams, you have to come. I'll pay you anything you ask. I'll give you anything you ask."

We both had heard that same conversation many times before. The conversation was frequently with people who had nothing to give.

As I've said, we had quinine. Though it was an import item and there was little available in the South, we didn't gouge people for quinine. We also didn't take all comers as patients. While it was impossible to take them all, turning away patients was stressful. People were dying with no chance of getting better. In spite of all that, I expected Henry to excuse himself politely and walk off, but he didn't.

Henry just stood there with a blank look on his face for a few moments, then said, "I don't suppose those were idle words you used, ma'am."

"Absolutely not," she said. "I never use idle words."

"Good," Henry said. "Give us directions and have your driver take you home. We'll be along behind you."

After drawing the directions and handing them to Henry, without speaking further she waved her driver on.

I asked, "Why are you going to help that pompous old hen? There are lots of other people who need quinine."

"Horses," Henry said. "Did you notice that carriage horse? Both of us are going to her place. You can help bring the horses back."

After renting a rig we drove the better part of two hours before coming to the plantation house. The same carriage and driver were standing in front of the house but a fresh horse was hitched up. There was no shortage of anything but quinine on that farm.

We were admitted to the parlor by a black woman of eighteen years and met there by Mrs. Whipmore. The younger woman from the carriage, Virginia, the children's mother, was also there.

After a brief examination, which wasn't needed because we had already been given the diagnosis, we returned to the parlor and Henry said, "It's malaria. Our fee will be two horses, their tack, and a one-horse wagon in good condition. For this you'll be provided six months' supply of quinine for the two children."

That woman puffed up and said, "Sir, that's outrageous."

She babbled on and on but Henry wasn't listening. Turning to me he said, "Ben, bring her driver in please."

Leaving immediately, I was back in less than two minutes. I don't know what was said in my absence.

As soon as we entered, Henry asked the driver, "What's your name?"

"Nathaniel, suh," he answered.

"Do you have a wife?" Henry asked.

"Yes suh. Her," he replied, pointing to the young woman who had admitted us.

"Do you have children?" Henry asked.

"No suh," he replied.

Turning to Mrs. Whipmore, who had not been standing quietly, Henry said, "Madam, you said I could name my price, anything I wanted. You then said they were not idle words. I'm going to give you a final offer, which has increased. If you don't accept, be damned with you and we're gone."

Following Henry's comments a white man in his mid-twenties who had entered the room said, "Sir, you've insulted my mother. You'll give me satisfaction."

"I'll shoot you dead where you stand," Henry replied, opening his coat and placing his hand on his revolver as he spoke.

That man wasn't armed but Henry was wearing his .44 caliber Remington revolver, which he always did. I thought Henry was going to shoot him on the spot until Mrs. Whipmore broke in.

"Hush, Tom." Turning to Henry, she said, "State your final terms."

"For fifty dollars in gold coin I'll provide enough quinine for your grandchildren for six months. You will sell me three horses of my choice, a wagon, and appropriate tack for a total of two hundred dollars in Confederate paper money, and Nathaniel and his wife for one hundred dollars each in Confederate paper money. I'll also need five bushels of shelled corn as part of the deal.

Virginia, who had been silent all that time, said, "But they've been here all their lives. We raised them. Sally lives in the house mostly."

Tom shifted around, but didn't say anything.

"Be quiet," Mrs. Whipmore said to Virginia. Turning to Henry, she said, "We have a bargain. You've robbed me but I'll say no more about it. We'll shake on it."

"No," Henry said. "We'll write out a contract and a bill of sale for each item and person. Bring pen and paper and I'll do it now."

Nathaniel and Sally had backed off in a corner and were whispering together.

Turning to them, Henry said, "Nathaniel, choose the three best riding horses on the place. Hitch one to the best one-horse wagon on the place, and load the corn."

Looking at Sally, Henry said, "Collect both of your personal things and put them in the wagon. We're leaving within the hour."

When Nathaniel and I got back in the house, the contract, bill of sale, and money were on the table. Reaching in his bag, Henry got out six months' supply of quinine for the two children and placed it on the table. In the same motion he put the gold coins in his pocket. After signing the papers he passed them around for everyone present to sign. I noticed that Nathaniel and Sally only signed their first names. It was a little surprising that they could write their names at all. Such skills were often forbidden for slaves. Having been raised in the big house, Sally had learned to read and write with the white children. She had also taught Nathaniel to read and write some. Due to being the carriage driver and hostler, Nathaniel had also been required, by Mrs. Whipmore, to speak properly.

As we mounted to leave, me in the rented rig, Nathaniel and Sally on the wagon, and Henry on one horse leading another, I heard Tom say, "Sir, there will be another day."

Henry said, "I've always been told there's no point in lifting a load you can't carry."

I thought about Henry's trade as we traveled. He had gotten $50 in gold for $400 in Confederate paper money, which was worth only $27 in gold. The corn, horses, wagon, Nathaniel, and Sally were a straight trade for the quinine. Henry had never taken advantage of anyone like that before. Mrs. Whipmore should have kept her mouth shut after the first offer. She just couldn't though—it was her nature to bully her way through everything.

Arriving at the house just before dark we found that Jolene had already gone for the night and Alice was back from Ringgold. Since it was the fourth day since Alice left, she was expected back.

Henry called everyone to the kitchen and asked Alice,

"What have you decided?"

"We'll do it," she said.

"Good," Henry said. "We'll fill out papers as soon as I get everyone ready to go. Things have changed. We're leaving for Florida at four tomorrow morning. Everything's ready. All we need to do is pack our personal things and go. After you're all packed, everyone get a few hours sleep. We'll be up at three. I want to be clear of Atlanta before daylight. Ben, why don't you talk to Nathaniel and Sally while Alice and I get our business taken care of."

With paper from his book of blank pages, Henry wrote some passes and a contract for Alice. He also gave her a letter to the banker and one to Jolene and gave her money to pay off our guard and Jolene. Additionally, he gave her Mrs. Whipmore's fifty dollars in gold coin for expense money and half of a Confederate ten-dollar bill. The banker in St. Louis had the other half. The bill was torn at a strange angle as an identification arrangement Henry had made in case a stranger showed up at the bank with papers from him. Jolene's letter asked her to rent out the house while we were gone.

Not really knowing what to say, I talked with Nathaniel and Sally about where we were from, something of our travels, about our families, and the fact that we had never owned slaves. All of us had known, and played with, black children though. About that time Henry returned.

"Nathaniel, do you know how to shoot a rifle?" he asked.

"Not well, suh," Nathaniel replied. "It wasn't something we were allowed to do openly."

"Then you'll be armed with a double barrel shotgun while driving the wagon," Henry said. "Don't shoot at anyone we're not shooting at."

"Yes suh," Nathaniel said, the amazement showing in his face.

After cooking enough for supper, breakfast, and dinner, we ate before everyone scattered around in the house to sleep. Alice and I were up the latest.

I asked, "Did everything go okay?"

"Yes," she replied. "It was good. Everything's going to be all right.

We sat talking for several minutes before I walked Alice home. I went to sleep instantly when I got to bed. The next thing I knew Henry's hand was on my shoulder and it was time to get up.

PART III

Taking up Arms

November 8, 1863

Traveling south-southeast toward Macon, we kept moving until well after daylight. We had five horses, including the two Henry had previously bought. Henry, Coon, George, and I were riding horses. Nathaniel and Sally were in the wagon.

We stopped nine miles south of Atlanta to rest the horses and eat breakfast.

As we were eating, Henry handed Nathaniel two pieces of paper and said, "Nathaniel, we're going to Florida. We don't own slaves and don't hold with it. Minding our own business, we don't usually bother others who do. These papers give you and Sally your freedom. I would still like for you to go to Florida with us.

We need a driver and a man with courage enough to use a shot-gun if needed. There's some valuable stuff in those bushel baskets so it might be necessary to use the shotgun. If you go, it would be good to teach Sally to handle the wagon so you can have the gun close at hand. You have until we finish breakfast, and the horses have eaten, to decide. Like I said, we would like to have a good man with us."

Going over by the wagon, they looked at the papers and talked back and forth for twenty minutes. Sally read the papers out loud three times.

While they were gone, I said, "You just didn't like Mrs. Whipmore, did you?"

Henry laughed and said, "No. But I didn't go there with the idea about the slaves. After she wouldn't take my first offer, which I thought was steep but reasonable under the circumstances, I decided to take her down a notch. I also figured we needed to exchange a little money and have a written record of each trans-action for legal purposes. The Whipmores probably didn't get where they are by being fair or honest."

I had to ask, "You wouldn't have shot Tom and him not even armed?"

His only reply was, "Well, it would have put us on the run again and that wouldn't have been any fun."

Returning to the group, Nathaniel said, "Suh, we feel we'll be better off with you."

"Good," Henry said. "Do me the courtesy of telling me when you start to leave."

"Yes suh," Nathaniel replied.

"That's another thing," Henry said. "My name's Henry. These three are Ben, Coon, and George. We have changed our names on occasion, even though the authorities don't want us for anything I know of. I'll tell you if we change names again. It would be preferable to call us by our names, but you can call us what you choose. You know the situation about slaves as well as I do. Sometimes you might wish to act like a slave, and sometimes like a free man. Let the situation and your own desires dictate your actions."

"We'll do that, suh," Nathaniel said.

Nathaniel rarely called Henry anything besides "sir" or "doctor" after that. I guess Henry was the only person he ever really wanted to call sir, black or white. He became quite accustomed to addressing the rest of us in various ways.

Sally soon became at ease around us all. She even became a little bossy at times. I think she and Henry both enjoyed it. They came to like each other quite a bit.

Though we were heavily armed, that alone wasn't cause for anyone to suspect we were carrying valuables. Our horses, on the other hand, were cause enough for us to be on guard against thieves even if we had no other valuables. The three obtained from the Whipmore plantation included two full-blooded Arabian mares and a thoroughbred gelding. I have never seen better horses. I don't believe any better existed in Georgia. The one that General Johnston was riding at Shiloh and the lineback dun, taken by General Bragg from Henry, were close.

The only reason the plantation horses hadn't been previously taken by the army was because of the size of the plantation where they were from. Having far more slaves than met the requirement, Tom and the rest of the males in the family were exempt from military service if they chose to be. Their property was also exempt from confiscation. Those kinds of plantations were needed desperately to supply the South. Anyone who owned twenty slaves was exempt from military service in most Southern states.

Expecting Tom to come riding up behind us, I kept glancing back as we traveled. We were also keeping a sharp eye out for any band of thieves or deserters that might want to take our horses and weapons. Henry and I were carrying Spencer repeating rifles, probably the only two of their kind in civilian hands in the state of Georgia. The CSA army didn't have any unless they had picked them up on the battlefield as Henry had. Ours wouldn't have been any good for very long except that Henry had gathered up four hundred cartridges that fit them. He could have gotten more rifles, but cartridges were more important. Being an import item, the .52 caliber cartridges that fit the Spencer repeater couldn't be bought in the South. Coon and George were armed with breech loading single shot Springfield rifles. All of us had revolvers. We were armed for a war. There were lots of people who would have killed for either our horses or weapons.

When passing through McDonough, Georgia, we met a small CSA cavalry detachment. Asked who we were, our destination, and cargo, Henry produced papers from General Bragg. The papers were orders for us to proceed to Jacksonville, Florida, which, with a population of a little over 2,000 people, was then the second largest city in Florida. Taking a boat from there, we were to carry out a mission vital to the Confederate States of America. Our papers showed Henry to be a colonel for the CSA and requested the assistance of all CSA units in helping us along the way.

The captain saluted smartly and said, "Sir, can we be of any assistance?"

Henry replied, "You could ride with us for a ways, Captain, and we can talk."

"Yes, sir," he said, before ordering his unit to fall in behind the wagon.

Being curious, I moved up beside Henry. He was now riding slightly ahead of the wagon. Henry and Coon had been riding forty yards in front of the wagon. George and I had been riding forty yards behind.

The captain said, "Sir, I can't help but admire your mount. I've never seen better."

"Took him off of a Yankee general at Chickamauga," Henry said. "We took these repeaters off of two men in that battle. The

Northern army had a brigade armed with these rifles but we routed them anyway. General Bragg provided the two Arabians. He wanted us to have the best possible mounts."

"Yes, sir. I can see they're the best," the captain said.

Henry asked, "Are you going to be in and around McDonough very long, Captain?"

"Only a couple of days, sir," he responded.

"That's just about enough. We had an encounter with a known Union sympathizer outside Atlanta. I'm not sure what last name he's using. He usually picks the name of an important local person like a plantation owner or politician, but mostly goes by the first name of Tom. His group might have learned of our mission, or for some other reason he might decide to pursue us. You could do me a favor by shooting him. I had the opportunity once and regret letting it pass. If he should decide to surrender, you could at least detain him and his band for three or four days and let us clear the area."

"I'll keep a guard posted on the road, sir," the captain said.

We rode without speaking until the captain said to me, "I see you're carrying a Remington .36 caliber revolver. That's a light and unusual weapon for an army officer."

"We had an encounter with a Union Navy unit in Pensacola in sixty-two," I said. "I took it off of a navy lieutenant and kind of liked the feel of it."

"I guess the whole war will pass and I'll not get in it," the captain said.

"Captain, we've kept you from your duties too long. If you'll watch the road behind us for a couple of days, I'll be in your debt," Henry said, dismissing him.

We were still riding near the wagon, and the captain was a half-mile away when Nathaniel said, "Suh, I think we made the right choice."

I was stopped to let George catch up and Henry was loping his horse to catch up with Coon when I heard Sally say, "They just flat out lied to that man. Serves him right, too."

Grinning, Nathaniel replied, "Yeah. We're gonna be all right."

We purchased some hay near Locust Grove, Georgia, and camped five hundred yards off the road. Not wanting to let the horses move about to graze, we fed them hay and corn. Having traveled thirty-five miles that day, they needed as much rest as they could get. Coon, who usually did most of the cooking and cleaning up around camp when we traveled, had some fine help from Sally. The rest of us felt kind of spoiled because Nathaniel wanted to take care of the animals' needs. That was a job Nathaniel had held since getting big enough to reach a horse's back. He has great skill with horses, the best I've ever seen.

Coon asked about our route that night.

Henry said, "Someone told me once that when running one should always go in a straight line or the dogs will catch you or you'll get shot. We'll bypass Macon to the west and go straight to Fitzgerald, Georgia. From there we'll go straight toward Lulu, Florida. It's three hundred miles as the crow flies, but it's three hundred fifty by road. Barring misfortune, we'll be there in two weeks. We should arrive just in time to help Aunt May cut cane and make syrup."

"I'd be proud to help with that. That's my favorite thing on the farm besides horses," Nathaniel said.

"I've helped with the syrup for two years," Coon said. "Henry did most of the work two years ago but I did it last year."

His talking about the time reminded me of something and I said, "You know what, I told that captain we were in Pensacola in sixty-two but it was sixty-one. I guess I lied. Time seems to slip away."

Coon retorted, "From what you told me everything else was a lie anyway. Henry took those pistols but never told us exactly how."

Everyone laughed.

I said, "Yes, but somehow I almost lost a year. I hate to lie by mistake."

Henry said, "I told you that I had a run in with some desert-ers who had the revolvers. They also had the dun and money. Not satisfied with what they had, they wanted my horses."

"How many were there?" George asked.

"Less than I had loads in my revolver," Henry replied.

I figured that to be four since we always carried our hammer on an empty.

Taking advantage of the opportunity, I asked, "Do you know where they got the money?"

"Not for sure," Henry answered. "One of them lived a few minutes and said something about them deciding to keep the money they were transporting to an army in Alabama. I asked to which army and what happened to the rest of the transport detach-ment, but he didn't get a clear answer out before he passed on."

Sally asked, "Did you all really attack the Union Navy in Pensacola?"

"No. It was Union soldiers from Fort Pickens on Santa Rosa Island," I said. "We only shot them because we couldn't get at the navy people who killed Henry's pa in Cedar Key. He wasn't doing anything but standing there when they shot him. Henry went after them for revenge and Coon and I joined in."

"How old were you?" Sally asked.

"We were old enough. I was fourteen," Coon said. "We got revenge too—fourfold."

Late the next day, near Forsyth, we stopped at a farm to buy a bale of hay for the horses. Meeting us at the gate, the planter held up his hand and blocked our way.

"I must ask a question before welcoming you. There's vario-la in the area. Have you been around any?"

"No we haven't," Henry replied. "Have you and your people been vaccinated?"

"My wife and I have," the owner replied. "Our younger chil-dren haven't. Due to the shortage of medicine caused by the war, some of the older ones haven't been vaccinated within the last four years as is recommended. If you haven't been around anyone with variola, dismount and welcome."

"We're just looking to purchase hay for the night and to camp a mile up the road," Henry said.

George, having never heard the words, asked Coon, "What does vaccinated and variola mean?"

Overhearing his question, I said, "You mean you've never been vaccinated?"

"I don't even know what it means," George replied.

Sally said, "I know what it means. Nathaniel hasn't been vaccinated either. They mostly don't worry about black folk. The milking girls and some others become immune because of catching the cowpox. I was vaccinated because I worked in the house. Variola is the smallpox."

Henry asked the farmer, "Do you know of a cow nearby that has cowpox?"

"Sure," he said. "There's some about."

"How long would it take to find and fetch one?" Henry asked.

"We could get one tomorrow morning," the farmer replied.

"Ben and I are physicians," Henry said. "I would like to vaccinate my people who haven't been. We could also vaccinate your children if we had a cow with the pox."

"Stay overnight," the farmer said. "You can have the best accommodations we have."

"No," Henry said. "We'll stay over, but would like to use the barn for sleeping. I would also like to turn our horses in a pasture to graze."

"Sir, I insist that you sleep in the house," the owner said.

Coon said, "You two physicians sleep in the house. The rest of us will sleep in the barn."

"Okay," Henry said. "Nathaniel, see to the livestock."

We all knew he didn't have to say that. He was just playing an expected game in front of the owner.

"Yes suh," Nathaniel said. "I'll sleep under the wagon tonight."

"What does vaccinated mean?" George asked, louder that time.

"It means to take some pustules from a cow or person with cowpox and put in on a cut place on your shoulder," I said. "It gives you a light case of cowpox. After that you can't catch small-pox."

"What if it kills me?" George asked. "I don't want to do that."

"When done with cowpox it's not going to kill you. You could be a little sick for a day or two at the worst. Henry asked for a cow to be sure that it was cowpox he was vaccinating every-one with. If you were vaccinated with smallpox you would almost surely die."

"I don't know," George said. "I never heard of that before. I'll watch it done to somebody else."

"If Doctor Henry says it's okay, I'll do it," Nathaniel said.

"Of course you'll do it," Sally said. "And there'll be no more talk about it."

Staying the night, Henry and I slept in a nice room in the big house. We were treated like visiting royalty—or maybe it was just the way they ate, drank, and acted every day. After a fine din-ner and a couple of drinks we were entertained at the piano by the very attractive eldest daughter of the owner.

At breakfast the next morning the owner tactfully brought up the sum he would owe for our medical services.

Henry said, "There'll be no charge for our services, but there is a service you could do for us. Being in need of a mule for the wagon, I would like to trade a horse for one. If there's a good mule in the area that could be acquired today, I would be indebt-ed if you would make the arrangement."

"I'll have someone look into that," he replied.

It took most of the morning for them to find, and fetch, a

cow with the pox. In the meantime Henry and I looked around the farm while Coon and George stayed close to the barn. Nathaniel and Sally mingled with the slaves as they did their work.

The owner, looking at our horses, said, "I'd almost give half the farm for those two mares. Did you raise them or buy them?"

"We purchased them," Henry said.

"They must have come high," the owner said.

"They did. Their former owner placed a great value on them," Henry replied.

"May I ask the price without offending?" the owner asked.

"Yes, you may," Henry said. "The price was two lives and almost a third, and a hundred dollars in Confederate paper money."

Any sane man would not have asked further. The owner didn't.

The same daughter who had played the piano said, "I would love to ride one of the mares. I've never seen such a horse."

"There are few Arabians in this country," Henry said. "If I had a sidesaddle, and your father's permission, we could ride for an hour."

"We have sidesaddles. Father, may I ride?" she said.

"Yes, but take the creek trail. Stay on our property," he said.

They were back in a little more than an hour. The daughter couldn't say enough about the mare. I got the feeling that she would have ridden off to Florida on one.

Soon thereafter a cow was brought forth that had cowpox. Having set up two locations outside to perform the procedure, Henry called for the first person. The daughter immediately stepped forward. Scraping a spot on her shoulder sharply enough for it to bleed, Henry put some pustules from the cow on it. He then rubbed it with the stick he used as an applicator. Wanting to impress Henry, the girl almost didn't flinch.

Finishing with the girl, Henry said, "Sally, line up the slaves. Ben can start on them at the other table."

Placing Nathaniel in front to act as an example, Sally organized and chastised the slaves into line.

Since it was afternoon by the time everyone had been vaccinated, the owner asked that we stay the night. Before we could accept or decline, and before the cow was released, a farmer from close by arrived leading two mules. It was no surprise that he had his family with him.

After introductions, he said, "Hoping they might be vaccinated, I brought my children. I've also brought two mules, either one of which I'll consider trading."

Henry said, "If you'll excuse me, sir, I need to speak to my man."

He then called Nathaniel to one side for a private conversation. I talked with the farmer during Henry's absence. In less than two minutes he was back. Nathaniel then disappeared into the barn.

"Either of your two mules is more valuable than either of the two horses I'm willing to trade," Henry said, "But I'll make you an offer. I'll vaccinate your children and give each a thorough examination for other afflictions. We'll then trade one horse for one mule even. You may choose from the two horses designated and I'll choose between the mules."

"Fair enough and done," the farmer said.

Nathaniel was back from the barn at that point in the conversation.

Henry asked the owner, "Sir, if you were choosing between the mules which would you choose?"

Without hesitation the farmer said, "The one on the right as they face us. The darker one."

Henry said, "I'll think about your advice. Coon, would you catch up the two horses so they can be examined while I start vaccinating the children? Ben, please take each of the children in the house and give them a thorough examination after I'm finished with them."

As everyone was either gathering horses or concentrating on the vaccinations, I observed Nathaniel examining the mules. I then went in the house with the first of the children and his mother. Frequently glancing out of the window, I continued observing Henry and Nathaniel as I worked. After finishing his examination of the mules, Nathaniel joined two nearby slaves in conversation. Henry didn't examine the mules except for a glance from a distance. I was certain the owner hadn't seen Nathaniel look them over.

Having vaccinated and examined everyone, we cleaned our instruments and stored them. The subject of the conversation then returned to the trade.

Henry asked, "Have you made a choice between the horses?"

"I have," the farmer replied. "I'll take the brown."

"A good choice," Henry said. "Though they are about equal, that is the prettier horse. You said the one on the right, the darker one, would be your choice of the mules?"

Following Henry's glance at Nathaniel, I saw Nathaniel scratch his left ear as he continued his conversation with the slaves.

Henry said, "Well, sir, not wishing to take advantage of the situation, I'll leave you with the one you like best and choose the one on the left." Turning to Coon, he added, "Would you turn our new mule in with the horses?"

Bursting with curiosity, I soon found cause to be near Nathaniel and say, "Tell me about the mules."

He replied, as the two slaves he had been talking with tried to keep from smiling, "Doctor Ben, that other mule would be lame in two days. He would have to rest five days out of seven. We got a fine animal."

The hour was so late by the time our work was done, and the trade accomplished, that the prudent course of action was to remain for the night. We then volunteered to examine every person on the place for any apparent affliction. Our mule's former owner and his family left during that activity.

Later I heard our host ask Henry, "What made you choose the other mule?"

He replied, "One has to assume that in an animal trade even your friend would try to best you."

As we were leaving, our host insisted that we take some parting gifts. We accepted a quart of molasses, a smoked ham, and a bushel of sweet potatoes. The molasses and sweet potatoes, in terms of those particular items, would satisfy our needs for the balance of the trip. Nathaniel, Coon, and a slave took only a few minutes getting the potatoes, which had long before been dug and banked.

Though we were delayed a few minutes in our departure to get the potatoes, our delay was made up a hundred times by information and a courtesy given by our host. We were advised of a system of wagon trails that were used weekly to secure rosin from pine trees by various owners to the south. Following that route allowed us to leave the main road and bypass Macon by ten miles to the west. Traveling to Perry, Georgia, by the most direct route, we would cover in one and a half days what would have taken two and a half. Taking a mule to ride back, an older slave who knew the area was assigned to travel with us for that segment of the trip. We thus recovered the extra day we had spent on the farm. Not only did we save more than twenty miles, but other than slaves chipping trees, we also avoided contact with any people for that segment of the trip.

As we camped near the community of Haynesville, Georgia, Nathaniel awakened me and said, "Doctor Ben, there are two folks who need some food. They're afraid to come to the wagon. I didn't want to take anything without permission."

Without becoming fully awake, I said, "I suppose they're runaway slaves. Take enough for several days and give them a blanket if needed. It's always cold at night in November."

Drifting back off to sleep, I didn't think of it again until Henry awakened me for my turn on guard duty. He supported the correctness of my response. We never did ask who they were.

Two days later, near Fitzgerald, we encountered a band of

twelve mounted and armed men. The situation suggested they had less than good intentions. Approaching us from the front, their guns ready, they were spread out across the road and into the woods on each side of the road. As was most land in the area, this was open pine woods with scattered palmettos about waist high. All of us were visible to them and they to us. Wearing no uniforms, and carrying no unit colors, they were obviously not soldiers. Further, leading no pack animals they were obviously not a group of travelers. Their intentions being suspicious, Henry and Coon, who were forty yards in front of the wagon, stopped. Nathaniel also stopped the wagon. George and I, who were at our normal position forty yards behind the wagon, began loping our horses forward to the right and left of Henry and Coon.

When they were at fifty yards Henry raised his left hand and shouted, "Hold your ground and state your intentions."

The line of approaching riders didn't stop until Henry fired a shot in the air. They were only forty yards from Henry and Coon at the time.

Levering a second round into the chamber of his rifle, Henry leveled it on the rider in the middle of the road. Though several words passed back and forth between Henry and the leader of the band, I heard none of them over the sound of my running horse as George and I moved forward into position. I stopped twenty yards to the left of Coon. George was twenty yards to the right of Henry. Henry and Coon had dismounted in the road and stood partially concealed by their horses. As we stopped, George and I dismounted and took shelter behind pine trees.

As I dismounted I heard the last sentence ever said by the leader of the group. "We'll take your animals, weapons, and wagon, and leave you with your lives."

Without verbally responding, Henry shot their spokesman out of the saddle with what the spokesman obviously thought was an empty rifle. I expect he had never heard of a repeating rifle. The skirmish broke out in earnest then. Though fewer in number, we had the advantage. Being on foot, we had a stable place to shoot from. We also had the superior weapons and some cover. They, on the other hand, were on horseback, which is a moving and poor platform from which to shoot a rifle or pistol. There being eleven of them left after Henry shot one, unless they had double-barrels they only had eleven shots total in their muzzle-loaders. Henry and I between us still had twelve cartridges in our rifles, Henry having fired one in warning and one into the chest of their spokesman. We also had six-shot revolvers. Additionally, Coon and George were armed with Springfield breechloaders and revolvers. Forty yards behind us, eighty yards away from them, and out of range with a shotgun, Nathaniel was initially out of the fight. We tumbled two more from their saddle immediately. I saw George and his horse, which was standing near him, go down in the first shooting.

Thinking we had empty weapons because we all fired imme-diately, they charged us. A few of them hadn't discharged their weapons at the first shooting. Thus, they thought to have the advantage of being the only ones with loaded weapons as they charged. They obviously didn't know about the Spencers. We took three more from the saddle before the group passed through us, and dropped two more as they scattered. Upon reaching our position, they had also come within range of Nathaniel. He took one, and a horse, out with the shotgun. They were not expecting a slave to be armed. I then noticed that Coon was down, though still moving. The mule had also been hit and soon dropped to her knees in front of the wagon.

Seeing the remaining members of the group scattering, the mule down, and George's horse down, Henry shouted to Nathaniel, "Take my mount and catch us some horses."

Henry got busy working over George so I went to help Coon. He was shot through the leg. An artery severed, he need-ed a tourniquet. Within the half-hour I had Coon's wound cau-terized and bandaged. There was no bone damage. He had much the same wound that General Albert Johnston died from near Shiloh Church. An artery having been severed in his thigh, and his personal physician on an errand, Johnson died from lack of a tourniquet. The only person with Johnston at the time, a journalist, didn't know how to apply one.

Henry was still working on George, who had two shotgun pellet wounds. Both were grievous, though not mortal. The pine tree George was behind, and his horse, had taken most of the load.

Returning with four spare horses, Nathaniel used two to drag the mule from the road. Nathaniel then hitched a horse to the wagon.

Hearing the pounding of hooves, I faced them and raised my Spencer. Happy to see the ragtag uniforms of some Georgia Militia, I lowered the rifle. The lieutenant in charge was extremely well outfitted in spite of the ragged appearance of his men.

Dismounting, the lieutenant said, "What's going on? I had a report of a battle here."

After filling him in on the battle, I added, "We are CSA officers on a secret mission for General Braxton Bragg. Colonel Williams has our papers to that effect. He and I are also physicians, which is instrumental to the nature of the mission."

Having finished with George and placed him in our wagon, Henry joined us and showed the lieutenant some papers. At that time the lieutenant saluted and gave his name and rank.

The lieutenant's sergeant, who had been scouring the palmettos for dead and wounded, reported, "Sir, we've found five dead and two others seriously wounded and have collected their weapons."

I said, "You might look closer, or look for signs where some crawled away. Only three of the twelve were still on their horses when it was over."

Pointing at my rifle, the lieutenant said, "I've never seen a weapon like that."

"It's a Spencer repeating rifle, fifty-two caliber," I said. "These rifles can be shot seven times without reloading. It's something new the Federal forces have. We took these off of some Union soldiers at Chickamauga. These men's ignorance of the rifle's capacity for rapid fire cost some of them their lives."

Our papers from Bragg, my speaking of Chickamauga, the Spencers, and the quality of our horses raised us to a level from which we could rise no higher in the lieutenant's eyes.

Henry said, "Lieutenant, we'll need a place to stay for a few days until our two companions are able to travel. It only needs to be an abandoned house or barn. We need nothing fancy. Preferably, it should be something that's away from town. It's also imperative that our rank and mission remain secret. We are simply two physicians traveling south."

"I'm sure my father would be proud to have you stay at our place. I'll confide in only him and mother the nature of your mission. You'll then receive the service you deserve," the lieutenant said. He added, "Sir, what shall we do with the wounded prisoners?"

"I'm afraid the wounded are hurt too bad to save. I'll give them something to ease their pain. They'll be dead by the time their friends come back for them, though I expect they won't bother. You might send some men with shovels to bury them," Henry said.

Upon arriving at the lieutenant's home, we were given a warm welcome by his parents and friends. Everyone was overjoyed with the result of our encounter and treated us as heroes. We were informed that our assailants were part of a group of riffraff who had been doing some raiding and pillaging throughout the area. In addition to open violence and looting, it was said that a couple of ladies had been detained and assaulted. Such an occurrence wasn't even condoned by most good thieves before the ravages of war descended on us. Units of the Georgia militia had spent considerable time hunting this particular group with little success.

Taking a group of militia and volunteers to search for those who had survived the attack, and some slaves to bury the dead, the lieutenant left shortly after introducing us to his family. Though we were left alone with the lieutenant's family, we were by no means ignored. Every comfort and courtesy was provided. Even though it required shuffling some people between rooms, Coon, George, Henry and I were given two rooms in the big house. Our wagon, said to be containing supplies vital to our mission, was placed in a locked shed. To insure that the wagon was secure, Nathaniel and Sally also slept in the shed.

Since we had little to do during our stay but be entertained, we offered to provide medical services to owners and slaves alike. We treated cases of diarrhea, worms, gout, and various other common afflictions. Soon people from nearby heard about the presence of physicians and came.

The day after leaving on the search for those who attacked us, the lieutenant returned and told of their search. Finding seven persons dead upon returning to the place of our attack, some slaves were left to bury those while the armed group followed the trail of the survivors. After tracking them for several hours, they were found holed up in an old barn. During a gun battle that followed, the militia sustained two casualties.

With dark drawing near and running low on ammunition, the lieutenant feared our assailants would escape so he set fire to the barn. Emerging under a white flag to escape the fire, one man said that another was too injured to come out. Two others were dead. One of the wounded from their attack on us had gotten back with his gang and there were four. The lieutenant, with the help of one other person, attempted to get the wounded person from the burning barn. Failing in that, he turned his attention to his prisoner. His prisoner was by that time hanging from a tree. Returning to the plantation, they brought the captured horses and weapons with them.

During our stay at the farm we managed to trade one of our

newly acquired horses for a mule. When the mule's owner asked an exorbitant amount for the mule, in addition to our horse in trade, Henry wrote a warrant on the CSA treasury for the additional compensation. The lieutenant confided to the owner our true identity and assured him of our authority to write the warrant. It seemed fair at the time. I thought the horse was of greater worth than the mule.

On our last night at the plantation a ball was thrown for us. The wealthy and their friends came from twenty miles around. Many of them stayed the night because of the distance. Because of the number of men gone to war, the women outnumbered the men by two to one. Coon and George were able to be up, at least to sit in a chair for some time, adding to the number of men present. There was no shortage of ladies who wished to bring them food and drink, and in general attend their needs. Tiring early, however, they were soon escorted to bed and tucked in.

Being the honored guests, Henry and I felt that we needed to stay up until the party was over. The party allowed all of us to momentarily forget our problems and concerns.

The morning of November 20, we pulled out from the plantation. The lieutenant, wearing his finest uniform and commanding six men, escorted us the ten miles to Ocilla. There, they wished us good luck on our mission and turned back.

Thinking about the other cavalry detachment as this one turned back, I wondered if Tom had indeed mounted a pursuit. Also thinking about the wonderful time I had the previous night, it came to me that we could continue riding about the country on a mission, frequently stopping off at a plantation. Passing that thought on to Henry, I got a big smile but no comment.

After fording the Willacoochee River for the second time as it meandered south, we camped near Lax, Georgia. Having gotten a late start, and taking it slow because of Coon and George, we made only twenty miles that day. We were still a hundred miles from Lulu, Florida.

Thankfully, there was little enough excitement over the next four days.

November 25, 1863

At noon, almost two years after leaving, we turned into the lane leading to Aunt May's house. Everyone was in the kitchen eating until Lilly's mare neighed and ours answered. Within seconds one head appeared at the door. It soon vanished to alert the others. They all rushed out, except for Lilly and Mary, and met us fifty yards from the house. Everyone hugged, kissed, and talked at once as we proceeded to the house. The younger ones danced about.

At that point Mary, then Lilly, appeared at the door. Rushing down the steps at first, they slowed to show some semblance of dignity. Having been dressed for work in the field, they had quickly changed to good dresses and further straightened their hair. They were both beautiful. I couldn't help but notice how lovely Lilly was, even for a sister, but my eyes were chiefly on Mary. Turning fourteen in less than a month, she was almost a grown woman.

Henry swept Lilly up in his arms, kissed her, and turned about with her. She was instantly over the need for shyness or restraint. I hugged Mary and gave her a small kiss. We were a long ways from establishing a relationship as committed as Henry's and Lilly's apparently was. I sensed such a thing at some time in the future, however.

At the house, Henry took charge long enough to introduce

Sally and Nathaniel and explain their status. He took care to say that Nathaniel had, using his shotgun, perhaps saved some of us in a fight back up the road. Close to recovering from that battle, but still showing some sign of it, Coon and George were evidence of what could have happened to all of us. Everybody wanted to hear about it immediately but Aunt May broke in and organized us.

"We can talk at the table; and for the rest of the day. There'll be no work this afternoon. You men strip those horses and wash up. Girls, unload the wagon. Henry, where do you want these crate baskets?"

"They best be put in the attic for now," Henry said. "Or wherever you put those other shipments. It's the same kind of stuff."

"Oh my goodness," Aunt May said. "You boys have been off taking advantage of someone. Go on and take care of the horses."

Nathaniel said, "Just tell me where the animals go. I'll take care of them."

Henry replied, "I'll go help. Everyone else can wash up. We'll be right in."

Grabbing his hand, Lilly went with him.

Knowing she would be hesitant, I got Sally's hand and pulled her toward the pump and wash basin. Though she had been raised in the big house, it was a rare occasion that she had been allowed to sit down at the table while the adult members of the family were there, and never with strangers. It also became apparent when Henry, Lilly, and Nathaniel came to the kitchen that Nathaniel was hesitant, even with Sally there. He had never eaten with white folk, other than at our house in Atlanta and on the trail with us.

Actually, the kitchen was a separate building away from the big house where all cooking and eating was done. Reached by a covered walk, it was designed to keep the house from burning if the wood stove got out of control and started a fire. During the winter it became a warm assembly place for everyone. The main house was used mostly for sleeping. Using Confederate paper money, Doctor Isaac had purchased the hundred-acre farm adjacent to Aunt May's farm. Though the farmhouse on the new property was used for sleeping by some of us, we all ate in Aunt May's kitchen.

George returned to his family the day after we arrived. Henry sent him off with one of the saddle horses we had taken from that gang in Georgia. He also paid George handsomely. I don't know how much, but George left smiling.

After a half day of talking and loafing, Aunt May had us all hard at work. Most of us worked at cutting cane and making molasses. Henry and Nathaniel got a wagonload of boards and started increasing the size of the horse pen and shelter. Sally was highly skilled in household activities of all kinds. She soon became an instrumental part of that work.

Henry asked his ma to teach Nathaniel about reading, writing, and numbers. She's the best I've ever seen at that. They were spending one or two hours every evening at it, but then everyone did. It was just a way of life in the house.

Doctor Isaac, Henry, and I discussed medicine during the study time. He was particularly interested in our experiences at Shiloh and Chickamauga. We confirmed his theory that the use of alcohol to clean instruments, hands, and wounds greatly increases the percentage of surgery patients surviving. Also, we continued learning from Doctor Isaac. Soon after the horse pen, shelter, and cane grinding was under control, the three of us began making medical calls together again.

Nathaniel spent an hour or two every day seeing to the welfare of the horses. He knew as much about treating horses as we knew about treating people, which on our part still wasn't something to boast about.

On December 8, we received a letter from Jolene.

Atlanta, November 30, 1863

Dearest Henry and Ben,

This morning Tyler left for Dalton. You might or might not know about the battle at Chattanooga of November 24. Ours was a defeat. The Confederate troops having withdrawn to Dalton, we all fear for Atlanta. We will forever be indebted to you for the medical leave that kept Tyler away from the slaughter of November 24.

Alice left for Dalton with Tyler. He'll assist her through our lines. You will not hear from her until after she arrives in St. Louis. Mother and I will remain here.

Having rented your house out, I'm living with mother. I'm taking a smaller fee in specie rather than a large one in paper. The value of Confederate paper money in Atlanta has fallen to twenty-one dollars to one in gold or silver. We pray that you are as well as we are.

Your lifelong friend,
Jolene

Henry posted a letter in return assuring her of our health and friendship. He also told her that she and her mother could keep any rent from the house beyond its taxes and upkeep.

As we were sitting at the table that evening discussing the St. Louis businesses, Henry turned the conversation to other business by saying, "Those Arabian mares are too valuable for just riding. We need to get them bred."

Nathaniel said, "Doctor Henry, they are bred. Two weeks before you got them they were bred to the only Arabian stallion that I know of in Georgia. They should have colts next October.

I just hadn't thought to tell you."

"Have you thought about what you would like to do in the future?" Henry asked Nathaniel.

"My dream would be to own a farm and raise some cotton and horses. How to get the farm is my biggest problem. I'll probably end up working for somebody, working with their horses," he replied.

"There's still a war going and we can't be certain how it will end. I firmly believe the Union will win. The South might sue for peace, but I don't believe the North will allow it. Ben and I have acquired quite a bit of property and money over the past two years. We've got a hotel and other property in St. Louis, money buried in Atlanta, money here, Confederate paper money that we won't ever get traded, and gold and silver pieces and art work stashed here. We also own the house in Atlanta that we were using as an office. Jolene's looking after it. Alice is probably in St. Louis by now looking after our property there. I guess what I'm trying to get around to saying, Nathaniel, is that I would like for you to consider working with us on a horse farm after the war. We have enough money to start one when the time's right"

"I'm ready. I don't have to think about it, suh," he said.

"What I have in mind is buying a farm, maybe five hundred or a thousand acres, and you running it. I doubt that any of us would be there very often. You would have to make the decisions about hiring and firing, and buying and selling. I'm sure that, over time, Sally could learn to handle the books. I know ma would help her," Henry said.

"Like I said, we don't have to think about it, suh. We'll be ready when the time comes. The only other thing I have to do is see to my ma and three sisters."

"Are they at the plantation?" Henry asked.

"My ma and two sisters are, suh. One was traded while young. We don't know for sure where she is. She's said to be around Macon."

Henry had plans for lots of things. Usually I learned about

them as they unfolded, which was fine with me. The way I saw it I hadn't brought very much to this relationship. Rapidly learning to be a physician, I was far better off than I had ever hoped to be. Henry considered Coon and me as full partners in everything.

With the cane grinding finished, Henry and I became more active in studying with Doctor Isaac. Day by day we discovered that he had a wealth of medical knowledge not recorded in any books. As fast as possible, he made all that available to us. We were also able to show him a few things learned while on the battlefield.

Though it was three hundred yards to the main wagon road from the farmhouse, we kept the gate to the lane closed. We were sitting on a fortune in gold, silver, and art, and another in horses. Afraid someone might try to take them for the war effort, Nathaniel put the two Arabian mares and the thoroughbred gelding in their stalls every time someone stopped at the gate. Those three horses were never ridden off the property. We probably would have had to go on the run again if the military had tried to take them.

It seemed we had only been home a few days when Mary's birthday and then Christmas came. As usual we had our gift giving the night before Christmas. It was a good Christmas. Though there were shortages of everything everywhere throughout the South, there were no shortages of food and good people on Aunt May's farm. I couldn't help but remember the Christmas two years before and sitting close to Ella Mae in the barn. Thinking about her made me wonder where Ella Mae was and how she was getting on. There was no desire to see her, just curiosity. I didn't know it back in west Florida, but it could have never worked between us.

Him being twenty, and her turning seventeen in a few days, we expected an announcement from Henry and Lilly around Christmastime, but none came. Though Mary had apparently decided on me, and I was thinking about her, it was far too early for us. I wasn't ready for that and I thought Mary was too young. Henry and I gave Mary and Lilly some nice silver for their hope chests, however.

Soon after Christmas Henry seemed to become restless again. On a trip to deliver a baby he spoke of his concerns to Doctor Isaac and me.

"We still have close to twenty-eight thousand dollars in Confederate paper money. The harder we work, the more we seem to get. Since almost no one has specie, there doesn't seem to be a way to get all our paper money changed. I need to be in Savannah, Macon, or Atlanta. The war's going to end soon and our paper money will be worthless. It might be best if we all go north."

"You're probably right about the war and money, but I don't think we need to go anywhere right now. There's enough money already. We only need to think about our safety until the fighting ends. This seems to be the safest place to be. It might be that the war will be over without us having to be in the middle of it," Doctor Isaac said.

"I think I'll agree with Doctor Isaac," I said. It was one of the few times I didn't come down hard on Henry's side.

Henry dropped the subject but it was apparent he wasn't satisfied with it. I decided to clam up and wait for him to make a decision about what we were going to do. Whatever it was, I would go along.

Other than for making house calls, we stayed on Aunt May's farm and kept our necks pulled in. Henry and I continued to learn a lot about medicine from our house calls and discussions with Doctor Isaac. Most everyone else stayed busy with the strawberries, either preparing the ground or preparing plants. Though Henry and I helped with the farm some, the women insisted that we spend most of our time studying with Doctor Isaac. Sally had taken over the kitchen and house duties. Having been raised on those duties, it was her choice of things. Miss Daisy worked with Sally mostly. The rest of the women worked with the strawberries, or turnips and collard greens.

At least every other day a load of farm goods was carried to the station at Lake City. Since Aunt May was mostly receiving Confederate paper money in payment, sometimes I didn't know why she bothered. The last value posted for Confederate paper was $21.50 to one dollar in silver. The value had seemed to stabilize a little at that point.

On January 23, a letter came from Alice.

St. Louis, December 15, 1863

Dear Henry and Ben,

This is the second letter I've mailed. Since all the mail might not get through, I'll mail one every two weeks after this. I've been in St. Louis for seven days and am well. Though the situation across Missouri is not yet stable, Union forces are in firm control here in the city. It's an amazing city and its size is almost overpowering. Prices are fairly stable, everything is plentiful, and business at the hotel is booming. I feel guilty because of occupying a room that would otherwise rent for $1.00 a day in silver.

There are many opportunities here for people with money. As you directed, I'm considering several small investments with funds that you left in the bank and those that accrue from your hotel and other property. I believe that buying the balance of the hotel might be one of the best possible moves. I've begun talks about that. I feel that I'm learning quickly and can soon be of value to you. I await further instructions.

Your obedient servant,
Alice

Henry didn't immediately respond. Having made a judgment about Alice, he was leaving it in her hands.

News of the fighting was sparse and inconclusive. CSA forces were still holding on north of Atlanta and Lee was active in the east. Fighting continued on a smaller scale in all the Southern states. The pattern of fighting we were hearing about, and the size of the heavily contested areas, left room for anyone who wished to move around and avoid the massed armies while traveling north or south. Various cavalry units on both sides were doing so.

General Forest, with 8,000 Confederate cavalry troopers, was striking behind the Union armies at will it seemed. Units of Union cavalry were also raiding throughout north Georgia and Alabama. Though things seemed to be at something of a stalemate between the large armies, both Henry and Doctor Isaac said the Yankees were just consolidating their holdings and improving their supply lines.

February 8, 1864

Having carried a load of greens to Lake City, Henry's ma and Aunt May returned with news of a massive buildup of Union troops in Jacksonville, fifty miles east of Olustee. After quickly taking complete control of Jacksonville, Union forces were moving west toward Olustee. Doctor Isaac and Henry immediately called everyone together to discuss the situation.

"We don't yet know what the Union plan is," Doctor Isaac said, "but there are some natural assumptions. Their goal could be to take Baldwin. The railroad lines to Fernandina, Cedar Key, and to here are controlled from that point. We have to assume they'll do that. They could then go north into Georgia or south into Waldo and Gainesville. We can't rule those out. I think their real goal might be to follow the railroad west through Sanderson and Olustee, and to take Lake City. If they occupy Lake City, that would effectively cut Southern forces off from Florida's cattle and other farm products. Assuming they are coming here, we must prepare for what we'll do."

Aunt May said, "I'm just going to sit right here. This has been my home for the last twenty years and will be until I'm taken away or die."

"That part's settled then," Henry said. "We must immediately bury the gold and silver pieces. If they take this place, they'll steal everything and burn the house. Ben and I've seen it before. Aunt May, you need to put enough preserved food in a place where it won't be found so that you can still eat for a month if everything else is destroyed. You also need to hide some seed."

Speaking to my ma, he said, "You and your family need to make arrangements to leave for the Suwannee if things go badly for the Confederate forces. Take the rig and the two Arabian mares, but don't leave unless necessary."

"What are we going to do?" I asked.

Henry replied, "I'm going to do what I can to stop them. Failing at that, I guess I'll be patching people up."

"I'm going with you," Coon said.

"I am too," I said.

"Okay," Henry replied. "If things go badly, one of us needs to bring word here, and go with our families to the Suwannee. Nathaniel, you'll be safest here. They'll just liberate you."

"I'm already liberated, suh," Nathaniel replied. "I feel obligated to help defend this place."

"The command under General Finegan has no black troops," Henry said. "You could be shot by the wrong people."

Doctor Isaac said, "I'll go to Olustee and offer my services.

Nathaniel, if you wish to be of service, you could help me."

"I'll go with you," Miss Daisy volunteered.

"I'll go too," Henry's ma said.

"I'd be proud to help you, Doctor Isaac," Nathaniel said.

Preparing that night, Henry, Coon, and I left the morning of February 9 for Olustee. Everyone else was busy burying our valuables and otherwise getting prepared. There not being an immediate need for Doctor Isaac's group in Olustee, they planned to report the next day and then be on call.

There wasn't a public show of affection as Henry, Coon, and I left. There wasn't a dry eye among the women either. Everyone understood the situation. There was a job that had to be done. In order to defend our home and families, Henry, Coon, and I were finally taking up arms on a side.

Well mounted and leading a pack animal loaded with our instruments, medical supplies, food for one week, corn for the horses, and our sleeping rolls, we arrived in Olustee before 9:00 A.M. Once there, we heard that Union forces had already taken Baldwin.

The source of our information, a colonel, asked, "Are you men here to enlist?"

"No," Henry replied. "We're just here to help keep them out of this area."

A militia sergeant standing nearby said, "Colonel, I know these men. Two of them are physicians."

The colonel asked, "Is that true?"

"Yes," I said. "We served as physicians at both Shiloh Church and Chickamauga. Henry also helped out when Quantrill raided Independence, Missouri. Due to a shifting of the lines and a series of other events at Shiloh Church, we served both sides there."

"Our need for you will be as physicians," the colonel said.

"When will that be?" Henry asked. "I've seen these things drag out for months before the serious fighting starts."

"General Finegan is fighting a delaying action and awaiting reinforcements. We only have six hundred men gathered at this time. They're reported to have seven thousand," the colonel replied. "We'll try to stop them short of Lake City if they come this way."

"We'll join those fighting the delaying action," Henry said. "We're well mounted and well armed. Also, there will certainly be casualties among those fighting the delaying action. We can help them."

"Three men can't make much difference in the fight. You could be of great service here as physicians," the colonel said.

"Sir, we have two Spencer repeating rifles and three hundred and seventy cartridges that fit them, and one of the latest Springfield Breechloaders. We have the firepower of a company, the reach of a Sharps rifle, and can move with the stealth of only having four horses. Still, we will be here to serve as physicians when the big fight comes. In the meantime you need time to prepare. We can help by providing that time," Henry replied.

The colonel said, "Good luck to you. We've lost telegraph contact with Barbers plantation and Baldwin, so we can only assume the enemy is headed for Sanderson."

Following the Lake City to Jacksonville road east as the Union force wound its way west, we started for Sanderson, some ten miles away. Occasionally seeing other armed men, both mounted and walking, we were keenly aware that we would not be alone. Others besides the military would be joining this fight.

Sparsely covered with longleaf pine, all of which had been chipped for turpentine, the area through which we rode had few buildings and little natural cover that would conceal a horse and rider. The ground was covered with grass, largely wire grass, and low palmetto bushes. The palmettos were mostly waist high, but higher near the swamps. The only cover tall enough to hide horse and rider was furnished by some of the small swamps where there were clustered cypress trees and the underbrush was tall.

Occasionally seeing refugees going west, we inquired as to the location of the forward Union positions. No one seemed to know. We had long since passed Sanderson when we met a scouting party of three CSA troopers who gave us our first information.

Raising his hand to stop them as they galloped their horses toward us from the east, Henry got them to stop and asked, "What's the rush? What's ahead?"

"Sixteen or eighteen Union cavalry are less than ten minutes behind us," was the reply. "We were sent out as scouts and are to report back with their location."

"Let's hide our horses behind the cover of that swamp and stop them here," Henry said. "You can then report where they are, not where they were."

"We're supposed to report back," the sergeant said.

"Do as you wish. We'll stop them here," Henry said.

"Just you three?" the Sargent said.

"We have two repeating rifles and one breechloader," Henry said. "They'll stop."

"Then we'll stay with you," the sergeant said.

"Fine," Henry replied. "Since you men only have muzzle-loaders, send one man behind the swamp to hide and hold the horses. We'll take up positions behind some pine trees and surprise them. Wait for me to shoot. I'll start the fight when they're less than a hundred and fifty yards away. If they withdraw we'll get in a few shots. If they charge, we'll have time to do some serious shooting. Either way they can't be one tenth as effective from a running horse as we are braced on a pine tree."

We took our positions and waited. I was on the left and Henry was on the right. Coon and the two soldiers with muzzle-loader rifles were in the center. The Union cavalry appeared in minutes. The troopers and the upper half of their horses came into view at three hundred yards. Standing behind a tree like the others, I slid my rifle barrel under a palmetto frond cut for concealment and braced on the tree for my first shot. Henry let them get to what I thought was 120 yards before he opened the fight. Without announcing our intentions, Henry took a captain out of his saddle. Three more went down in the volley that followed.

The smoke from our rifles clearly marked our position, and the fact that there were only five of us. Thinking to reach us before we could reload, some young lieutenant shouted charge, drew his saber, and started for us. Henry and I both must have shot him because he's the only one who fell when we fired our second rounds. Two more fell from our third shots. Wheeling their horses at less than eighty yards, all but one of those still left in the saddle charged the other way. Having got a second round in the breechloader, Coon shot him down. It was over and our new companions hadn't finished reloading their muzzleloaders for a second shot. Without reason, both Henry and I held our fire or another two or three would have gone down. That dead lieutenant's mare kept right on charging after he fell. Coon got in front of her and caught her.

After most of a minute had passed, and the Union detachment was out of sight, the sergeant came over and wanted to see my rifle.

Following a brief look, he said, "How about you boys hanging around with us through the rest of this."

As I was explaining our situation, Henry came walking up. The horse holder also brought our horses. In the meantime, Coon adjusted the stirrups of the Lieutenant's mare to suit the length of his legs. He then changed some of our load to the mare he had been riding. We could move better in a running fight if the horses were more lightly loaded.

The sergeant then said, "Maybe we should go pick up those Yankee's weapons and horses."

Henry replied, "Be careful, Sergeant. You can step on a dead snake's mouth and get bit. There's a good possibility some of those men are just lying quiet."

Taking their weapons, stray horses, and one wounded man

as a prisoner, we followed the sergeant west and bivouacked with his unit. Being with them, we wouldn't have to post a guard that night. The prisoner was rushed to the rear for questioning. Every man in the unit came by to look at our rifles and talk. Everyone was far more interested in our fighting and our rifles than in us being physicians. Unfortunately for them, we would see some of these men again when they would value us more for being surgeons.

Staying with the sergeant's cavalry unit, we hit some advance Union units twice the next day. In spite of our efforts, and those of others, the Yankee's advanced units were reported to have reached Sanderson by that afternoon. Their main force, however, had still not put in an appearance. It was my understanding that cavalry raids on the main Union force were slowing it.

Though only fourteen miles from Aunt May's when we bivouacked that night, we again spent the night with the cavalry detachment. Riding twenty-eight miles round trip would have nearly killed our already tired horses, and would have taken all night.

We learned from a messenger that Union raids were extending in several directions from the railroad track. It was no longer certain where the main body would go. Logic told us it would be to Lake City. The Union general would then want to advance to the Suwannee River and destroy the railroad bridge that crossed it.

To that point our medical skills had been needed only to patch up a few men and to get them in a boxcar to Olustee. Since we still controlled the railroad west of Sanderson, the train was in use.

During this same time every able-bodied person who could be mustered was building breastworks near Olustee. Extending between Ocean Pond on the north and a large swamp on the south, those breastworks formed a line that was one and a half miles long. The line crossed the Jacksonville to Tallahassee railroad and road. Since Union forces seemed to be advancing along those roads, this was the logical place to build breastworks. Also, Ocean Pond isn't a pond, it's a big lake. The location of a lake at one end, and a large swamp at the other, would make it impossible for the Union forces to turn our flanks. Their options would be to attempt to breech our lines, leave the road and maneuver through bad terrain, disengage and return to Sanderson, or build up their own breastwork and remain in place near Olustee. The last of these would leave them open to a flanking movement from CSA Forces. It appeared the enemy would have to fight in a place of General Finegan's choosing or retire from the area.

To provide time for construction of the breastworks, and time for reinforcements to arrive, a number of cavalry raids were conducted. Never, however, did the Confederates attempt a major engagement.

On February 11, we were asked to support an infantry company that was set up in a blocking position west of Sanderson. There was an early morning fight in which a small unit of Union soldiers withdrew back toward Sanderson. Our side sustained a couple of injuries. Those injured were given emergency attention and sent back to Olustee. The day then passed without further encounters. It was reported, however, that a larger Union force had entered Sanderson.

Lying in the shade of a pine tree at mid-afternoon, Henry said, "Coon, you're the lightest of us, why don't you go to Aunt May's house and check on them. You can give a report on us and tell us how they are when you get back. Take three horses and switch off riding them. It's only twelve miles. Barring the unforeseen, you could be there before dark. We're also almost out of grain for the horses. You can bring some, and bring more supplies."

Because of the Yankee lieutenant's captured horse, Coon taking three mounts still left mounts for Henry and me.

Coon replied, "I'll be back before daylight."

Henry said, "There's no need to rush. Rest the horses overnight and start back tomorrow. We're probably going to be doing the same thing we're doing now."

I said, "Bring baked sweet potatoes and a smoked pork

shoulder, and kiss Mary for me. On second thought you don't have to since she's your sister."

We were at the same place when Coon returned the next afternoon.

Riding in, he said, "Everyone was fine but worried. They were glad to get news. Everybody sent their love and prayers."

Coon's horses were loaded. Aunt May had sent a bushel of already baked sweet potatoes, two quarts of strawberry preserves, syrup, corn meal, two smoked hams, dry grits, and some fresh-baked cornbread. The women had got up early and baked before Coon left.

I asked, "What about Nathaniel? Has he gone to Olustee?"

"No. He's at the house," Coon replied. "He tried to come with me but I told him to stay. If he hears cannon fire he's to join you at the breastworks in Olustee. I heard back down the line that some reinforcements are in Lake City. Some of them will be in Olustee tomorrow. More are due in a couple of days. Doctor Isaac's in Lake City at the hospital. Nathaniel wanted to go with Doctor Isaac but was asked to help you two in Olustee when the battle starts there."

"Where are the reinforcements from?" I asked.

"Mostly from Georgia and South Carolina," Coon replied. "General Colquitt and twenty-eight hundred Georgia men are supposed to be on the way from Charleston. Five hundred Florida and Georgia troops with artillery are on the way from Savannah."

Having walked toward us, the captain who was commanding the unit we were supporting heard the last part of our conversation. He said, "If we have enough men we'll whip them."

Not responding to the comment, Henry said, "For tonight you can pass out these things to your men. Yours being a small unit, there should be enough for supper and breakfast, and maybe noon tomorrow."

Aunt May had caused us once again to be raised to the status of hero. Most of those men hadn't eaten anything but cold cornbread for a couple of days.

While there was little change in our situation, on February 13, a Union cavalry force of several hundred was reported to be near Waldo, some thirty miles to the south. Though the Union raids were penetrating deeply to the south, it was still thought those were diversionary.

Leaving the small infantry unit, which was receiving no action, we rode to the sound of gunfire. On two occasions we found situations where our medical skill was useful. During the process of evacuating the wounded we also received word that some reinforcement units had already arrived in Olustee.

The next day found us riding with a small cavalry detachment between Sanderson and Lulu. At that location we were only nine miles east of Aunt May's farm. Her farm was directly between Lake City and us. Lake City was only sixteen miles away.

Encountering a Union cavalry patrol, we had a brief, but intense, exchange of gunfire before they retired at a gallop to the east. Since a couple of our men were wounded, and one of their wounded was captured, we gave no pursuit. Shortly after placing his command in a defensive position, the captain came to see his wounded as we attended them.

"I was in doubt as to the value of us patrolling this area," he said. "I couldn't understand why I was sent this far south of any roads."

As he continued tending his patient's wound, Henry replied, "If they don't go through Olustee, this is the most probable route for the Union force to use in reaching Lake City. Of all their choices, there are two that are most likely. First, they can attack your breastworks at Olustee. Second, they can swing around the swamp at the south end of your line. Though it's a longer route and rough traveling, once at Lulu they have a straight shot to Lake City. They could also turn north from Lulu and engage you in the open woods behind your breastworks. Those last options have the disadvantage of leaving the railroad, which is their best supply line, and the best escape route in case they're defeated.

Having finished with the patient, Henry drew a map in the dirt.

Pausing to consider the map and Henry's words, the captain asked, "On what military experience do you base your opinions?"

Henry replied, "I've commanded no troops. Ben and I did observe some brilliant maneuvers, and some blunders, at both Shiloh Church and Chickamauga Creek."

"You were at both of those?" the captain asked, a new respect in his tone.

"Yes," Henry said. "And with three times as many casualties at both battles as there will be total number of men fighting here. I fear, however, that the fighting here will be no less fierce. It matters little to a dying man that there are two thousand others or twenty thousand dying.

"If you were the Union General, how would you do it?" the captain asked.

"I'm not sure," Henry replied. "But, with five thousand men on your side, and seven thousand on mine, I would not make a frontal attack on your fixed positions. Our families are close by and we'll leave you now to see to their safety. If you get these wounded men to Olustee, they'll be fine."

Riding cautiously, we arrived at the farm well before dark that Friday afternoon, February 14. Nathaniel looked to the horses' welfare. We had little to do but take a warm bath in a tub in the kitchen, then talk well into the night. Taking a bath in the kitchen was nice. It was the first time I had been warm in five days. February in north Florida gets mighty cold sometimes. It was dipping below freezing on some nights. The cold weather isn't all that bad unless you're out in it twenty-four hours a day, which we were.

Cold or not, Henry and Lilly walked off from the house shortly after dark. It wasn't anything unusual, and it didn't slow the talking as we sat around the table in the kitchen. Their return, almost an hour later, didn't slow the conversation either.

When the buzz of the conversation grew dim around the table, Lilly silenced everyone momentarily with an announcement. She said, "Henry and I have decided to marry."

Everything got quiet for a couple of seconds. Lilly had certainly taken the women's mind off the hostilities. Since Lilly was wearing a nice ring, it was obviously something Henry had been planning for some time.

Ma was up and walking toward Lilly when Aunt May said, "We all knew that was coming, child. When?"

"In a month or two. We haven't decided yet," Lilly replied.

Ma had got to Lilly by then. First grabbing Lilly up and hugging her, she then hugged Henry. Far from ready for that step, I avoided Mary's eyes.

The women looked at, and talked about, Lilly's ring for some time. Ma also listed the date and time in her bible: February 14, 1864, at 8:30 P.M. The women naturally took on about it being Valentine's Day. They all stayed up and talked about it until almost 10:00 P.M.

Following breakfast the next morning, Henry kept all the adults at the breakfast table and said, "We have to decide what to do about the fight. The only reason I joined in was because Aunt May lives here. I was hoping we could keep them out of this area until the war ends. With that Yankee patrol headed this way yesterday, I'm not certain the Union general isn't going to take this route. Even if he doesn't, there still might be other Union patrols coming this way. They could burn the buildings and do no telling what else."

"There's lots of good boys at Olustee ready to fight," Aunt May said.

"Yes," Henry said. "At least one from every family within fifty miles, and others from beyond that. Their being in Olustee won't do you any good if the Union force comes this way. Though it's not a war of my choosing, I'll also do my part in it because you live here. I don't condone the cause of either side, however.

Sometimes I'm not certain what either side's real cause is."

"Maybe we should hang around here for a few days and patrol our own area," Coon said.

"That's kind of what I was thinking," Henry said. "What do you think, Ben?"

"Well," I said, "I'm concerned about everyone here. There is likely to be a Yankee patrol this way. What do you think Nathaniel?"

"As a free man I chose to take shelter and eat here," he replied. "I'll do what I can to help. Whatever Doctor Henry says."

"I'm not sure any of us have the answers," Henry said. "For today, I think we should stay and patrol this area. Two of us can ride the surrounding area while the other two fort up in a building. Everyone else should also stand by with weapons. We won't fight a big force, but we can keep a patrol from burning the buildings and pillaging."

When everyone nodded, Henry said, "Nathaniel and I will ride this morning. Coon and Ben can patrol in the afternoon. We'll not be more than a mile from the house and can respond to gunfire. If we hear cannons from Olustee we'll go there. That'll mean the main forces have engaged. We'll be needed to help the wounded. If all's quiet at the end of the day, we'll talk again."

I positioned myself in the attic with a Spencer and a shotgun. Coon positioned himself in the barn loft with a Springfield and a shotgun. Only going outside to tend to essential chores, the women mostly stayed in one or the other of the buildings, their shotguns in hand. Exchanging duties with Henry and Nathaniel for the afternoon, Coon and I patrolled within one mile of the house. As dark settled in, and having seen no CSA or Union troops, we gathered at the house for the night. Coon and Nathaniel slept in the barn that night to be close to the horses.

At breakfast the next morning, Henry said, "I'm going to Olustee to see if our help's needed and gather news."

"I'll go along," I said.

"Okay," Henry replied. "But Coon and Nathaniel should stay here. We'll return tonight, conditions permitting."

Upon arriving at the Olustee station it became apparent that good progress was being made in preparing fixed positions from which to do battle. We also learned that Gainesville, thirty-seven miles to the south, had been taken on February 14 by a Union cavalry force. That event cast doubt on the intentions of the large force facing us. Some of the reported behavior of those taking Gainesville also increased our concerns about our families.

There being no casualties at Olustee, we left in mid-afternoon and returned home. While there had been no sighting of Union troops at the house that day, a CSA patrol had been there. It being a unit that we had ridden with, the patrol members recognized Coon. After having been fed by Aunt May, they promised to return every time the opportunity occurred.

Seeing no need to return to Olustee on February 17, we again patrolled and guarded the house. It occasioned no result other than our peace of mind, and the opportunity for me to flirt with Mary.

Again on February 18, Henry and I rode to Olustee, with the same result as on the sixteenth. It was very clear from the work in Olustee that General Finegan was determined for the enemy to come to him.

Reinforcements and volunteers had then increased Finegan's force to 5,200 men. I couldn't help but think of Shiloh. We had seen as many as thirty lines of that many men between the two sides. In spite of the smaller number at Olustee, this somehow didn't seem like a less dangerous place.

Returning to the house, we spent February 19 there. We were constantly alert for the sound of cannon fire to announce the main event. When the CSA patrol returned on that day, the men were again fed. Knowing the members of the patrol, we talked of their events and ours since last we rode together.

The next day Henry and I again rode to Olustee. Arriving there at 9:00 A.M., we received word the main Union force was advancing. As they approached, shortly after noon, General Finegan ordered his cavalry forward to engage them. Once engaged, the cavalry was then to retreat, drawing the Union force toward the prepared positions. As the battle heated up, and not sure the Union troops would be drawn all the way to the breast-works, General Colquitt called several brigades forward and the entire engagement occurred in front of the prepared positions. Henry and I, along with some other physicians, moved up with them. Without the benefit of a prepared position on either side, it was a bloody battle for both.

At one point, an hour after the first cannon fired, I looked up to see Coon and Nathaniel standing beside me. Nathaniel remained to help me. Taking my Spencer, Coon moved forward to join the battle. Henry, Nathaniel, and I were too occupied with our bloody duty to participate in the battle.

The battle ended for the day about dark. As the Union troops rapidly withdrew, it was apparent that there was a complete Confederate victory. As in previous battles in which we were involved, it was total carnage. Figures later released showed almost a thousand Confederate dead or wounded. Union losses were more severe. They listed 1,400 killed or wounded and five hundred missing. We knew that of the five hundred missing, almost all of whom were our prisoners, over four hundred were wounded or dead. The enemy wounded and dead under our control raised the total on the Federal side to 1,800 plus. While the raw numbers were not as staggering as the Shiloh or Chickamauga numbers, it should be said that in terms of the per-cent of those participating who were killed or wounded, Olustee was reported to be the third most vicious battle of the war. As was the case with most battles during the war, everyone knew there could be no accurate count of the casualties. Like Henry, Coon, Nathaniel, and me, many volunteers from the area would have gained no official recognition unless identified when counting the dead.

The wounded who were left behind by the losers became prisoners. It turned out that a large number of the Union wounded we cared for were soldiers from the Eighth United States Colored Troops (USCT), a famous all-black unit that earned its reputation at Olustee. That unit lost 310 of its 575 members there. That they, the Fifty-Forth Massachusetts USCT, and the First North Carolina USCT were there was surprising to us even though we had heard of colored units in the Union army. It was just as surprising to those men to see Nathaniel serving as a physician's aide for the CSA. Receiving better treatment at his hands than at the hands of most others, they were very happy to see him. There was talk of some black prisoners being summarily executed. Those who survived had the bad fortune of being shipped off to Andersonville prison. Fortunately for them, they were shipped around on trains so long that they never got to Andersonville.

Interestingly, not being regarded as legitimate soldiers by the Federal government for which they fought, the black units were given the nonstandard designation USCT. As an additional affront, they only received seven dollars a month instead of the thirteen paid to white Federal soldiers. Upon hearing about the seven dollars a month, it caused me to wonder as to the real motives of Lincoln and the Federal government. Since many of us were fighting for no pay, it wasn't difficult for me to understand why they would fight for seven dollars a month, however.

Soon after the Union force was in full retreat, we received another surprise. Returning to where we were working, Coon said, "Pa was there in the fight."

"How do you know?" I asked. "Did you see him?"

"I thought so one time in the smoke and haze from the guns," he said. "He's in the Seventh Connecticut and they were right in front of me. Strangely enough, their unit is armed with

Spencer repeating rifles. If it hadn't been for them holding us back, we would have killed or captured most of the Yankees. Some of their other units made massive blunders. A couple of units were even marched into battle formation before they loaded their rifles. Many of them never even got their rifles loaded. I picked up a few spare Spencer cartridges from the dead when we finally forced the Seventh back. We might not have been able to push them back except that most of them were running out of cartridges. Some of the dead that I checked didn't have any. After they fell back, the Fifty-Fourth Massachusetts USCT slowed us enough for the rest of them to escape."

Later, as I worked on those battered bodies from both sides at the Olustee station, I had time to wonder what it was all for, brother fighting brother and son fighting father. At that time I heard a small child cry. Looking to see its plight, I saw a two-year-old child whose toy had been taken by a larger child. Therein I got my answer.

March 1, 1864

Having pursued the Union forces to Jacksonville, the Confederate side began digging in twelve miles from that city. Our work with the wounded done, we then reassembled at Aunt May's house. There was great jubilation over the victory among the Southern population, not only in Florida but all throughout the South. Jubilation was not the atmosphere at our gathering around the supper table. Having seen the wealth, huge cities, and the massive armies in the North, Henry and I knew and soon communicated the realities of the situation to the others. Though brutal, this was but a small battle. It could have little influence other than to extend the war.

As we sat at the supper table Henry said, "We need to move north. There might still be worse times ahead."

Aunt May said, "I'm not going to leave here."

"I know," Henry replied. "Since there might come a time when things will be very bad and your Confederate money is worthless, just as you've helped us, when we leave I'm going to leave specie in a sum that will get you through those times."

"Henry's right about the money," Doctor Isaac said. "I'm not so sure about going north, though. There could be considerable danger in that."

"Less, I think, than staying here," Henry replied.

"I'm going if Henry says go," Lilly said.

"Of course you are," Ma said. "We'll go too, John, Ivy, Mary, and I. I can't speak for the others, but Mary was left in my charge. Coon's old enough to know his own mind."

"Doctor Isaac, you need to go," Henry said. "Ben and I had a good practice started in St. Louis. We also own property there. It would be a great place to open your office. Counting refugees and garrisoned soldiers, there are two hundred thousand people living in the city. I hope Ma and Miss Daisy will go, and Nathaniel and Sally."

"You've been there and back. How would we go?" Doctor Isaac asked.

"Ben and I slipped through the lines. We've sent a representative through also," Henry said. "With a larger group, we'll need to avoid the battle areas. That's where the troops are concentrated. There has to be hundreds of miles that aren't under the control of anyone. General Forest goes and comes to the rear of the Union armies at will with eight thousand men. Surely we could go in a small group with little notice. Our biggest danger would be from groups of riffraff. We could arm the women and children with shotguns, and hire George and some others as riders."

"What about the valuable things you've buried here?" Henry's ma asked.

"They're worth little or nothing because no one here has money to buy them," Henry said. "We'll have to leave them where they are until the right time. Those things need to be in New York or Boston where people have money. There are several million people in that area of the country, almost a million in New York City alone. Our items would be of considerable value in those cities, but we'll not be concerned with that now. We could use the money buried in Atlanta, however."

"It's just too far, and too hard of a trip on your mother and Daisy," Doctor Isaac said.

"I'll give that some thought and we'll talk again," Henry replied. "Just keep it in mind. I feel strongly that going is the best thing."

Things returned to normal over the next couple of days. That is, if you call picking strawberries and bundling turnip greens normal after the recent battle. Henry, Doctor Isaac, and I returned to the more mundane practice of medicine. We also made calls on some of those who were injured at Olustee.

One week later Henry left on his mare for Lake City. Stabling her there, he took the train to Tallahassee. The train stopped overnight at Lake City so it would make little sense to catch it at Olustee and then have to spend the night in Lake City. Henry didn't announce his purpose and we didn't ask. Since he had long ago started confiding things to Lilly, I'm sure she knew but she didn't say.

Henry returned on March 11. Ordinarily he would have brought trinkets for the kids, but there was little enough to buy beyond what could be grown in the soil. He did bring a squirrel rifle for John. John, who was then twelve, didn't have one of his own.

After supper, and over coffee, Henry told of his trip. "I've been to Tallahassee, and north into Georgia nearly thirty miles.

The Florida railroad still ends at Quincy. It's only thirty miles from there to the nearest Georgia tracks. That's the closest the Florida and Georgia tracks come to joining at any point. From here straight north to the Georgia tracks it's sixty miles. It's a longer route through Tallahassee than going the route taken by George and Coon to Atlanta, but less of it is without riding a train. Taking the train and hiring a rig in Quincy, one could reach Atlanta in five days, and with only one day by wagon."

"This has to do with us going north?" Doctor Isaac asked.

"Yes," Henry said. "I propose to travel with you, Ma, Miss Daisy, Lilly, and Sally. Traveling as doctors, nurses, and servant, we'll have priority passage. Taking the horses, wagons, and every-one else, Ben, Coon, Nathaniel, George, and three other riders can take the route we took to Atlanta two years ago. We have friends along the way who know Ben. The wagons will travel to Duluth, about twenty miles northwest of Atlanta. We'll meet the wagons in Duluth. After that, we'll all travel north and then north-northeast. We should find a Federal train station within a hundred miles of Duluth. Doctor Isaac and the women can go from there to St. Louis by train. The rest of us will bring the hors-es and wagons. Along the way we might find property that's suit-able for a horse farm. I don't have a particular location in mind."

"That's quite a plan," Doctor Isaac said.

"Yes," Ma said. "And it's a good plan."

Henry said, "I don't know who wants to go, but it's the best I can come up with. Things might change. We'll have to keep track of the major battles and troop movements. I've ordered a couple of papers sent here by train so we get the best possible news."

Ma said, "When do you propose to go?"

"April twenty-sixth, for the wagons," Henry replied. "By the middle of April the grass should be up enough for the horses to graze a little. We'll leave by train from Lake City on the second of May."

"That leaves us some time to decide," Doctor Isaac said.

"Nathaniel and I don't need any time," Sally said. "We've already decided to go."

"We're going too," Ma said.

There was no question about Coon and me. We would go wherever Henry went.

What we learned from the newspapers, and from rumors, was that there seemed to be one continuous moving war in Virginia. In Georgia there were several separate battles going on. Sieges, skirmishes, and constant raids conducted by both sides made for a battlefield that was not clearly defined, other than for the situation between Atlanta and Chattanooga. There, they sat with armies numbering 55,000 for the Confederates and over 65,000 for the Union. Neither side was willing to massively engage the other at that time.

The value of Confederate paper money kept falling. It then stood at twenty-five paper dollars to one of gold or silver. Still having over $25,000 in Confederate paper, it seemed we had missed the best opportunities to divest ourselves. We had, however, traded or spent well over $35,000 of our Confederate paper money. The problem was that we kept acquiring more. Having services that were required by many, and perishable goods that had to be sold, Confederate paper money was pretty easy to acquire at its current value. Though we didn't trade in perishable goods routinely, we were sometimes left with some in payment for our service.

A lift in spirits was provided for everyone when Lilly announced her wedding date as April 15. After that the women had fodder for conversation every time they gathered. Even with shortages of everything, a common cause ignites ingenuity like no other thing. A white gown was retrieved from its storage place and alterations began. All other appropriate things were also retrieved from attics and storage rooms of friends and neighbors.

The battle of Olustee was not long past and Henry's participation in it was well known throughout the area. Many local residents had sons or husbands who had felt his probe in search of a minié ball, and his knife and needle in repairing their wound. Aunt May and Doctor Isaac were also well regarded in the community. Additionally, everyone was looking for a celebration to rally around. Ma announced there was an open invitation and the wedding soon became a community affair. Though Henry had thought to have a small wedding at Aunt May's house, he didn't have the heart to say so except to me, so it was planned for the church.

It seemed that every able person within a four-hour buggy ride came. Though the wedding occurred on Tuesday, it soon took on the atmosphere of a Sunday dinner on the grounds at the church. All the women brought food.

As had been prescribed by Henry, the ceremony itself was brief. Perhaps as an omen of things to come, I stood up for Henry, and Mary for Lilly.

Shortly after the reception started it became obvious there was more to drink than cool lemonade. Within an hour two fiddlers were called forth. The party continued in earnest then. I recall hearing the preacher comment that he would like to see all these people on Sunday morning. It was a vain wish. Less than a half of them had been able to get in the church for the ceremony. Pausing only for Lilly and Henry to depart three hours after the ceremony, the party continued well into the night.

April 26, 1864

We pulled out of the lane that morning headed north with two wagons pulled by mules. Nathaniel drove the lead wagon and Mary the other. Coon, George, and I, along with three riders hired for the trip, were on horseback. Being seven months pregnant, the two Arabian mares were tied behind a wagon. Nathaniel, Mary, John, and Ivy were armed with shotguns. Those of us on horseback were armed with revolvers and rifles. Additional long guns were in the wagons for Henry's party that would meet us in Duluth, Georgia, on May 10.

Well-armed with passes bearing the names of general officers of both the CSA and Union, we should go unchallenged by local marshals and the state militia. Also well armed with weapons, and with no apparent wealth beyond our animals, we would be avoided by most of those seeking ill-gotten personal gain. When joined by Henry's group for what would be the most dangerous part of the trip, our armed presence would increase.

Our first few days on the trip passed without an event worthy of reporting. Our route was roughly the same as Henry's and my flight of two years past. We crossed the Florida railroad near Olustee and the Georgia railroad to Savannah two and a half days later. Those were the same tracks that Doctor Isaac's group would travel on from above Quincy to Savannah before going north to Atlanta. Having concluded that the bold and open way was the safe way, we stuck to the roads and traveled during daylight. That way it would appear we didn't have anything to hide, which we didn't. For the security provided by other people, we camped mostly on large farms or plantations. I provided occasional medical services, which made us welcome at a number of places. By May 2, when Henry would have been leaving, we had passed through Hazelhurst, Georgia, one of the places we already had friends.

Later, Henry told me of their trip. As always he told it briefly.

They left from Lake City by train. Aunt May's family didn't go. Traveling as physicians and nurses, with Sally as a servant, they were given priority access to the train. Henry had written them orders to report to the army of the Tennessee north of Atlanta. After taking one day to get to Quincy, Florida, they hired a rig for transportation to the nearest Georgia railroad terminal. Due to some delays, and the roundabout route they had to take, they arrived in Atlanta on May 8. They went directly to Jolene's mother's house. Since our house was rented, Jolene and her mother agreed to put them up for as long as was needed.

Henry and Lilly spent the following day retrieving the $8,000 in specie we had secreted in Atlanta. A goodly part of it was in silver, causing it to weigh over two hundred pounds, so retrieving the money was a hard day's work. Additionally, the money was buried in five different locations. While retrieving the money they learned that Sherman's forces were on the move in Dalton, sixty miles north of Atlanta. Sherman had been placed in charge of all Union forces to the north of Atlanta. Late in the day word was received in Atlanta that advancing Union forces had engaged Confederate forces in Resaca, fifty miles north of Atlanta.

Leaving Atlanta at first light on May 10, Henry directed their driver on a detour in order to visit the plantation where we had acquired Nathaniel and Sally. He was greeted at the door by a black servant, and shown in to see Mrs. Whipmore.

"I see you have ladies traveling with you. Perhaps they would like to rest in the shade of the porch," she said.

"Thank you," Henry replied. "Yes, that would be nice. I also have Sally with me. There might be friends and relatives she would like to see. My business, however, will be direct and our visit brief. But first, I would inquire as to the health of your grandchildren."

"They're well, thank you. Their health makes the price of their medicine seem smaller as time passes. Others, however, have become afflicted. Tom and my older son's wife, Virginia, are among those. We have no quinine. If you have some I'll pay the price," she said.

"I'm sorry for your grief," Henry said. "I had no knowledge of your plight. There's an eminent physician from Florida in my group. We could invite him in to examine them."

"Please do," she said.

Turning to her maid she ordered refreshments for Henry's group. She then led us to where Henry and Doctor Isaac could examine her son and daughter-in-law. Returning to the parlor after the examination, Henry came to the point of his visit.

"You have some slaves I would like to acquire," Henry said.

"We don't have any we wish to sell," she said. "Who were you interested in?"

"First let me say that General Sherman now has forces attacking Resaca, only fifty miles north of here. I've also heard that units of the Union cavalry have raided some nearby plantations. They were burned and the slaves freed. The same could happen here. You could lose all your slaves. In answer to your question, I'm interested in the mother and sisters of Nathaniel and any husbands and children they have."

"One is married, if you call their voodoo ceremony marrying. They have one child, and I fear another on the way. The other girl, Sarah, hasn't taken up with anyone. What would you say their value is to you and how would you pay?" she said.

"They have little value to me," Henry said. "It's of concern to Nathaniel. He needs to have his full wits and skills focused on a job ahead of him. They'll soon be set free. As to payment, I still have a supply of quinine. It would bring a good price in Atlanta. I could then pay in specie. Or, you could be paid with quinine. You could then do with it as you wish. Before we came I didn't know you were in need. Also, you might consider that your slaves might soon have no value to you."

"How much quinine?" she asked.

"I'll not bargain," Henry said. "It'll do as much good here as anywhere. I'll give you most of what I have. Three times what you received before. Given the current situation, it's far in excess of the value you would get for the five slaves. For purposes of our written agreement I'll also pay you ten dollars in Confederate paper money for each of the five."

The price of Confederate paper having rebounded to twenty to one, he was giving her some very scarce quinine and the equivalent of two and one-half dollars in gold for the lot of them. Though their marketable value was decreasing as rapidly as was Confederate paper money, they would have brought $150 to $600 each, in gold, three years earlier. Also, once in St. Louis, we could buy more quinine at a reasonable price.

"You have a deal," she said. "I'll get pen and paper." Turning to her maid she said, "Bring Nathaniel's relatives and have them bring their things. Doctor Williams wants his stay to be brief."

Henry said, "Sally, go with her. Mrs. Whipmore, I'll also need the use of a mule, wagon, and driver for the balance of the day. The wagon should be back by noon tomorrow."

They arrived at our encampment near Duluth several hours later. It was only after Henry talked to Nathaniel's relatives, and the reality settled in, that they openly talked and sang around the campfire. Henry said much the same thing to them that he had said to Nathaniel and Sally.

"I've written papers that set you free. You can take the wagon back to the plantation if you so choose, you can stay here, or you can leave for any other place. I secured your freedom as a favor for Nathaniel. Though I don't own slaves, I don't usually interfere with those who do. Nathaniel and Sally are going with us to Kentucky where we're going to buy a farm and raise cattle, horses, corn, and sweet potatoes. Nathaniel will be in charge of the farm. He was concerned about your freedom and safety so it was in my interest to ease his mind by securing your freedom. You're free to go with us and stay on at the farm temporarily or permanently. For your efforts there, you will be provided adequate housing and food, and a small income for clothing and other needs. If you stay, and work hard, you'll be placed on a regular wage when the farm begins to make a profit. In case you don't wish to stay, you're still welcome temporarily. Nathaniel will be responsible for deciding who his visitors are just as I am mine. Does anyone have a question?"

When no one said a word, Henry said, "If you go with us I'll have two sets of papers on you, one as my slaves and the other as free people. If we're required to show papers, we'll show the papers we need to show at the time. Having two sets of papers might prevent us from having trouble with people who have feelings either way. You should know that there could be trouble along the way, just as there could be trouble if you stay here or return to the plantation. I think there's a better future for you at the end of the road we travel. Talk with Nathaniel and Sally. If you want to go with us, have your things in our second wagon tomorrow morning."

Without comment Nathaniel's mother carried her small bundle and placed it in the second wagon. She was followed immediately by her youngest daughter, Sarah, and a few seconds later by the others.

Looking at Nathaniel, Henry said, "Show your brother-in-law how to load and use a shotgun. One should be close at hand, but not obvious unless trouble arises. Also, please instruct everyone about the procedure to be used should there be an inquiry about our identity, business, or destination. You know the process."

Nodding, Nathaniel proceeded with his assignment.

Henry's ma said, "You've decided the slaves need to be free?"

"No," Henry replied. "I decided Nathaniel will be a better partner because of this. He also fought with us and I owed him. I think of this as a business investment. How hard will these people work on our farm as compared to the one they were on?"

"I seriously doubt that Nathaniel feels you're indebted to him," Doctor Isaac said, to which everyone laughed.

As we traveled north from Duluth, everyone we met watched us openly. Miss Daisy, the ultimate lady, was sitting on a wagon seat. Lilly, the epitome of young womanhood, was astride her mare. Our party, black and white, some on horses or wagons and some walking alternately to rest the animals and stretch themselves, was armed to the teeth except for the new black women. Having never previously held a firearm, they were only now receiving instruction. The composition and demeanor of the group was, in itself, enough to catch the eye.

My first thought was that Lilly would be placed at extra risk when riding as an outrider with Henry. People would be less likely to shoot a woman in a wagon than as an outrider. At a glance from a hundred yards, however, it could be seen that she was a woman. Rounded off in all the right places, she looked just like Ma. Anyone who would hold his fire because of her gender couldn't easily mistake it when she was either riding or walking. Having received instruction from Henry, and having the mare all this time, Lilly could both ride and shoot as well as most men.

Counting John and Ivy we had eighteen armed people. While it wasn't an excessively large group, it was one that would give pause to even the stout of heart who intended us harm. Providing his usual foresight, Henry had gotten us to install an extra layer of boards around the interior of the wagons, thus providing some protection for those riding and shooting from there. The boards wouldn't stop all bullets, but would stop a minié ball fired from a distance, or a pistol or shotgun charge fired from more than forty yards.

It was our second morning out, and near Dawsonville, Georgia, that the road was blocked by armed riders. There were seven mounted white men. One black man, who was on foot, was holding the leashes of two hounds. I thought we would have a dogfight since Coon's two blueticks were with the wagon at the time. They were frequently off hunting. John soon had them on leashes and tied to a wagon. Riding out front, I was confronted first.

"We're looking for runaways," their spokesman said.

"You'll find none here," I replied as Lilly, Henry, and another rider came up beside me.

"We'll need to see in the wagons," the spokesman said.

"No. I guess you'll have to take my word on it," I said.

"We'll have to look in the wagons," the spokesman said, without making any effort to do so.

"I expect you better clear the road, at least out of shotgun range," Henry said.

Their spokesman was not only a man of pride, but he had also taken a stand. It would be hard to back off even though the odds were not turning out to be in his favor as others came on line beside me. After turning in the saddle and looking at his companions, he decided to take a new approach.

"Those two black men have shotguns," he said.

"And are very proficient with them and quite loyal," I said.

I should have given him an out but I didn't like his demeanor. A cooler head prevailed.

Lilly said, "With Ben's permission, sir, I'm going to save your life and possibly some others. If you'll hand your shotgun to a friend, and if they'll ride off to the side of the road at least fifty yards, all on the same side, you can ride by the wagons and glance in to see if you know anyone. Please know in advance that there are people in the wagons with shotguns trained on you. Is that all right, Ben?"

"That's fine," I said, nudging my horse to the side to create a gap between us for him to pass.

The spokesman sat without moving for a full ten seconds before handing his shotgun to a friend. Then, waving his friends away, he tipped his hat to Lilly and rode through.

"Thank you, sir," Lilly said as he passed.

"Anything for a lady, ma'am," he said, happy to escape with pride and body intact.

We hadn't traveled two more miles when there was a rifle shot no more than three hundred yards in front of us. Within three minutes I spotted a boy of fifteen years who was gutting a deer beside the road. Riding out front alone, I spotted him before he spotted me or I probably wouldn't have seen him at all. Having committed two unpardonable sins, one of failing to reload his rifle, the other of standing it against a tree out of reach, he stood glancing about like a cornered fox as I approached. Though having considerable concern about being confronted by me, he couldn't very well run and leave his deer and rifle.

I said, "Looks like you got a good one."

Nodding, he remained silent. As Henry and Lilly rode up behind me he looked somewhat relieved. Perhaps it was at having a woman present, and a beautiful one at that.

I said, "Looks like you forgot to load your rifle."

I was pretty sure because there was no cap on the nipple.

He grinned then, and said, "Yeah. Pa would thump me."

"Is your pa nearby?" Lilly asked.

"Over to Resaca with Captain McCoy, ma'am," he replied.

"Do you live nearby?" she continued.

"Yes, ma'am, 'bout a mile," he said, pointing in the direction we were going.

It's amazing how women can get information out of men. Had I asked those questions he would have told me anything but the truth. He would have then vanished in the woods with his deer and rifle. It's the same thing I would have done as a boy on the Suwannee.

Stepping down from his horse, Henry said, "Here, I'll help you put your deer on a wagon tailgate. We'll give you a lift to your house."

Had Henry asked him, he would have said no thanks, even if he had appreciated the help. But he didn't, he just helped load the deer.

Lilly dismounted as Mary walked over from the wagons. They walked with the boy, and talked, until we came to the cabin. With Lilly and Mary walking with him, the boy was over-powered. He answered every question asked. They learned that the cabin was a one room, dirt floor, log arrangement, which was about fifty yards off the road. His pa was fighting for the Confederates at Resaca but wouldn't let him go. His ma and four younger brothers and sisters were alone at home with him. Having no horse, mule, or money, they ate what he could kill, fish they could catch, and what they grew in a garden they could tend using a hoe and shovel. Coming off of a hard winter, things were pretty bad. There hadn't been much in the garden for awhile, and this was the first big animal he had killed in months. It was a story I knew well.

After arriving at the cabin and exchanging introductions, Henry said to the boy's ma, "Ma'am, it's time for our noon stop. Would it be all right if we stopped here?"

"Why sure," she said. "But we don't have any food to offer but venison."

"We have enough," Henry said. "We would be offended if you and the children did not join us."

Blushing, she said, "Sir, we wouldn't want to offend."

"You have lovely children," Miss Daisy said. "Have they been vaccinated for smallpox?"

"The smallest three haven't," she said. "There's been no vaccine since the war started. We didn't get a chance before it started."

"My brother's a physician. We'll let him do it," Miss Daisy said without asking permission.

Lifting a scab from Nathaniel's young nephew, Doctor Isaac vaccinated them. The boy was immune, having been vaccinated with a scab from a milking girl at the plantation. While Doctor Isaac was vaccinating them, he also gave them a general exam and provided worm medicine.

As we were eating, Henry said to the woman, "Your son tells

190

me he knows every road and trail for twenty miles. We could use him for a guide this afternoon and tomorrow. I'll leave you some supplies and pay you a dollar in silver if you'll loan him to us for a couple of days."

Value given and value received, she accepted. Though she would have sent the boy for nothing, she would not have accepted charity.

Henry had intended it as a generous gesture but it turned out to be one of the best investments he ever made. The boy knew the best fords, the shortest routes, where every mud hole was, and where there were trees across the road that had to be removed or detoured around. He saved us half a day over the next day and a half, and lots of work. Travel with the wagons would have been virtually impossible over those mountain trails without his knowledge. Telling our guide that we had only partially paid his mother, when in fact she had been overpaid, Henry gave him fifty Confederate paper dollars and sent him on his way home. Having learned a valuable lesson, we made use of a local boy as a guide quite often after that.

At Ellijay, Georgia, we were thirty miles east of Resaca, and almost clear of the battle. We learned that, though there was sharp fighting near Resaca, Confederate forces were holding firm there.

After calling us together, Henry said, "We can continue north, but we might have to abandon the wagons in the mountains. It's a long hard trip. I think we should change the plan and go almost west by northwest to Chatsworth. Chatsworth is fifteen miles north by northeast of the battle, and twelve miles from Dalton. I'll take a wagon and carry Doctor Isaac, Ma, Ben's ma, Miss Daisy, and Sally to the railroad in Dalton and put them on a train to St. Louis. Leaving the wagon if necessary, I'll ride the mule to Tennga. You'll wait for me there for no more than one day. That'll put you twenty miles northwest of the battle and away from any potential involvement."

"How do you propose to get permission to put us on a train within twelve miles of a raging battle?" Doctor Isaac asked.

"Wounded," Henry said. "Your head will be bandaged. To make it look good I'll draw blood from a mule to put on the bandage. I'll splint and sling Ma's arm and bandage Ben's ma's arm. Miss Daisy and Sally can attend you. I'll also write papers good all the way to St. Louis. You need to take half the money and put it in the St. Louis bank. The money you carry will be in gold so it's light enough."

"What if you aren't back in a day?" Lilly asked.

"Go on to Cleveland, Tennessee, and wait another day," Henry said. "Don't worry. I'll be there, riding or walking."

"I want to stay with Nathaniel," Sally said.

"All right," Henry replied. "Does anyone else have a suggestion?" No one did.

A Union cavalry detachment stopped us in Chatsworth. When Henry showed them some papers we were allowed to proceed. Henry then split one wagon off and headed for Dalton. Stopping five miles short of there, he applied his already prepared bandages and put on his blue captain uniform. His group then proceeded to Dalton.

Encountering two Union privates outside Dalton, who seemed to have nothing to do, Henry ordered them to get in the wagon. His party then drove directly to the train. Those privates were probably stragglers trying to stay away from the front. They seemed happy to be kept busy in the rear.

It being an hour after their arriving at Dalton before a train was leaving, Henry took advantage of the wait and had supplies loaded on the wagon. He picked out what supplies he wanted and had the privates load them. The wagon was soon half full of medical supplies, cartridges for our Spencer and Springfield rifles, powder and shot for shotguns and pistols, flour, corn meal, salt, a box of hardtack, some blankets, oilcloth ponchos, lanterns, condensed milk, and even five pounds of coffee. We had been short on Spencer cartridges ever since Olustee and short on blankets and ponchos ever since Nathaniel's relatives joined us. Doctor Isaac later told me the Union soldiers were bringing in supplies on trains and unloading them on the ground. Things were stacked everywhere.

Ordering one of the privates to drive and the other to sit on the tailgate of the wagon with his rifle ready, Henry sat on the seat in command and ordered them out of Dalton. When they reached Spring Place, five miles away, he told the privates they were to return to their unit, gave them a few days' supply of hard-tack, and drove off. Supplied with hardtack, I seriously doubt if those soldiers got back to their unit before the battle was over. Tired himself, and with a very tired mule, Henry caught up with us the next morning near Tennga.

After hitching a fresh horse to the wagon, and with Henry asleep in it, we headed for Cleveland, Tennessee. We traveled the main roads during the day and camped in the edge of communities at night. Those were the safest places. Since we had a large group and were well armed, we were relatively safe once past the major combat area.

Holding almost north to cross Tennessee as quickly as possible, we reached Albany, Kentucky, without unusual incident several days later. There were still both Southern and Union sympathizers everywhere in Kentucky. We were careful not to antagonize either. Since we were told that there was a railroad from Lexington to Louisville that was operational, and which connected with lines to Illinois and Missouri, we continued north.

On May 28, thirteen rather uneventful days after Henry left Doctor Isaac's group in Dalton, we reached Louisville, Kentucky, and set up a camp. A major city, Louisville then had a population of 70,000. Henry immediately sent a wire to St. Louis, which advised everyone there about our wellbeing.

After paying George and our other riders and dismissing them, Henry, Lilly, Coon, and I cleaned up and rode into

Louisville to place the money in a bank.

As we dismounted in front of a bank, the city's marshal, a shotgun across his arm and two deputies trailing him with shotguns pointed in our general direction, said, "Hold on, folks. You look mighty well armed to be going in a bank."

Holding his hands in clear sight, Henry said, "I'm glad to see you so alert, Marshal. We have considerable money to leave with the bank and now we'll know it'll be safe. You can help us carry it in if you will, and stand close until we get it in the vault. Four thousand dollars, mostly in silver coin, weighs close to two hundred pounds."

The marshal's attitude changed immediately. We instantly became some of the leading citizens of Louisville.

After seeing our money safe in the bank, but not on deposit because we wanted the same coin back, Henry talked to the banker about some property.

"Sir, we want to buy a farm of five hundred to a thousand acres. We'll want to know the status of taxes owed on it and other debts against it. Though the appearance of the buildings isn't important, preferably they should be usable buildings. Hopefully, this can be done quickly. Faster is better. I trust you have knowledge of available land and can expedite a purchase if we find a suitable farm. If not, we'll soon move on to Lexington."

We were not about to go to Lexington. Even though we had, Henry wanted the banker to think that we hadn't settled on the Louisville area.

"I'm holding past due papers on several places, a couple of which are that big. We can take a buggy tomorrow and look at them," the banker said.

"It'll take a six-person rig to carry the party I want to see any property. We're camped at the south edge of town. You can have us picked up tomorrow morning," Henry said.

"You should be in a hotel. I can arrange rooms," the banker said.

"We have friends at the camp and will stay there tonight," Henry said. "We might check into a hotel at a later time."

Sending Coon for Lilly, Mary, Sally, and Ivy, Henry rented a room that day. He also had warm water brought in so they could take a bath and fix up. They then walked the town and bought some things they hadn't seen in stores in Florida in a long time. Not being sure the letters we sent from Florida had arrived in St. Louis, we also sent a wire to Alice telling of our location, health, and route. The women spent the night in the room. Henry just didn't want to be in debt to the banker, even for small favors.

We looked at two farms the next day, one of seven hundred and one of a thousand acres. The asking price for both farms was $2.50 an acre in gold or silver. Additional money was wanted for the improvements and building. We didn't buy one, but told the banker we would think about it and would probably go back and look at one or both places again.

After looking at the larger farm the next day, we decided to make an offer on it. In addition to a few hundred yards on the Ohio River, it had a small stream and a pond. Other than that, it was high and dry and the buildings were in good repair. While the farm was operational, it wasn't making much profit. The owner wished to divest himself of it. Apparently there were some war casualties among his children and his ambitions were now as small as his profits. Also, he owed the bank money and owed some taxes.

On the third day Henry, Nathaniel, and I called on the banker. "We like the thousand acre farm enough to offer a dollar seventy-five an acre in silver. We'll add five hundred dollars for the building and all existing livestock," Henry said. "The only things the current owner can take are his personal things. Even the furniture, the preserved food, whiskey jugs, and boats have to stay. Within hours of his accepting I'll have people on the place to be sure nothing leaves. We've already done a livestock count. He can take his dogs and cats. We don't want them."

"That's over a thousand below his request," the banker advised us.

"I know how to count a little," Henry said. "I can even add and subtract some. He had an asking price he would almost certainly accept in greenbacks. I'm paying in silver. As you know, silver's thirty-five percent more valuable than greenbacks at this time. The other reductions he'll just have to live with. We both know people don't come along with two thousand two hundred and fifty dollars in silver every day. There might not be another such offer in years. The property also has to be certified to be free of taxes and mortgages. We'll hold half the money until you can guarantee it's clear."

"I'll take him your offer," the banker said.

"It's good until five o'clock tomorrow afternoon," Henry replied. "You'll find me at our camp or the hotel."

The offer was accepted and we set up camp in the farmyard at dawn the next day. That same day a letter arrived from Doctor Isaac.

St. Louis, May 28, 1864

Dear Henry and Ben,

We were glad to hear that all of you are safe and in good health. Alice required the tenants to vacate your house before our arrival and we're situated there. It's truly a great city.

I've opened an office and am already busy. Word soon spread of my connection to you and Ben. I've already had visits from a couple of your former patients. They hold you in great favor. Advise us of your arrival date so Alice can arrange accommodations.

Your professional colleague,
I. S.

He had given us a status neither of us felt worthy of.

Henry wired back. "Have purchased farm—Everyone is well—Arrive St. Louis after two days future notice—Need Ma to help with books—Inquire marshal's office for transport."

Henry's ma arrived three days later. In the meantime, Henry called in the farm workers, told them how things were going to be run and who was in charge, and fired all of them. He then announced that we needed some help. Those who wanted to be hired back had to talk to Nathaniel about a job. Counting Nathaniel's relatives, he got all the help he wanted.

Soon after Henry's ma arrived, Mary, Ivy, John, and I left on the train for St. Louis. Coon agreed to stay on at the farm for an indefinite period of time. The coon hunting was good there; and Nathaniel said it would be good to have a white man around until things settled in. That made Coon feel real good. He was only sixteen and hadn't developed his full growth.

Henry was a grown man back when he was sixteen. Other than for putting on some more weight, I was at seventeen. Coon, still having the appearance of a boy, even at sixteen, could have easily passed for thirteen. He was small, didn't shave, was very polite and unusually quiet. He was intelligent enough though and had been reading and doing numbers regularly ever since meeting Henry. He thought Henry was the greatest person that ever walked and would do anything Henry suggested.

Coon had just developed physically to the point that he seriously watched girls. I don't mean that he pursued girls. He just watched. I'm sure he hadn't really ever been with a girl, other than if she initiated hand holding, or maybe if she kissed him. He was about getting to that point, however.

PAUL VARNES

June 4, 1864

hough most folks wouldn't have counted Coon for very much unless they had seen him in action, he was certainly not lacking in whatever it took. Henry and I had learned about his courage at Pensacola. Folks around Louisville were about to. Coon had gotten good with his revolver. He was almost as smooth and quick as Henry. I wouldn't want to stake my life on the difference between them. Still unpretentious, Coon didn't show off any though.

Like most places, Louisville had a few rather seamy characters at the time. Maybe seamy is too soft a term. These men's form of letting off steam frequently lead to the flash of a knife blade or an explosion in a handgun. While on a trip to town with Henry and Henry's ma, as he frequently did, Coon bought some licorice candy.

He was sitting on the bench in front of the store sucking the licorice when three young men came out of a saloon across the street. Spotting Coon, one of them started twitting him. All three of them considered it sport. The focus of the twitting was the revolver on Coon's hip.

"What did you do boy, steal your pa's pistol? You best get on back home before he finds it gone and gives you a whipping," he said.

Smiling, Coon politely replied, "No. It's mine. My friend Henry gave it to me for Christmas. He took it off of somebody."

"You don't know how to say sir, boy?" the drunk said.

"Yes, sir," Coon said politely. "I mostly say sir and ma'am to older people though."

"You trying to be smart, boy?" the drunk asked. "I'll take your pistol and give you the thrashing your pa ought to."

Coon stood up then. The drunk, who was about four feet from Coon, reached to pull his pistol and it was halfway out when Coon moved. Stepping forward with his left foot, he

198

caught the drunk's pistol with his left hand and pulled his own revolver with his right. In the same motion Coon slammed the barrel of his pistol against the drunk's left ear. He went down like dropping an old pair of pants, his pistol still in Coon's left hand. Also under the influence, the drunk's two friends reached for their pistols. They sobered up real fast when Coon's revolver lined up on them. Making a smart decision, they just stood there.

Henry had stepped out of the store in time to see and hear the end of the confrontation.

Standing there with his pistol also leveled on the men, Henry said, "Well, boys, don't just stand there. Pick your friend up and go."

Coon had sat back down and was still sucking on the licorice. It had remained protruding from his mouth the whole time. His right hand still held his revolver level on those two.

Another voice broke the brief silence. "You boys bring your friend over to the jail. I'll let the three of you rest for a few hours."

The marshal had also observed the last few seconds of the altercation, but it had unfolded too fast for him to step in.

Coon was still sitting and sucking his licorice when the marshal returned a few minutes later and said, "I saw you pull that pistol, son, or I think I did. Where did you learn to do that?"

"Watching Henry mostly," Coon said. "He played with his revolver some to figure it out. I'm almost as quick as he is, but he can do it with a forty-four. His wrists and forearms are bigger and stronger than mine."

"I suppose you can shoot, too," the marshal said.

"Yes, sir," Coon said. "As good as some."

"Better than anybody other than Henry," Henry's ma, who had just come out of the store, said. "Though it's not something I encourage them about, I'm afraid it's useful. Maybe someday it won't be needed."

"How old are you, son?" the marshal asked.

"Going on seventeen," Coon said. "I just got a slow start growing. Worms probably."

After that the marshal often commented about our first appearance at the bank, saying he was sure glad we hadn't had a set-to. He figured his life might have been a little shorter.

It was two days later when the marshal called at the farm and asked to see Henry's ma. Hat in hand at the door, he asked if she would have supper in town with him.

"No," she said. " But you're invited to supper here tomorrow night. Later we can sit in the swing and talk."

He was there for supper the next night. As long as Henry's ma was at the farm he was there once a week for supper after that. Henry's ma and the marshal also got to where they went on a buggy ride every Saturday afternoon for a picnic. They would spend several hours down by the river.

Afraid there was going to be a jailbreak, the marshal sent for Coon and Henry to help him one time when he had a couple of dangerous prisoners. The break was nipped in the bud when two of the gang members were killed in a shootout outside the jail. Having been in the middle of the shooting, and holding their end of it up, Coon and Henry were frequently called on after that when the marshal needed help. Henry mostly declined. Coon stayed on as a special deputy on call. Given his innocent appearance, Coon could walk right up to someone and disarm him before he knew it had happened. His working as a deputy wasn't because he needed the money. We were all partners and had most of what we wanted. I think Coon just liked the excitement.

After a few weeks, Henry and Lilly came to St. Louis. His ma stayed on at the farm, supposedly to teach Sally about bookkeeping. She did, too, but I think the marshal had something to do with it.

In July, Henry told us that the value of Confederate paper money stood at twenty dollars to one dollar in silver. He said the value of Confederate money was determined by the probability of the Confederacy being able to make good on it. I took that to mean the chances, as things stood at that particular time, of the

CSA winning the war or getting a stalemate. We still had over $25,000 in Confederate paper that he wanted to trade for gold. There didn't seem to be much chance of getting that money traded, and we were still getting more.

We occasionally went to the farm to see that Nathaniel was getting things going. On one such visit Nathaniel commented about Coon's women friends, or lack of them. "I just don't know if Coon has a woman friend. I don't know of any. He's started shaving though, and always keeps himself neat and clean. Sometimes I think he and my sister, Sarah, have a case on each other. She's got to where she stays neat as a pin all the time, too. She doesn't ever come to the table without fixing herself up. They're also around each other a lot of the time," he said.

"Sarah's a mighty attractive young woman," I said. "Though she looks lots older, she's the same age as Coon."

"Yes, she is," he said. "Well, I'm not going to fret over it. I mentioned the possibility to Sally and she just said, 'Oh hush. You just have to leave young people alone.' I haven't mentioned it since then. It's just a troublesome curiosity. We don't know anything for sure anyway."

"No," I said. "We don't."

I then turned the conversation to the two Arabian mares. Henry, Coon, and I never came down on each other about anything. Also, we didn't really know anything.

Coon wound up staying at the farm all winter. He also got a girlfriend later that winter. Oh, some of the girls around town had shined up to him all along, and he got to where he would square dance a little, but he never went off on a buggy ride with anyone until this one girl ended up at the farm. It was a strange way to get a girlfriend, too. But I'm getting ahead of the story again.

Returning to St. Louis, I stayed in the house with Miss Daisy and Doctor Isaac in what was ordinarily Henry's ma's room. She was still in Louisville. Soon after returning, I was questioned about everything at the farm as we ate supper one night.

After considerable conversation, Miss Daisy asked, "And how's Ida?"

Ida, that's Henry's ma's name. We young people never called her by her first name.

"She's well," I said. "In fact, she looks the best I've ever seen her. It could be because of the marshal sparking her."

"Marshal?" Doctor Isaac said.

Detecting a disturbed note in his voice, I tried to change the subject but they wouldn't let me.

"Tell us about the marshal," Miss Daisy said.

"Oh, he's around lots. Coon helps him as a special deputy sometimes."

"No. Tell us about the sparking."

"Well, he eats supper at the farm once a week. They also go buggy riding on Saturday afternoons."

"Every Saturday afternoon?" she asked.

"I'm not sure. I think so," I said. But I had let the cat out of the bag.

Doctor Isaac didn't say another word, but two days later he told me he was going to the farm and asked if I would take his patients for a few days. Having never been to the farm, he said he wanted to see it. Miss Daisy didn't go with him. It's the first time I ever knew of that they hadn't been together. Within the week Doctor Isaac was back. Henry's ma came back with him.

Within a short time everyone established their own routine. My ma went to work at the hotel. She was in charge of socials and food service: the restaurant, weddings, banquets, the bar—stuff like that. She loved it, and needed something to do. It's a real classy hotel and lots of interesting people stop there. The best rooms went for up to two dollars a day in silver at that time. That was two days' pay for those with real good jobs.

Henry's ma started teaching John, Ivy, and Mary every day when she got back from the farm. They went to regular school the five months it was open. They had classes with her the other seven months of the year.

Miss Daisy kept the house spick-and-span and did some social and humanitarian things around town. She also made over Henry every time she had a chance. He has been special to her ever since back in Cedar Key.

Lilly was around with Henry or Miss Daisy all the time. Miss Daisy spent time showing Lilly about being a society woman. They went lots of places together.

Being in charge of everything, Henry only spent mornings, three days a week, practicing medicine. Because of only working at it three days a week, Henry had to limit the number of patients he took. Other than that, he was always working on some financial deal. Though staying busy and getting along great with Lilly, Henry was soon restless again. I asked him if there was anything I could do.

"No," he said. "We still have over twenty-five thousand dollars in Confederate paper money and no way to change much of it here. Here it is August and the value against gold is twenty-one to one. People ask for specie. There would be a way to trade it further south of here. I also think about going back to Florida and the things we have there."

"It's not worth it," I said. "We've got plenty of money. If we didn't have, I'd be the first to go. I think about going to Florida, too. We should wait until after the war for that."

"That's not all," Henry said. "The war is dragging on. Sherman has Atlanta almost cut off. I'll bet he's in Atlanta within a month. We've got a house there, and Jolene and her ma are there. I thought the South would call it quits but it seems they're going to fight until the end. Flour must be three hundred dollars a barrel in Atlanta by now. Jolene and her ma are better prepared than most. Though it's none of my affair, I can't help but think about them. I also worry about Aunt May."

"You could send for them," I said.

"None of them would come," he said. "I'm also concerned about all the things we have buried at Aunt May's house. Those things need to be changed into money. To do that we've got to get them to where the money is. That stuff needs to be dug up, carried up north, and sold. For those who have money, there will be fortunes to be made when the war ends. I've been thinking lots about that. When the war ends, or a little before, I'm going to Florida. As it stands now I don't think it'll end until the spring or summer of next year. One way or the other, I'm going in the spring."

I sat thinking about that for a few seconds before I said, "Give me two weeks' notice. I'll need to notify my patients and make arrangements. We'll have to give Coon some notice, too. He'll want to go."

By the first of September, Sherman was in Atlanta. The papers were full of it. It wasn't a complete victory, however. General Hood, who had been placed in charge of Confederate troops in the area, evacuated the city with his army before he was cut off and trapped there. His evacuation of Atlanta helped extend the war. After evacuating Atlanta, Hood moved behind Sherman and attacked the troops holding the railroad from Chattanooga to Atlanta. Sherman then had to go back and fight over the very property that Hood had recently retreated through.

Another event of great interest to us occurred in September. Doctor Isaac and Ida were married. Just as Hood had danced and feinted around Sherman to distract and delay him from his course to Atlanta, Ida had danced and feinted around the farm and the marshal to remove Doctor Isaac from his long held position of bachelorhood. It was a small wedding. Nathaniel, Sally, and Coon came up from the farm for the event. Only family members and close friends attended.

A couple of days after the wedding the businessman, Lee Greystone, checked in at the hotel. Hearing that Henry and I were in town, he called on us.

"This is mostly a social call," he said. "I also have an eye to the future. The government's need for people like me will likely decline as the war ends, which it seems can have but one conclusion. I'll probably have to find something different to do. I've spent considerable time thinking about it. It would seem that my experience in buying should be useful somewhere. As the blockade of Southern ports ends, there will be a need to get Southern farm products moving north. I thought we might discuss this and see if we could devise some business plan we could all profit from."

"I don't see a very high volume of goods moving right away," I said. "There are no trains connecting out of Florida to any other state's rail system and the rest of the South's railroads will be in shambles. More people will be trying to do business than there is transportation to move the goods."

"You men overcame the obstacles of moving cattle to Sedalia. I thought you might develop ideas for overcoming other transportation problems," he said.

"The heaviest traffic will be by ship," Henry said. "Cotton and other durable goods can be shipped that way. Cattle, on the other hand, can only be transported in small numbers on ships. Food would also have to be carried for the cattle, making that method less profitable. The biggest supply of cattle is in Florida and Texas. Florida has more cattle than any other state east of the Mississippi River and Texas the most of any state west of it. In addition to Florida's rail system not connecting outside the state, Florida has no rail system south of Gainesville. Texas has no rail system at all. Sedalia is the closest train station to Texas that could be used for shipping cattle east. That's over eight hundred miles."

"But cattle can walk," I said. "We've driven herds before."

"Small herds for short distances and on level land," Henry said. "Also, the price has stabilized. There's no profit in buying high and selling high."

"I'll bet you could buy cattle at one or two dollars a head in south Texas and sell them here for fifteen or twenty," Lee said.

"Yes, and have to drive them through Texas, Arkansas, and Missouri. That route would increase the distance to a thousand miles. There are also groups of men still contesting all three states. We would have to move a huge herd, maybe as many as a thousand cattle, to make it profitable. Also, that country is too hilly to drive cattle over. The only way would be to come straight north through Indian territory. The unsettled war situation, the Indians, and the hard trip makes it not worth the risk at this time. I'm thinking more about operating out of Florida."

"Ah, you said the magic phrase," Lee said. "At this time. Take away the hostilities, and find a way across Indian Territory, and you could do it from Texas. But Florida might be the best bet for some time to come. I would like to be involved with you men in such an enterprise if the opportunity occurs. I'll leave a forwarding address in Sedalia and at your hotel. You can reach me at anytime in the future. I've dealt with no others who've had the vision and success in anything that you two did in bringing cattle to Sedalia last year."

"We'll keep it in mind," Henry said. "But we've got a big project already planned in Florida for the coming spring. That project will require all our efforts for awhile."

On October 16, as we were having supper in the hotel, the waiter brought Henry a letter that had just arrived for him. After staring solemnly at it for a full minute, he read it to us.

Columbus, Ohio, October 10, 1864

Dear Henry,

I pray that you get this letter. I'm sure that by now you've heard of the white slave trains that Sherman sent north from Atlanta with women and children. I'm told there are thousands of us. Our group, over 200 of us, passed through Chattanooga and Louisville. Sherman ordered that we be sent north of the Ohio River. Many of the women he sent were working in the factories in cities around Atlanta. My only sin was being near some of the factory workers when they were rounded up. We were sent without spare clothing or money and were sold into bondage to pay for our transportation and food while they brought us here. We were advertised in the newspaper like cattle for sale. All of us must work twelve or fourteen hours a day for seven days a week. We hardly get paid enough to buy food for sewing in the garment factory. There's no hope of ever paying off our debt or escaping. It has taken four of us three weeks to save enough to post this letter, and then only by going hungry.

The dire humiliation of my circumstance has almost killed me. It is nothing, however, compared to the conditions under which we live. While sleeping five to a room, what little sleep we get, some of us have been molested by our overseers right in front of the other girls. I cringe at having you see me in this condition, but I pray you will come. You must come.

Fearing that I have omitted something of importance, I close.

Warmest Love,
Jolene

There were tears in everyone's eyes at the table. If we had been paying the hotel's normal price, the cost of our meals would have kept her from being in servitude.

I said, "We must catch the first train."

Henry replied, "No. We'll inform ourselves about this first.

Does anyone know about these white slave trains?"

Miss Daisy said, "I've heard rumors. There are so many rumors that I believed none of them, and little of what I read in the papers."

Henry said, "Tomorrow morning first thing we'll inquire at the newspaper, the mayor's office, and with the military. Miss Daisy, if you will, go to the newspaper. I'll take the military. Ma, you can inquire at the mayor's office. We need to know the extent of, and the legal standings of this, but don't mention Jolene. We'll meet here as soon as we gather the information. Ma, if a person has committed a crime such as theft or murder while spying for the South, I also want to know what standing the military would have to arrest that person in a civilian jurisdiction. At least get the mayor's point of view. While looking at some of the military's papers, I'll get their point of view."

The next morning when everyone was at the hotel, Miss Daisy said, "It would appear there's truth to the rumors, and to what Jolene wrote. Close to three thousand white women and children were sent north from the Atlanta area with orders that they be taken across the Ohio River. They were to be placed in bondage to merchants who would pay their transportation debts. Those who no one wanted as workers were to be turned loose without resources. The paper has sent off wires to further verify the accuracy of this."

"I don't think we'll wait for further verification. What did you find out Ma?" Henry said.

"The mayor's office had also heard about it, though they don't know the details. As to a Southern spy, he or she would be turned over even if having committed no other crime," she said.

"It seems the military people here are also aware of white women and children being shipped north from around Atlanta. Many of them were factory workers in Marietta and other places nearby. In addition to burning the factories, Sherman gathered up the women who had been working in them and sent them north. Other women and children were sent for any number of reasons, and some for no reason. It's said there have been quite a number of women and children turned out in Louisville because no one further north wanted them. It was the commandant's opinion that there would be no trouble in arresting a spy. If there was, he said he would order a squad to take the person," Henry said.

"So when are we going?" I asked.

"Only Lilly, you, and I are going. We'll leave tomorrow morning. Since we have to go through Louisville, Coon can join us there."

Henry immediately sent a wire to Coon, telling him to join us at the station with a bag of clothing that would make him look young. Coon was also to bring a spare set of clothes for a boy about his size.

Turning to me, Henry said, "Have your blue uniform pressed as neat at it can be. We'll put them on in Cincinnati."

Unlike Florida trains, Federal trains ran day and night. We were in Louisville in twenty-six hours and in Cincinnati in another fourteen. Actually, the railroad ended at Covington, Kentucky. The bridge wasn't finished across the Ohio River at that time. We had to get a ferry across and then catch the Ohio train system from there.

Cincinnati was overwhelming. There were 190,000 people living there, about half of whom were from Germany. Because we had trouble finding someone who could give us directions in English, it was late when we finally got to a hotel room and slept for the night.

Wearing our Union uniforms the next morning, we caught the 7:00 A.M. train for Columbus. Arriving at Columbus as dark descended, we hired a hack and dropped Lilly at a hotel. Henry then had the driver take us to the garment factory.

"Have you been in Columbus long?" Henry asked the driver.

"Been here all my life," he replied.

"It looks like a large city. What's the population?"

"Eighteen thousand. Give or take a few."

"You're familiar with the garment factory?"

"Yes, sir, Captain. It's been in the same place for some time."

"How many girls work there?"

"More than a hundred. They all used to be local girls. Some of those Southern tramps have recently caused some of our local girls to be fired."

"How did they do that?" Henry asked.

"I mean they just filled up some jobs. I reckon the owner fired those other girls to save money," he replied.

"Oh," Henry said. "My wife's with me, but my two friends are alone, and we kind of thought . . ."

"I don't know if it's possible. This isn't the first time I've had a request like that. They watch those new women pretty close I'm told. I can take you to the right place though," he said.

"No. Just show us around the factory. Do you know where the Southern women sleep?" Henry said.

"Yes, sir," he replied. "A hack driver has to know everything."

"We would like to see their place, and the factory. I would especially like to see where they go and come from the factory," Henry said.

The girls were just getting off work as we drove by the factory at 8:00 P.M., so we saw them leaving. The Southern girls walked in a group, twenty of them, a pitiful sight. Seeing Jolene, I almost went to her but Henry caught my arm.

Speaking to the driver, Henry said, "We'll go back to the hotel. If you used the most direct route, and traveled at the same speed we are now, how long would it take to drive from here to the train station at noon on any given day?"

"Oh, I don't know, Captain, fifteen or twenty minutes," he said.

"How long if you trotted the horse a little, but not enough to attract attention, and if the passenger was giving you a silver dollar tip?" Henry asked.

"Ten minutes, Captain," he said.

At the hotel Henry said to the doorman, "See the driver in that hack?"

"Yes, sir," the doorman said.

"I want a six-person carriage standing at the door tomorrow morning at six-thirty sharp, but I don't want that driver," Henry said.

"Did he do something wrong, sir?" the doorman asked.

"No. In fact I gave him a good tip. I just don't want my business talked about. He already knows all I want him to know. Can I depend on you?" Henry said, as he dropped a silver dollar in the doorman's hand.

"Yes, sir," he replied. "If I didn't have to work here, I'd drive."

"Six-thirty sharp," Henry said. "We need a man who doesn't babble on. We'll need him straight through until noon."

"Yes, sir," he said, while holding the door.

Though Henry told Coon and me that we could sleep in, I couldn't sleep and joined them in the carriage. Lilly was dressed funny. In addition to wearing a bonnet, something she never did, she had obviously padded her waist, and other places she didn't need to. I wouldn't have recognized her if I had seen her walking down the street.

Arriving at the factory, Henry showed the driver where to park. Within ten minutes the women came out of their sleeping quarters and walked toward the factory, two blocks away. Lilly immediately stepped out of the carriage and walked toward them. The driver remained in his seat. He didn't even help her out of the rig. As Lilly came abreast of Jolene, Lilly stumbled and fell into her and then fell on the ground. Jolene and another woman helped her up, and helped her brush herself off. I could see Lilly's mouth move as she said something. Departing them, Lilly then walked around the corner. Our driver clucked his horse on and we picked her up a couple of minutes later. We then headed straight back to the hotel.

I said, "OK, let me in on everything."

Henry said, "Lilly just handed Jolene a note telling her that we are going to arrest her and three others who she's to identify. She's not to recognize us and is to agree with everything we charge her with. After a few minutes she'll break down and identify the others."

"Why didn't you tell me before?" I asked.

"If we hadn't been able to get the note to her, we would have had to buy her. If that didn't work, we would have had to take her. I didn't know what the plan was until I saw if we could get her a note. At ten today, we're going to the local marshal's office and seek to enlist his help. At eleven-ten, we're going to arrest Jolene and her three friends on the charges of spying and killing an officer, with or without the marshal's assistance. I've got Sherman's signature on a document. We'll be on a train for Louisville at noon. Lilly saw the women and is going to guess at the sizes of the three who were walking closest to Jolene. After buying three nice dresses and bonnets, she'll meet us at the train. She'll also purchase our tickets in advance."

"But we're getting four women," I said. "Why only three dresses?"

"The flattest one will dress as a boy. Anyone looking for us would be looking for one boy, two men, and four women. Since there's also Lilly, we'll split up and travel as four couples," Henry said.

Walking in the marshal's office, Henry said, "I'm Captain Walker. We're here under orders from General Sherman to arrest four Confederate women spies who murdered a colonel in Marietta, Georgia. They slipped away and were accidentally sent here on one of Sherman's white slave trains. I'm taking them back to Marietta where Sherman will surely hang them. We can handle it, but would appreciate help from you and a deputy until we get ropes on their arms. We're on our way to get them now."

Pointing at Coon he added, "We brought this boy from

Atlanta to identify one who usually goes by the first name of Jolene, and a couple of the others. They're all sought on an open warrant. I don't know what last names they're using. Whatever it is, it's false."

The marshal and a deputy went along with us. The situation was a little too complicated for smiling or laughing, but I figured it was worth a smile if we got out of there alive and safe.

At the factory office the marshal took over. He said, "Bedford, we've come to arrest four of your Georgia girls for spying and the murder of a Union colonel."

"Wait a minute," Bedford said. "I've got money tied up in those girls. I've paid out good money."

Henry said, "If you have receipts where you paid the Army, I'm authorized to reimburse for those receipts only."

"I don't have any receipts," he said.

"How much do you think you paid?" the marshal asked.

"Ten dollars each," Bedford said.

"No receipts, no money," Henry said.

"I've got to have something," Bedford said "It's not my fault they were sent here."

"I was told to be reasonable," Henry said. "We don't want to cheat civilians. You've had them working several weeks, so you've gained from that. I'll pay you fifteen dollars in gold for the four, but you'll have to sign a receipt."

When that was done, Henry said, "Okay Marshal, let's go get them."

Coon walked straight to Jolene, pointed at her, and said, "She was the chief one. Dressed like they are, the others all look pretty much alike."

Henry said to Jolene, "You're charged with spying and murder. We're returning you to Georgia for a trial."

Jolene protested at first, then she broke down crying and confessed. She was then threatened, cajoled, and promised leniency until she pointed out the other three. I couldn't believe the fight one of the other three put up. We had to hog-tie her to get her in the carriage. Even then she tried to bite. The other two protested loudly, and cursed Jolene for a lying bitch, but they didn't fight us.

When, during the scuffle, Bedford slapped one of the women, Henry said, "Here now, there'll be none of that. These are Federal prisoners. They'll be treated with respect right up until they're hanged."

As we were nearing the train station, Jolene said, "Girls, these are my good friends from Florida. They're the ones we sent the letter to. I think we're headed for a hotel in St. Louis, Missouri."

Henry said, "I want you women to act sullen, but not unco-operative. We're going to have to keep your hands bound so you look like prisoners. You're going to have to continue playing the part for awhile. Don't be so vicious though. You put on too good of an act back there."

"It wasn't an act," Jolene said. "I thought it best if they acted natural, so I didn't tell them."

She had sure matured a lot since we last saw her. Sometimes traumatic experiences will do that.

"What about your child?" Henry asked.

"I'm saddened to say I lost her," she said.

Lilly was waiting at the station. The train being on time, and Lilly already having our tickets, we didn't have anything to do but wait ten minutes.

At the first thirty-minute stop down the line Lilly took our prisoners to the privy. Three of them came out dressed up, bon-nets and all, and looking like different people. Jolene had her hair under a cap and was dressed as a boy. In those loose clothes and having lost ten pounds, which she didn't need to lose, she looked like a frail boy with a case of worms. Coon changed into clothes that made him look older. We then entered different cars and sat as couples. It was almost like our group had vanished.

214

Since we had to pair up anyway, I picked Norma, the fighter. I liked her spirit. It turned out to be a good choice. She sure did clean up good. After changing out of his little boy clothes, Coon almost looked the seventeen years old he had just become. Naomi, also seventeen, caught his arm and they sat together. That left Jolene and the other woman together.

We were less than six hours out of Columbus, and stopped at a station, when Lilly brought up a subject that had been bothering her for some time.

She said, "Coon, what do you know about the Atlanta women and children who were released in Louisville?"

He replied, "I know there are more than fifteen hundred of them in Louisville. They've been there for over a month. Though a few of them have been hired for pitiable jobs, most of them have no jobs, no income, and no hopes of getting either. They sleep in stables, barns, and any other place they can find shelter from the rain. Some of them have been begging for food. There doesn't seem to be much hope for them. There was an article in the paper that was critical of the Federal government for giving assistance to the freed slaves but giving none to our white Southern women."

Lilly said, "Henry, we have to do something. It's mid-October. Some of them could be freezing to death soon."

"There's not much we can do for that many people," Henry said.

"We can do something. You can think about it," she said. "You could give some of them something to do on the farm, or at the hotel. There are also people in St. Louis who could provide jobs."

"Not for that many people," Henry said. "I will think about it though."

Once across the Ohio River, Henry sent two wires, one to Louisville and one to St. Louis. The one sent to Nathaniel said, "Arriving Louisville October 22, in the afternoon. Bring a wagon." The other, to Doctor Isaac, said, "All parties safe—Layover at farm—Arrive St. Louis October 28."

Even as these things were happening to us, the last attempts by the Confederacy to revive the war carried on. It even swirled around us. In late September of 1864, Confederate General Sterling Price with an 8,000-man cavalry unit briefly approached St. Louis. As we settled in at the farm for a rest on October 23, Price, who had turned toward northwest Missouri, ran into some major units of the Federal army and was routed. He retreated all the way back to Texas. Price's adventure, which was the last serious effort by the Confederacy to retake Missouri, turned into just a cavalry raid.

Upon arriving in Louisville, Lilly put a notice in the paper to the women and children who had been brought from Atlanta. The notice offered assistance in finding work, or in moving to another city in which there might be work. Lilly also rented a room in a hotel to use as an office in helping those displaced women. She was overwhelmed by the response. Within three days over three hundred women called on her. There probably would have been even more if more of them could read and had access to a newspaper. The hotel owner was ready to evict Lilly because of the disruption caused by all the traffic in the hotel until Henry rented all the rooms on the floor that her room was on.

A pleasant four days were spent on the farm by the rest of us. Nathaniel's ma didn't allow the women to do anything but pick up around their rooms. The women virtually went into culture shock from contrasting their past several weeks' experience with the time they had on the farm.

Coon and Naomi hung around together most of the time. They rode to town and down by the river in a buggy a couple of times. Their hanging around together seemed to make Nathaniel happy. It kept Sarah from being around Coon. Nathaniel told me that mixing just didn't work for a permanent situation, even for free people. I agreed with that, but I also pointed out that we didn't know anything for sure. Sarah seemed a little stiff around Naomi, but she never said anything about Naomi to Coon that I know of.

Nathaniel's last words on it were, "Don't take me wrong, neither Coon, Doctor Henry, nor you could ever do anything wrong from where I stand. My whole family owes too much to repay."

I replied, "Among friends, it's not about repayment."

It didn't seem possible that only nine days had passed since Henry got Jolene's letter or that we had been on the farm for three days when Henry called us together late that afternoon and said, "Ben and I are leaving for St. Louis tomorrow on the noon train. I don't know what you women want to do. You can't very well go back to Atlanta. I'll pay your fare to St. Louis and see you get a job if that's your wish. Or, I'll pay your fare anywhere else you want to go."

Jolene said, "I'll go to St. Louis."

Henry said, "Good. Ben and I were thinking you might run the office and cook and clean like you did in Atlanta. We'll pay you the same as in Atlanta if you'll take the job."

Like always, he hadn't said anything to me; but we could use her. Naturally she took the job.

Naomi said, "I was raised on a farm before I did factory work in Marietta. Is there work here I could do here?" It seemed that she was taken with Coon.

With a blank face, Henry said, "Nathaniel does the hiring here," scratching his right ear as he said it. "Farm work is hard, and there's no day off but Sunday. There are even some things, like milking, that have to be done on Sunday. It doesn't pay as well as most work in the city either. You'll have to speak to Nathaniel."

I had seen them use the signal several times since the mule trade, left ear for no and right ear for yes. It was kind of fun always knowing the answer in advance.

Nathaniel, who had been watching Henry to see if he would

express an opinion, said, "We can always use a hard worker on the farm. But Doctor Henry's right, it is hard work and six days a week."

Nathaniel couldn't quite conceal his smile. Naomi staying on would almost certainly end any flirtation between Sarah and Coon.

Looking at me and then Henry, Norma said, "Do you suppose there's work in the hotel? I can cook and clean. I don't have any experience in a hotel, but I'm a quick learner."

The fourth woman said, "Me too. I'd like to try."

Henry didn't respond directly, but looked at me. He wasn't sure what relationship had developed between Norma and me and he always let me make my own trouble.

I said, "A hotel's just like a farm. It's hard work and it's every day and everyone has to wear a constant smile. I'm sure Alice can find something though."

When we left for St. Louis, Lilly stayed on for a couple of weeks to help those Georgia women who had been dumped in Louisville. Several of them wound up working on the farm. Actually, there isn't as much work on a farm in the winter as at other times of the year, but they at least had shelter and food. And they were great help when spring came. Some of the other women went with Lilly to St. Louis and eventually got jobs there.

PART IV

The Final Trade

November 30, 1864

Word came that, after burning most of Atlanta and the surrounding towns and farms, Sherman left Atlanta marching south with 60,000 men on November 15. His army had vanished into Georgia. Hood, who had avoided Sherman, was now marching his army north toward Nashville. It made little sense. Hood obviously didn't have the force or supply lines to sustain a drive to the north, especially in the winter. Sherman had no supply line going south.

Again becoming restless, Henry said, "In the past few weeks the price for Confederate paper money has declined to twenty-eight dollars for one in silver or gold. It's almost worthless. I need to get ours changed into specie."

I replied, "The farm's turning enough profit to buy better breeding stock and pay all its help, the hotel and other properties are profitable, we have more patients than we want, and you still have the Federal warrant for the cattle that has never been cashed. Forget about the nine hundred dollars you could get for the Confederate money."

"Nine hundred dollars is more than the average worker makes in three years," Henry said. "For ten dollars each, Jolene and the others were placed in virtual bondage for life. For nine hundred dollars we could have placed ninety women in bondage and then freed them. For thirty cents I can buy a gallon of rum. It's not easy to forget nine hundred dollars. Only four months ago we could have gotten twelve hundred dollars in gold for the same amount of paper. Though it will probably be too late by then, I will wait until spring when Sherman's location is known and when there's grass for the horses."

"We should take the train," I said.

"Yes, as far as it goes," he said. "But Hood's army might have torn up the track as far north as Nashville by then. We'll need good horses."

By December 10, word came that Hood had moved his forces to the outskirts of Nashville. The press assured us that Hood's army was so depleted of both men and supplies that they couldn't attack the city's fortifications. No word had been heard of Sherman and his army of 60,000. They had just disappeared into Georgia. According to the Northern press, Sherman had departed toward Macon after pillaging and burning Atlanta and everything else within twenty miles in all directions. What Sherman had not confiscated for his army's use before leaving Atlanta, his forces had destroyed in order to deprive the Confederates, both civilian and military, of food and shelter.

On another trip to Louisville Henry again heard of Nathaniel's concern for his youngest sister, whom he thought to be near Macon.

"There's no hope of ever seeing Reva again," Nathaniel said.

"There's always a little hope," Henry said. "If we knew where she was, we would make a try for her sooner or later."

Nathaniel said, "All I know is that she was traded to a friend of the Whipmores over around Macon. She could have been traded again. Or she could be right in the middle of Sherman's army."

"The Whipmore Plantation was almost certainly burned with everything else. Our house in Atlanta was probably burned too. There's no telling where the Whipmore family is. If Sherman went to Macon, which is possible, he might have burned the plantation where your sister is," Henry said.

"After the war ends I'd like to look for her," Nathaniel said.

"I would offer to help," Henry said, "but I wouldn't know her if I saw her, or she me. Ben, Coon, and I will pass through Atlanta and Macon when we go to Florida in the spring. If we can locate Mrs. Whipmore, I'll inquire as to which family Reva was traded. It's a slim hope, but it is a possibility."

"It's probably the best hope I've got," Nathaniel said.

On December 20, we got some interesting war news. General Thomas had attacked Hood's Confederate army and driven him from his position near Nashville. Hood, then in Alabama, was in full retreat toward Mississippi.

Sherman had also surfaced. His army was in Savannah. After occupying the city, Sherman made his location known through the Union gunboats blockading the port. He reported having marched his army through Georgia on a forty-mile-wide front. They had foraged for supplies along the way. Having taken about twenty percent of everything for his supplies, Sherman had destroyed all else. He had left nothing in his wake but dead and bloated sheep, hogs, cattle, and mules. His stated purpose was to leave the Confederates to starve. Sherman's soldiers had gone into a feeding frenzy—raping, burning, killing, maiming, and looting at will. This behavior was encouraged until they occupied Savannah. There, his army returned to their normal behavior.

It was also reported that over ten thousand slaves followed Sherman in hope of freedom. We later learned that over ten percent of those died from hunger, disease, or exposure. Sherman chose not to feed or care for them.

One piece of joyous news was received. Lilly announced that she was with child. Having waited three months to tell us, she was sure. It was an occasion for a gathering at the hotel. Her announcement was a good Christmas present for everyone.

Soon thereafter, Henry said to Doctor Isaac and me, "I've been planning to leave for Florida in late April but a number of circumstances have caused me to want to go earlier. I'm going as soon as travel by rail is possible to Atlanta. Union forces will be repairing the railroad damage done by Hood and trains will soon be running. I still have Confederate money to trade. I also want to inquire as to the whereabouts of Nathaniel's sister, Reva. Though there's little left of value in the area Sherman marched through except land, he couldn't very well have burned the land, rivers, or lakes. Now's a good time for people with money to buy land. There'll be a rush to do so when the war ends. I would like to be ahead of those people. We have a warrant for $19,000 in greenbacks from our last cattle deal, and a couple of thousand dollars left unused from the specie we brought from Atlanta. Money also comes in regularly from our investments here in St. Louis. The time will soon be here to invest those funds."

While we could both see the logic of his thoughts, we also knew the dangers. There were no objections raised, however. I did provide my usual advice.

"The value of Confederate paper money has fallen to forty-five dollars to one in silver. It's hardly worth the trouble when compared to the problems and dangers it might present."

He said, "I've changed lots of it into large bills—hundreds, five hundreds, and thousands. I can carry it in a pocket. Sooner or later an opportunity could present itself to make a profit."

"When do you propose to leave?" I asked.

"When the railroad and winter permits," he said. "Hopefully, by March 30. It might take a month to blunder about Atlanta and Macon and complete our search and business. Hopefully, we can get to Florida by the middle of May. I want to look at acquiring land in Florida and to find a way to move the buried things. I would also like to check on Aunt May."

"I'll be ready to go when the time comes," I said.

"I was thinking of taking Coon," he replied. "Two could be better than three in terms of not attracting undue attention. It might be better if you wait to hear from us. Given the fact that you have patients, and he has only himself, it's probably best that Coon goes."

"You're forgetting about Naomi and Sarah," Doctor Isaac said.

"No," Henry replied. "I was thinking about them. Although I haven't heard any more about it, the situation at the farm might be better if Coon goes with me for awhile. Unless you hear from me otherwise, it would be good if Ben joins us in Atlanta by the first of May. We'll need all the help we can get in Florida."

"That all sounds reasonable," I said. "Do you have a plan to move the stuff from there?"

"No," Henry said. "But somehow we need to get it to here, or to Boston or New York. A water passage to New York could be best. I was mostly concerned with giving both of you adequate notice so our patients could be cared for."

Upon hearing about this plan, Jolene and another of the women we had rescued asked to go to Atlanta.

Henry said, "You're free to go anywhere you choose. But I won't be responsible for you going to Atlanta. The place was burned. There's no place to live and nothing to eat."

Jolene replied, "I'm concerned for my mother. Though I've posted letters to her and Tyler in Atlanta, I've heard nothing. They don't even know where I am."

"There's probably no post office," Henry said, "I'll inquire about your mother and send you a message."

Sending Coon a letter, Henry apprised him of the plan. He soon received a reply that Coon would be ready.

Lilly wanted to go, but being pregnant she didn't request to. If she hadn't been pregnant, Henry would have taken her. She could ride and shoot as well as most, and they enjoyed each other a great deal.

Mary still hinted about marriage off and on and I thought about it. She especially got cuddly when Lilly announced being pregnant, but I wasn't ready for that.

Signs that the war was rapidly coming to an end were frequently in evidence. In mid-January Union troops captured Fort Fisher. With its capture, the last safe haven for Southern blockade runners was closed. Fort Fisher, which was located at the mouth of the Cape Fear River, protected Wilmington, North Carolina. The cordon around the South had been effectively sealed. No longer able to get supplies, even Lee said the end of the war would not be long in coming.

In mid-January General Sherman's army was still in Savannah. Bogged down there by heavy rains, it was unknown what he would do next. It appeared that he wanted to march north through the Carolinas. Since the Savannah River was two miles wide due to the flooding, Sherman seemed boxed in for some time.

As the time approached for Henry to leave, Lilly expressed a desire to accompany him to Louisville and further assist the Atlanta women there. Henry's ma and I made plans to accompany her.

March 25, five days before we were to leave for Louisville, Jolene got a letter from Tyler.

Atlanta, March 10, 1865

Dearest Jolene,

 I have just received your letter of three months past. After being grievously wounded while serving with General Hood near Nashville, I was captured and lost my left arm by amputation. I later signed an oath of loyalty to the Union and was paroled.

 Upon arriving in Atlanta in search of you, I found your mother's and Henry's house burned. Your mother has been living, along with several others, in an improvised tent shelter throughout the winter. Regrettably, she's seriously ill. Because your mother's in need of me, and since I'm not sure where you are because your letter's three months old, I'll remain here with her. Also, I fear it isn't safe to travel in any direction. If I don't hear from you within thirty days, however, I'll come looking for you. Having no money or horse, I shall have to walk. There's little to eat and considerable sickness here. Many are dying of starvation and disease. Though you are far better off wherever you are, my heart wishes you were here.

 Give Henry and Ben my blessings. I find from your letter that we are again more deeply in debt to them than we can ever repay.

Yours in deepest love,
Tyler

After letting Henry read the letter, she said, "I have to go with you. I have money for the trip. It was saved to repay you for your expenses in rescuing me. The others have also been saving for that purpose. There's enough to pay my way if you'll let me delay that debt."

Lilly said, "You will not pay us. We would never accept payment from you or the others."

"There's no food or shelter in Atlanta," Henry said. "But I guess you must go."

"We could help them, Henry," Lilly said. "You said you would purchase farmland and there's our house that needs rebuilding in Atlanta. You'll need someone to look after your affairs, whether in Florida or Georgia. It's not like it would be charity."

"She can go with Coon and me," Henry said. "We'll see what develops after that."

Arriving in Louisville on March 31, Henry stayed there for two days before leaving. During those two days we received word that a Union cavalry unit had raided the iron works in Alabama, and destroyed them. That was a devastating blow to the Confederacy's ability to continue fighting.

Coon, Henry, and Jolene boarded the train and left the morning of Sunday, April 2. They left prepared for the cold. Adequate blankets were taken to remain warm, as were oilcloths to wrap in and break the wind while riding in the cattle car. The cattle car we rented carried Henry's thoroughbred gelding, Coon's favorite riding horse, and three large mules. A three-hundred-pound pack was taken for each mule. Medicine, food, weapons, grain, and several bags of seed made up the bulk of the load. The travel plan was for one of them to ride in the cattle car and one in an enclosed car. They would change places at every stop. Riding in the cattle car was necessary to insure that the packs didn't vanish even as the train moved. Since the train stopped frequently, it was also possible the animals could have been stolen. Having been almost continuously with Henry for forty-one months, I had mixed feelings about their departure. It didn't seem right for me to remain behind. I consoled myself with the fact that Coon would fill me in on every detail later, that I wasn't needed for what they were going to do in Georgia, that I had responsibilities here, and that I would be joining them in Florida to move our cache. Having to ride in the cattle car in early April, especially at night, was also a point in favor of being left behind. As it was Sunday, we attended service and said a prayer for them before returning to the farm.

Since Coon was gone, and because Sally continued to need assistance with the books, Nathaniel prevailed on Henry's ma to stay on at the farm and help for awhile. Saying she would soon be unable to ride, Lilly stayed on to have a last opportunity to ride her mare. She also wanted to help any of the Atlanta women who still needed it. I took the noon train to St. Louis and arrived there the following afternoon.

Meanwhile, Henry's party was traveling south toward Nashville, Chattanooga, and Atlanta. Soldiers stationed at every bridge and trestle provided evidence that the area through which they were traveling was still contested, if only by small groups. Delayed only by the regular need to load firewood and take on water, a chore with which able bodied-travelers assisted, they arrived in Nashville at midnight the same day they left Louisville. Being delayed a number of times, and having to ferry across the Tennessee River in order to switch trains, it took three days to make the trip from Nashville to Atlanta.

Atlanta was in shambles. Burning several thousand homes in the area, Sherman had left little but ashes. At least the stench of the animals that Sherman's army had shot had long since vanished. Also, some efforts at rebuilding were underway. With few available building materials, and exorbitant prices for everything, little was being accomplished.

The value of Confederate paper money stood at seventy dollars in paper to one silver dollar. Even Henry abandoned his efforts to exchange it. He did not abandon the money. Saying that it might rebound a little as it had in the past, and that it weighed almost nothing, he kept it.

Jolene wanted to immediately search for Tyler and her mother. Knowing the danger of traveling about at night with the great wealth they had in the form of animals and supplies, Henry chose to set up camp. Choosing a location that could be easily defended, Henry and Coon alternated on guard duty until daylight. They then began the search. In less than two hours they found Tyler. He was still living in the temporary structure that had been their home for the winter. Jolene's mother had passed away several days before Jolene arrived to see her.

After introductions to Tyler's friends were over, Henry drew Tyler aside and said, "Is there anyone among your companions who you trust like a brother, one in whom you would trust your life and wealth, who also has no deep attachments to any others in your group?"

"There are two men who served with me. Somehow we came together here."

"Other than yourself, I need only one. Pick the one you would choose to stand beside in a fight ahead of the other and bring him here. There should be no humanitarian consideration, only trust and ability."

Choosing one, Tyler brought him and reintroduced them. "This is Mathew. He's a good man from Alabama. He has no wife. Given the situation there, he has no other reason to return to Alabama. As I said before, this is Henry. I owe him my own life twice over, and for the freedom of my wife."

Henry said, "Mathew, Tyler's going to work for me and I want to hire one other good man. The salary will be one dollar a day in silver, and food. You'll eat the same as I do. Your job is to help as directed. You might have to use a shotgun in our defense. Are you the man?"

"I'm your man, sir," he replied.

"Good," Henry said. "Do you have anything you need to carry with you?"

"Only my blanket," he replied.

Arming Tyler and Mathew with a shotgun each, Henry said,

"Get your blanket and say nothing beyond goodbye to anyone. We're leaving."

Beset frequently by those who wanted to beg or buy food, they passed through what had once been a proud city as they proceeded toward the Whipmore Plantation.

Upon arriving at the Whipmore plantation, they observed that the big house and barns had been burned and most of the farm animals had been taken or destroyed. Of the buildings, only the slave quarters had been spared and those at the begging of the slaves. Having had some slave quarters improved, Mrs. Whipmore, her daughter-in-law, and two grandchildren were living there. A black man showed Henry to Mrs. Whipmore.

"We meet under bad circumstances, Mrs. Whipmore," Henry said.

"Yes. I'm afraid the worst possible," she said. "Thanks to your medicine, Tom and Virginia recovered from their illness. But the Yankees killed Tom when he refused to lay down his pistol and leave the porch. Over half of my slaves have left. Those who remain do little work. Actually, there's little work to do. We have no seed for planting. Everything was taken, killed, or burned by Sherman's troops except for the slave quarters. Because of the pleading of my slaves, they also spared a few milk cows."

"There are no slaves, Mrs. Whipmore," Henry said. "Lincoln announced them free on January first, eighteen sixty-three. Sherman brutally enforced that order some months past."

"Lincoln is not my master," she said.

"No, but his law will be your demise if you don't adhere to it and work within it to salvage something," Henry said. "You need to put your people on a salary, even a meager one, and get your fields planted. There's money to be made as the South recovers from this."

"Sir, I have a few milk cows, no mules, no seed, and no money to buy seed if it was available. My oldest son, William, who was Virginia's husband, was killed in the war, my husband died of consumption twenty years ago, Tom and my overseer were shot here, and some of my thankless slaves showed the Union soldiers where I buried my gold and silver pieces. The only way I could get money for animals and seed would be to mortgage the entire five thousand acres. One crop failure and the place would be gone."

"There are ways it could be done," Henry said. "But I didn't come here to discuss that. I came to try to locate Nathaniel's youngest sister, Reva."

"I know of no Reva," she said.

"She was a small girl you traded to some friends ten years ago," Henry said.

"I remember her," Virginia broke in. "She was the same age as my son, Josh. She was given to the Rileys. They're acquaintances of mine who live near Macon. Though it was small, I fear their place is burned now, along with all the others."

"Thank you, ma'am, we'll be going," Henry said.

"Wait," Mrs. Whipmore said. "It's close to time for the noon meal. We have little enough, but there's always something to eat on a farm. You'll join us I hope. I'd like to talk some more. You said there were ways. Perhaps you would share your thoughts. I never have liked you, but I do admire your method and results."

"If you'll point out an older man who's knowledgeable about the farm, and if we can contribute some food for the meal," Henry said. "But first I'd like to ride about the farm with the chosen man."

Coon rode with them to look at the farm. It took more than three hours for Henry to look over the five thousand acres close enough to satisfy himself. Two thousand five hundred acres were cleared, including five hundred in pasture and two thousand under cultivation. The other half was in pine trees that had been chipped on one side for turpentine. That land was also used as forage for animals. The farm buildings, other than the slave's quarters, were burned. While almost all the farm animals had been killed or stolen by Sherman's troops, the farm equipment was not significantly damaged, in many cases not damaged at all. Since some of the slaves had left, there were less than a hundred people living where there had been almost two hundred. There were more than enough buildings for living and storage, even if they were only slave quarter quality structures.

Upon Henry's return to the house, Mrs. Whipmore said, "I'm afraid we ate without you. After you've eaten we'll talk."

After eating, and talking to Tyler and Mathew to make the proper arrangement with them, Henry said, "Mrs. Whipmore, I plan to buy land and immediately begin plowing. Most people in the area won't be able to get a crop of any size in the ground this spring. The first crops in will go for a huge price. I expect to pay for the land I buy in one year, and make a profit. I'm willing to offer you one dollar an acre in gold, five thousand for the whole place."

She replied, "It's worth three dollars if I was willing to sell, which I'm not."

"It was worth one and a half dollars four years ago when things were different, and the buildings and animals were in place," Henry replied. "One dollar's more than fair at today's depressed land prices in this area. But you've stated that you don't plan to sell anyway. If you wait another year, you'll probably have to sell for fifty cents an acre. If you wait three years, you might lose it for taxes. Still, I want to put a crop in the ground starting this week so I'll make you another offer. If it's not acceptable I'll move on and buy land from those willing to sell, even though I don't wish to lose the time. Time is money in this case."

"It costs nothing to listen," she said.

Henry said, "I'll put in all the planting we can get done as quickly as possible. We'll keep planting until at least a thousand acres is planted in one thing or another. If things go well, we might get the entire two thousand acres that was previously cultivated planted. I'll see the crop planted, tended to maturity, and harvested. You'll get ownership of half of the proceeds from the crop's sale. After the crop's sold, you'll repay me for half the labor charge for planting, plowing, and harvesting. I'll furnish mules, seed, and pay the labor."

Interrupting, she said, "What do you get out of this other than half of the crop?"

"I get title to twenty-five hundred acres—half cleared land and half timber," he replied. "In one crop you should get several times the income you would from the sale of twenty-five hundred acres. Also, in case of a crop failure, which is unlikely, you would only lose half of the place. If you borrowed money and had a crop failure, you would lose the entire place."

"What if the Yankees come and burn the crops?" she asked.

"They won't. I'm working under authorization from General Grant," he said, producing a paper. "You probably need to think about this overnight. We'll camp here and talk again tomorrow after you've thought it through."

"Where will you get the seed?" she asked. "Not only is the price of seed beyond reason, seed isn't available here. The price of seed and labor would negate any profit on your part."

"That very price is what should make this impossible for you to refuse," he said. "Thinking to sell some and plant some, I brought seven hundred and fifty pounds of various kind of seed from Louisville, mostly cotton and corn. Though the seed isn't enough, or in the right proportions, that error can soon be remedied. More seed will be shipped from Louisville. We have three mules now and can have another seven within the week."

"You have seven hundred and fifty pounds of seed with you?" she asked.

"Yes," he said, "and there'll be more by the time that's in the ground."

Taking up residence for the night in an empty slave shanty, Henry asked Mrs. Whipmore, Virginia, and Virginia's two children to join him for supper. Mrs. Whipmore respectfully declined, saying she needed to talk with Virginia.

Virginia showed up at our camp as dark set in and said to Henry, "I'm to gather some information. Would you walk with me?"

"Sure," Henry said, wrapping his blanket around his shoulders. It was cold at night in early April.

Returning two hours later, Henry said, "They're going to take the offer. We have some fine points to hammer out tomorrow morning but it's pretty much settled. Tyler, call a meeting for tomorrow at ten for everyone who lives here. We need to get people hired and start plowing immediately. You and Mathew are employed as agreed. Mathew, your first job will be to take an order for goods and animals to Louisville. I'll expect you back within ten days. If your other friend's still where you were camped, you can put him on at one dollar a day for the trip as a guard and helper. If he's not there, choose someone else. Jolene, you're on the payroll as a bookkeeper."

Henry didn't talk about what he had negotiated during the two hours with Virginia other than to say, "She tried everything to get the best deal she could. I guess Mrs. Whipmore thought Virginia could be more persuasive than she could. But, business is business."

At 10:15 the next morning Henry spoke to the former slaves. "I've made an arrangement with Mrs. Whipmore to own half the place and farm the whole thing. Those of you who want to stay here and work are welcome. Everyone else has until tomorrow morning to be gone from the property. Those who stay will be used for work only as needed. There won't be work all the time for everyone. Anyone twelve years old, or older, who is chosen to work will be paid twenty cents a day or ten cents a half day, in silver, at the end of each week. If you put in a good day's work you'll be paid. If you put in a poor day's work you'll be paid for that day, but you'll be sent away. If you're still with us when the crop is harvested and sold, you'll be paid an additional ten cents for every day you've worked. Everyone who stays may live where they live now and can grow a common garden for food. I'll provide your seed this year. Miss Jolene will keep the books based on your supervisor's report on your work. Mr. Tyler will be in charge of the farm and will be responsible for everything."

"Masa Williams, what be the punishments," one young man asked.

"There'll be no punishment. If you don't work a good day's work when called upon, or if you cause unreasonable trouble, you'll be sent away, with force if necessary."

There were no other questions, so Henry added, "We're going to start plowing now. Mr. Tyler will need to get some people started today. Those of you who don't want to be involved must go to your quarters now and start gathering your things."

Turning to Mathew, Henry said, "Let's get you some things and go to town. I want you on the first train to Louisville."

After getting Mathew on the train with an order to Nathaniel, and a letter telling me to arrive in Atlanta by May 1, Henry contacted a couple of physicians around town and sold some medical supplies he had brought for that purpose. He sold most of it on credit. It was after dark when Henry returned to the plantation.

While helping with Henry's horse, Coon said, "Virginia came to see you at first dark."

"I can talk to her tomorrow," Henry said.

"Just thought you might like to know," Coon said. "You had the three mules and seed with you on purpose. You had this planned, didn't you?"

"No," Henry said. "I planned to buy a smaller place and have it farmed by Tyler, along with a few helpers. I was thinking to leave the mules there. If I had been thinking this big, I would have brought more mules. Enough seed was brought for a modest-sized farm, and to have some to sell. My real plan was, and is, to buy a large farm in Florida. How did the work go?"

"Good," Coon said. "According to one of the supervisors, people are working harder than ever before. They're making something instead of nothing. Other than here, there's not much work to be had. The word got out fast about what's going on here. We had several strangers, black and white, show up before dark wanting work. Those who were not assigned to work today got started on planting a common garden. They seem to have some focus now."

"We'll stay here ten days and see that there's no trouble, and wait for Mathew to get back. I then plan to go to Macon and look for Reva," Henry said. "We'll also see what other opportunities might be available as we travel."

After only one day of plowing with three mules, Henry realized that ten mules were not enough to get the full two thousand acres planted in a timely manner. He then wired Nathaniel and changed Mathew's order from seven to twelve mules.

After a few days a Union cavalry unit showed up. When shown Henry's papers from General Grant by Mrs. Whipmore, they departed without incident. She was so impressed that she invited Henry to supper. He declined, saying he was tired.

It was nine days before Mathew got back. Having received a wire two days earlier, Henry and Coon knew he was coming and met him with a wagon. Mathew brought twelve mules and a saddle horse, and all the supplies. He also brought letters from everyone.

While in Atlanta, Coon and Henry received some interesting news that was, then, several days old. Lee had surrendered his army on Sunday, April 9. They also found out that the value of Confederate paper money had dropped to eighty dollars to one in silver.

Some people thought the hostilities were over when General Lee surrendered but they were wrong. Johnston, still roaming around in the Carolinas with his 40,000-man army, didn't surrender his army until April 26. Confederate General Richard

Taylor didn't surrender his army until May 4. General E. Kirby Smith didn't surrender his Trans-Mississippi army until May 26. Tallahassee, Florida, was the only state capital that hadn't been taken by the end of the war. Union officials then arranged to enter Tallahassee without soldiers. Even so, smaller units continued fighting in Florida and Texas until the end of the year.

April 22, 1865

Satisfied the farm work was going well, Henry and Coon left for Macon in search of Reva. Flitting when necessary to avoid armed groups, which could have been from either army, or neither, they made forty miles the first day and camped near Jackson, Georgia.

The path of destruction Sherman left was marked by chimneys that were still standing from burned-out houses, the bleached bones of dead animals, and a diseased and starving population. Typical of the population was a family they stumbled upon the second day at noon. Ordinarily they avoided contact with people, but in this instance they topped a ridge and were within fifty yards of a young mother with five children before knowing they were there. Their house was burned, and they were living in a lean-to made of salvaged materials and pine boughs. That they were starving was obvious at a glance. The woman weighed no more than eighty pounds. Her oldest child, a boy of ten years, had the weight of a six-year-old. The woman immediately approached them and asked for work.

Henry said, "Ma'am, I'll leave you some food and five dollars but we have no work."

"I'll not take charity," she said. "All I want is some honest work to feed my children."

Dismounting, Henry said, "Very well then, you can cook for us." It being near noon, that was all he could think of.

After they ate, they left half of their supply of food. It was enough to last the woman and children for several days.

Henry also gave some advice. He said, "Hide what food we leave. After resting a few days, so the children can become stronger, travel straight west for fifteen miles. Being out of the strip the Union soldiers burned, you can find work and assistance."

"I can't leave," she said. "My husband will return here after the war."

"Ma'am, I hate to paint a bad picture but I think there's no more than one chance in four that any one person will return. Why don't you leave him a message," he said.

"I can't leave" were her last words as Henry and Coon rode off.

Twenty miles from Macon they started inquiring about the Riley farm. Though most of the places at which they inquired were inhabited by people similar to the mother with five children, there were places where good fortune or a swing to the east by Sherman, short of Macon, had spared some houses. Those who were fortunate enough to have had their house spared often had a garden and other food to eat. Some did not. After Sherman had passed them by, stragglers or other groups had raided some farms. The Riley farm turned out to be one of those. The house was there, but stragglers from Sherman's army had been by and stripped the place of its food and animals. Having hidden some seeds and other supplies, they now had a garden up and were managing to survive.

Even as Henry and Coon arrived, the Rileys were having

new problems. Approaching the place with caution, as was their custom, they heard some shouting while still out of view. At almost the same time they flushed a black boy from the bushes. The boy ran like a rabbit until he realized he was not being chased. After some quiet persuasion, he approached them to talk.

"What's the shouting about?" Henry asked.

"Dat's some men. Dey's bout dis many," he said, holding up ten, then five fingers. "Some of us hid."

"Is there a black girl here named Reva?" Henry asked.

"Sho' is," he replied. "She be in duh bushes close to duh house."

"What are the men doing, stealing things and messing with the women?" Henry asked.

"Dey sho' is. Dey be doin' what dey wants to," he replied.

Leaving their horses, Henry and Coon approached until they could see over the ridgeline. To reach the main house from where they were, one would have to cross a seventy-yard plowed area. Other than a hundred-foot-wide strip that had been cleared on one side of the house to prevent wildfires from reaching it, the area around the other sides of the house had grown up in weeds. All the other buildings also had large clearings around them. Eight men were visible outside. If the boy had counted right, that should leave seven in the house or another building. Some of their horses were in the horse pen and others were staked out. Three horses stood, still saddled, in front of the house.

Henry said, "Coon, there seems to be only one thing to do. You move twenty-five yards to the right and I'll do the same to the left. When we start shooting, keep shooting until your rifle and revolver are empty but move after every couple of shots. Never shoot at the same target twice. Assume you've hit it and go on to the next. I'm betting they've never been under fire from repeating rifles. They'll think there are ten or twelve of us. You start with the man farthest to the right. I'll start on the left. After our weapons are empty I'll order a cease-fire loud enough for them to hear. While we reload I'll offer to talk."

Coming under fire without warning, three of the men went down before they realized what was happening. One more fell as they ran for shelter. Some of the men didn't have their weapons in hand at the time of the attack. Many then found themselves crouched behind some form of cover without weapons. Firing at the men's hiding places, Henry and Coon emptied their weapons.

Henry then ordered as loud as he could, "Cease fire." He and Coon then began reloading as he shouted, "You in the house."

Receiving no reply after fifteen seconds, Henry repeated, "You in the house."

A voice from the house replied, "What do you want?"

"We want John Williams!" Henry shouted.

"There's no John Williams here," the voice said.

"I don't believe you," Henry said. "We're looking for John Williams."

"He's not here. If you don't quit shooting I'll kill these people."

"I don't care about those people. I'm looking for John Williams for the murder of my wife."

"He's not here I tell you."

"We'll have to see, or kill you all."

"We can't very well let you see us."

Already knowing what he was going to say, Henry sat quietly for a full minute before he shouted, "I've got an idea."

"Go ahead," the voice said.

"I know John Williams when I see him. We'll let you come out one at a time with your hat off so I can see your face. If you're not John Williams, you can each take one horse and leave," Henry said.

There was silence from the house for the better part of two minutes before he was answered. "That's no good. You would shoot us down as we came out."

"We can't very well shoot you all down and you leaving two

minutes apart," Henry said. "We'll kill you all if you don't." With that he shouted, "Open fire."

Henry and Coon again emptied their rifles and pistols, twenty-four rounds in all. They again darted from place to place in order to represent more people than they were.

Their weapons again empty, Henry shouted, "Cease fire."

After waiting for the smoke to clear and to reload his weapons, Henry shouted. "What will it be?"

After a brief pause the voice said, "What about our guns and horses?"

Henry replied, "You can take one horse each, and can carry one rifle or shotgun each. If anyone takes more, or turns the horses out of the pen, we'll shoot him down. If one of you is John Williams we'll shoot him down. You are to ride straight south. We've got two men in that direction. If you delay, you'll be shot. Make sure you leave your head uncovered so I can see if you're John Williams."

They chose one, or he volunteered, for in a minute a voice said, "I'm coming out," and a young man of about sixteen came out. His hands raised, he held a rifle in one hand. Walking to a staked-out horse, he threw a blanket and saddle on the horse and rode south without looking back.

Henry shouted, "One more," and the same procedure was followed. Within a half-hour we were down to the last of them.

The last man shouted, "My brother's down in the yard. Can I see to him?"

"Go ahead," Henry said.

After checking over his brother he shouted, "He's bad hurt."

"Put him on a horse and leave. You walk and lead the horse," Henry replied.

"He'll die," the man said.

"Or he'll die here, along with you, and we'll keep the horse," Henry replied.

After the men were gone, Henry shouted, "Is anyone in the

buildings? If so, come out."

They came out then—a white woman, two black women, and a couple of young girls.

"Are there any more of those men here?" Henry shouted.

"No," the white woman said, not knowing if she had been saved from one gang only to fall into the hands of another.

Approaching the house with caution, Henry found three dead men and two more soon to be.

Speaking to the white woman, he said, "We're in search of a young black girl named Reva. We're here on behalf of her mother and brother. She was three years old when traded to you ten years ago."

"She's here," the woman said. "She and some others who were outside managed to hide in the bushes when those men came."

"Call her in," Henry said. "We're taking her back to Atlanta to be with her family. Also, gather up the weapons from the dead. Are there any men here?"

"Only some young boys," she said. "We have no weapons."

"You have now," Henry said. "Which of those horses are yours and which belong to the men who were here?"

"We don't have any," she said. "All of ours were taken weeks ago."

One by one, children were coming in from the brush. Spotting the young boy they had first seen, Henry said, "Up on the house with you and watch for anyone coming." Pointing to another, he said, "You. Get on top of the barn and keep a lookout."

Confident that the men were all gone, Coon then approached the house.

The woman said, "What happened to your other men?"

"I'm afraid there are only the two of us," Henry replied. "We just make a big noise."

"God bless you," the woman said.

"We have enough supplies to make a meal for all of us. If we can find Reva, we'll then be going."

"You two are more than welcome to stay here for an hour or forever," the woman said. "Anything I have is yours. The Lord took my husband at the hands of Sherman's desecraters. You're the first good men I've seen since."

A voice from the edge of the yard said, "I'm Reva."

Hugging Reva, the white woman said, "Yes she is.

"Where are your black men?" Henry asked.

"One took his family and followed after Sherman. Another was hung. The third is in the brush someplace. I expect he'll be back any time," she said.

While waiting for a meal to be cooked, Henry and Coon told Reva the story of her mother and siblings, and that she would be leaving with them for Atlanta. They also instructed everyone in the loading and firing of the newly acquired weapons.

Offering no price for Reva, and being asked for none, they took six of the eight horses left by the gang and departed. Having exhausted their food supply, they traveled southwest. They found that, as had been reported, Macon had been outside Sherman's line of march. Sherman had only feinted at the city. Without a supply line, or the possibility of reinforcements, he could not put Macon under siege without putting his army at substantial risk. Sherman had no way of knowing the strength of the Macon garrison. He also couldn't know if Hood's, or some other army, was following him.

Upon finding a farm that hadn't been raided, they bought more supplies. Turning north from there, they arrived back at the Whipmore farm on April 28. Reva was then assigned to Jolene until such time as someone was going north and could escort her to Louisville.

The extra horses, except for two, were put to work in the fields. The best two saddle horses were held back, one as a saddle horse for me when I arrived, and one as a pack animal for our trip to Florida.

Henry told Tyler to arm and train eight of the former slaves who worked for us against the time that deserters or other riffraff showed up who were up to no good. Having led a company in battle, Tyler would do a good job with that. It was Henry's experience on the trip to Macon that brought that about.

Though the value of Confederate paper money dropped to $800 to one silver dollar on May 1, Henry still said he would carry ours with him. It was as if he just couldn't put it down. He also carried the warrants given for his horses and weapons by General Bragg. It was the one illogical thing Henry did.

May 2, 1865

As we were leaving for Florida we received news that General Johnston had surrendered his 39,000 soldiers to Sherman on April 26, in Durham, North Carolina. Open warfare was now confined to Florida, other parts of the Gulf Coast, and those Southern areas west of the Mississippi. The overall status of the war meant little to our safety, or lack of it. There were bands of soldiers, state militia, deserters, and thieves everywhere who were seeking to profit from the lawless situation. Since it was a dangerous time, we would consider everyone the enemy unless there was evidence otherwise.

At the time of our departure the value of Confederate paper money had fallen to a thousand to one dollar in silver or gold. I spoke with Henry about delaying our trip for a year or two until the fighting had stopped everywhere, but he had his mind made up about going. He wanted to buy a Florida farm while the time was ripe. Though he hadn't shared it, I was sure he had a plan for the money we could get from selling the buried things. Henry still carried our paper money and warrants with him.

Our first camp of the trip was near Locust Grove, Georgia. An unusual thing happened there. A lanky man approached and asked for food as we set up camp. That alone wasn't unusual but what followed was.

Henry said to the man, "Sorry. If we fed everyone we would soon be out of food ourselves."

The man said, "I've got something to trade but it'll take more than a little food to get it."

"I'm always willing to trade," Henry said. "What do you have?"

"I've got one of those Spencer repeating rifles," he said. "Picked it up off the ground at Chickamauga."

"Is that so?" Henry said. "If you were at Chickamauga, why are you here now?"

"Deserted," he said. "Got tired of it and walked off. My wife and kids were alone and needed me. I used all my Spencer cartridges when Sherman came through here. We hid in a swamp for days after that. "

"What unit were you with?" I asked.

"I was with Bragg the whole time, from Pensacola through Chickamauga," he replied. "Where did you get your Spencers?"

"We were at Chickamauga," I said. "As battlefield physicians, we frequently found ourselves in the middle of the fight. Henry picked ours up."

"I'll be damned," he said. "You say you're physicians?"

"Yes," Henry replied. "You mentioned a trade."

"Sure did. It's the only valuable thing I've got. I don't have any cartridges for it though."

244

"Where is it?" Henry asked.

"Back there. When I saw two of you with Spencers, I started following you hoping to trade. The rifle's no good to anyone without the fifty-two caliber cartridges that fit it. You can't buy them except up north."

"We'll trade," Henry said. "Bring it in pointed backwards. We're a little touchy."

"Sure will. Can I bring the kids? You said you were physicians and a couple of them are a little sickly."

"Bring them in," I said.

He was back in fifteen minutes, a wife and four kids in tow, with a Spencer held backwards in one hand. Squatting at the fire, he and Henry talked while I examined the wife and kids and Henry examined his Spencer.

"What'll you take for the rifle?" Henry asked.

"All I can get. I'm kind of at your mercy. Nobody else has cartridges that fit it so you're the only ones I can trade with."

"Your family's eaten up with worms," I said. "I'm going to treat them and leave you some medicine to finish the job."

"I don't have any money," he said.

"There'll be no charge," I replied. "You just worry about trading with Henry."

"We'll be eating soon," Henry said. "There's beans, onions, and salt pork in the pot and I've doubled the cornbread. There'll be enough for your family."

Looking at me—Coon had done so well with the Spencer that I had left it in his hands—Henry asked, "How many cartridges do you have for the Springfield?"

"Close to two hundred," I replied.

"I'll trade you Ben's Springfield breechloader and cartridges for the Spencer and I'll throw in a slab of salt pork, three pounds of beans, and five pounds of corn meal," Henry said.

"That's lots more than I expected," he said.

"We're all lucky to be here after Shiloh and Chickamauga," Henry said.

"You were at Shiloh?" he asked. "I was too."

"We were there. We had our field hospital set up at the church toward the end of it," Henry replied. "I assumed you were there when you said you had been with Bragg all the way. We were also at Pensacola for one small encounter. We weren't acting as physicians then."

"I remember you now. We came off the line late at Shiloh. You showed us the right road and stayed at the church with some of those who were badly wounded. How did you ever get out of there?" he said.

"Henry and I stayed on and helped the Yankees fix up our boys and theirs," I replied.

After eating, they excused themselves and returned to wherever they came from. As a parting remark, our guest said, "I'll be out in the woods with this Springfield. You boys sleep well. No one will bother you tonight."

We did, however, still keep a guard posted all night. As good as his word, he walked into camp at daylight. Obviously he hadn't slept. After having a cup of coffee, beans, and cornbread with us, he left.

We had to buy supplies that day. Though Henry had been too generous in the trade, it felt good to help out every once in a while.

Near Macon, we had another unusual encounter. We met two riders who were northbound on the road. Had there been more of them we would have left the road to avoid the meeting. Since there were only two, we stayed on the road.

When they got within fifteen yards, they stopped and one said, "I know two of those horses. They belonged to Pete and Jake. Where did you get those horses?"

The one I was riding and the pack animal were the two to which he referred.

Pulling his horse sideways, Coon blocked the road. Suddenly, as if by magic, his revolver was in his hand. The motion was so quick as to leave no time for reaction by any of us.

"Drop your weapons and reins," Henry said, his Spencer hammer pulled to full cock.

They didn't try to bluff it. They dropped their weapons and reins immediately.

"Tell us about Pete and Jake," Coon said.

"Nothing," the original speaker said. "I just thought I recognized those horses."

"You should, we took some of those you left at the Riley place," Coon said.

"I was mistaken," the rider said.

"You were mistaken to be involved at the Riley's," Henry said. "Get down off your horses slow and easy, and on the near side."

"It wasn't us," he said as he dismounted.

"It was you, all right," Coon said. "I was hoping none of you would take that bay mare you're riding. I was kind of partial to her."

"You were there?" the other rider said.

"Shut up, Irvin," the first speaker said, knowing they had already revealed too much.

"I was there," Coon said. "You were the third one out of the house. Your friend was hiding out behind the corner of the house while we were shooting. If there had been more of us, you would have never been allowed to ride off."

"There must have been fifteen of you," the first rider said.

"Only two, and these Spencer repeating rifles," Coon said. "That's enough talk, down on your belly."

Once they were tied, I asked, "What are we going to do with them, Henry?"

"Hang them," he said.

At that time Irvin put in to begging until Coon kicked him in the ribs. He still said, "Please, mister, we split off from that bunch after that."

Coon would have recognized them even if they hadn't told

on themselves. Even with that we still didn't like hanging them. They would have been turned over to the law but there wasn't much law then. Henry left a note pinned on each of their chests, "Thieves and Rapists." Though it couldn't be helped, hanging them wore on me for several days.

We took the two horses and their weapons and almost two dollars from their pocket. I considered taking their things as payback from Henry's generosity in trading for the Spencer.

We hadn't ridden very far when Henry said, "Someday we ought to tell Mrs. Riley."

"I plan to after we get through with our business," Coon said.

Swinging southwest to be further from the coast, we planned to go through Moultrie and Quitman, Georgia, and Madison, Florida, before swinging over toward Lake City and Lulu. Not being known in those areas, and being in no particular hurry, that route would be safer even if it did take one day longer.

Food being plentiful at the farms once we got away from Sherman's trail, we traded the saddles from the two spare horses for food and a couple of packsaddles. Two extra horses with regular riding saddles on them created an unusual situation that generated questions, even if not asked. The people we traded the saddles to made offers on our spare horses. Thinking they might come in handy, we declined. All the things buried at Aunt May's couldn't be carried on a couple of extra packhorses, but having the horses at least presented alternative possibilities.

We spent a night in Moultrie and Quitman, Georgia, but were bypassing Madison, Florida, to the east when we saw the wagons. Our saddle horses were walking faster than those pulling the wagons were so we were slowly overtaking them. As we caught up, it became clear that there were Confederate uniformed officers in the group. Ordinarily we would have avoided people, but those with the wagons were obviously not riffraff. There were also some slaves and a sprinkling of women and children. Since they posed no apparent threat to us, we continued at our normal fast walk and closed the gap.

They had pulled over to rest and water their animals when we overtook them. We also stopped to water our horses. Even before Henry spoke to him, one of them looked familiar.

"Captain, I haven't seen you in a long time. How's your wife?"

Startled, he responded, "Oh yes, you're the physician from Atlanta. What are you doing way down here?"

"The war takes us to strange places," Henry said. "Do you have news from the fight?"

"There is no fight, I'm afraid," he said. "You haven't heard about what's happening?"

"I've heard about Lee and Johnston," Henry said. "Is there more?"

"I'm afraid so," the captain said. "It's all falling apart."

"That's too bad," Henry said. "We've been traveling and didn't know. We're about to swing east to Jacksonville or we would accompany you."

My ears perked up then. Rather than say nothing, Henry had just lied to him about where we were going.

We were out of hearing and I was about to ask Henry when Coon did.

"Who was that?"

"One of President Davis' aides. I treated his wife for dysentery in Atlanta."

"Why did you tell him Jacksonville?"

"I didn't want him to know where we were going—I wanted to give him a chance to tell me where he was going. He didn't. There's something interesting about that wagon train. As soon as we get out of sight, we're going to swing around behind them and follow."

"How far?"

"Until we know what they're doing."

Well, there we went again. But I really wasn't in a hurry to dig up those things at Aunt May's anyway. As far as I was concerned we could wait a year or two on that. It would be lots easier after all hostilities had ended.

We stayed well back. Riding a horse of a different color each time, one of us moved up far enough every couple of hours to see them. I don't believe they ever saw any of us again. Making over thirty miles in a day, they were going somewhere in a big hurry to be pulling what appeared to be heavily loaded wagons. It was full dark before they camped. We camped more than two miles beyond them so we could have a small fire for hot food and coffee without being seen. That location also allowed us to see them as they proceeded the next morning.

Saddled up and ready at daylight, we were watching from a half-mile away when they went by us the next morning. We played tag all day. They seemed to be headed straight for Newberry or Archer.

It was well after dark and we were camped again when Henry said, "I've got it. They're headed for a plantation at Archer. They couldn't be going anywhere but there. At least they'll be passing through the plantation."

"How do you know," I asked.

"The most powerful man in Florida owns the plantation," he replied. "I've got a childhood friend that's a slave there. I'm going to take two horses and alternate riding them tomorrow. If I leave at three in the morning, I should get there by noon. It'll be almost dark when they get there with the wagons. I'll have time to alert my friend before they get there. He can get his friends to find out what's going on. One of you should come with me. The other can trail them from close enough to see if anything unusual occurs."

"I'm going with you," I said. "Coon can follow them." Having missed out on the Riley farm incident, I wasn't about to be left behind again.

"What am I looking for?" Coon asked.

"I don't know," Henry replied. "There's just something strange going on."

"What does it mean to us?" I asked. But I was already getting mighty interested.

"There's no telling," Henry said. "Maybe nothing."

Up at 2:30 A.M., we left right after Henry diagrammed the plantation and showed Coon where we would camp near it. The moon had already come up, so there was a little light. I let my horses follow Henry's. Henry seemed to know exactly where he was going. We stopped every hour to change our saddles to fresh horses and at daylight for the horses to rest. Already fourteen miles ahead of the wagons by the time they got started, we would gain a little more because their wagons would be slower than our saddle horses. Also, the wagons would have to stick to the roads.

Though I still didn't know where we were, at least I could see where we were going after the sun came up. Henry wasn't using any roads, only horse and animal trails. Frequently, he would cut straight across the woods where there was no trail at all. A little before 11:00 A.M. we came to an abandoned house with five acres around it that had been farmed. At that time the place was grown up in weeds and bushes.

Henry said, "This is where we lived."

It wasn't much better than where we had lived on the Suwannee River.

While resting our horses, Henry said, "The plantation is an hour by horseback from here. My friend Jacob is a slave there. I hope to call him out and get him to have his friends listen to the conversations around the plantation. He can let us know what's going on without it being known that we're here."

"How can you call him out?" I asked.

"While hunting and fishing together we always used a quail assembly call as a signal. We got pretty good at it. Good enough to pick ours out from others."

I replied, "What did you use at night? Everyone knows that quail don't call after dark."

"Three owl hoots," he replied.

He gave me a demonstration of both.

Proceeding to the plantation, we approached the fields through a thickly wooded area. After tethering the horses to some trees, we then crawled forward to observe. There were lots of workers in the fields, and an encampment of people with wagons near the plantation house. Some of the people wore Confederate uniforms.

"At the rate we traveled, and because of the head start we got, the wagons we were following are a good five hours behind us," Henry said. "I wonder who those people are?"

Not having an answer, I kept quiet.

Within minutes Henry spotted Jacob, who was plowing, and gave the quail assembly call. Lifting his head, Jacob looked straight at the woods where we were crouched. When Henry gave the call again, Jacob scratched his head.

"He knows it's me," Henry said. "He'll come as soon as he can. We'll wait here."

Our wait wasn't long. In less than half an hour everyone started to the house for the noon meal and break. Jacob spoke to someone, then walked to the woods fifty yards from us. He joined us within minutes.

"Lord, Henry, I thought it was you. Where've you been for the past four years? You were going to Pensacola the last time I saw you," Jacob said.

After introducing us, Henry filled Jacob in on his travels. While they talked, I went to the horses and got some cornbread, fried pork, and water for all of us.

When I returned, Henry was asking, "How long before you have to be back?"

"I'll stay here and rejoin them when they return to the field," Jacob said. "I told Missy to bring me some food, but I've already got some now."

"Tell me about the people camped here," Henry said.

"It's big time stuff," Jacob said. "That's some of President

Davis' people. They've been here five days. They buried some silver and gold coin in the stable. Twenty-five thousand dollars was the sum mentioned. I'm sure it's true. There's also supposed to be some more folks coming soon."

"They'll be here before dark," Henry said. "We've been trailing them for most of three days."

"Why?" Jacob asked.

"I'm not sure," Henry said. "Just a hunch."

They talked for another half-hour about what they had both been doing. Jacob must have had a hundred questions.

Finally, right out of the blue, Henry said, "I'm going to take that money."

After Jacob and I were tongue-tied for almost a minute, Henry continued, "I have over twenty-five thousand in Confederate paper money that I'm going to swap for it. They printed that money and it's their fault I have it. I've also got warrants from them for seven horses and twice as many weapons. Counting interest, I figure they owe us close to thirty thousand."

I said, "You're crazy." But my heart was pounding and I had already decided to help.

Henry said, "Jacob, we'll need your help. Since the war is nearly over, you'll be free before the year is out. When they free you, you won't have ten cents or a way to make any money. We'll give you a good stake for helping."

"You know we've done almost everything together," Jacob said, "but this sounds crazy, Henry. I'd be hung from the closest tree."

"Can you come back here at first dark?" Henry asked.

"Sure I can, but I don't want to steal any money," he said.

"I'm not going to steal it," Henry said. "It's owed to me. I'm going to trade for it, hopefully without them knowing."

"How are we going to do that?" I asked.

Smiling at me for including myself, he said, "I don't know yet. The other wagons have to get here first. After we see how they organize, I'll think of something. Jacob, I wouldn't have you do anything more dangerous than you've done before now. What I'd like you to do is find out about the new wagons after they come in—how long will they be here, where are they going after leaving here, and are there others coming? Get someone who's around them to listen and tell you. After you find out, I want you to get back as soon as possible and let me know. But mostly, I want to know where the money is."

"I can do that, but you've got me scared," Jacob said. "I already know where the money is. It's buried in a little pony's stable."

"Well, don't be scared," Henry said. "I'm not going to do anything stupid. By the way, why haven't I seen any dogs around?"

"They're all in the pens because of all those strangers being here," Jacob said. "Except for old Bossy, they never pen him up. He don't ever bark anyway."

"How many are in the pen?" Henry asked.

"Five," Jacob answered.

"We'll camp over by the opossum tree," Henry said. "Get there when you can."

Having done all we could at the time, we pulled back about a mile to the opossum tree. Henry soon returned to where he could observe the plantation while I waited for Coon. Coon arrived before dark and I filled him in.

Then I asked, "What do you think?"

"Henry's been the general of this army ever since I joined up and we seem to be doing better than the Yankees or the Rebs," he said. "I'm sticking till the end."

"Me too," I replied.

Because Coon wanted to see the area, we walked to where Henry was as we talked. The wagons we had been following were already at the house. Counting slaves, family members, and the wagon train members, there seemed to be two hundred people visible at any one time. I didn't see how we could get the money from the stable with all those people around.

While the new arrivals at the plantation made camp, Henry drew diagrams in the dirt and showed both of us where the dog pens, barns, hog pens, horse stalls, and everything else was. He seemed to know the place like the back of his hand.

Moving back to our camp, we waited on Jacob. He announced his arrival by hooting three times. Henry answered.

"I didn't want to get shot, so I gave notice," Jacob said as he sat down.

Handing him a cup of coffee, Henry asked, "What can you tell us?"

Sipping the coffee, Jacob said, "I can tell you this coffee sure is good. I don't get any coffee."

We waited for him to go on. For almost a minute he seemed to be contemplating something.

Finally, he said, "Henry, you said I would get a fair stake. What is a fair stake?"

"What do you want?" Henry asked. "What's your ultimate wish in life?"

"You know what that is. We've talked about it before. First, I want to be free. After that I want a farm—two hundred acres and enough mules to work it. A man should also have money for expenses—seed, tools, money to pay his help, and such. There are probably expenses I don't even know about. You taught me how to read, and gave me books, but I need to know more. I need to know more about numbers," he said.

"You're going to be free in weeks or months," Henry said. "Or you can be free now. We have a good horse that no one's riding. You could leave with us."

"I have family here," Jacob said.

"Leave them here and come back and get them. Or, stay here with them until the end and then leave. I'll leave money for all of you to travel on," Henry said.

"We want to stay in Florida," Jacob said.

"If we pull this off," Henry said, "I'll buy you three hundred acres within a hundred miles of here. We'll stock it with four mules, two saddle horses, and twenty cattle. I'll also leave you five hundred in specie to make sure you get a good start."

We could get all that done for less than $2,000 in silver. Thinking back to my life on the Suwannee River, I couldn't have imagined what that much money looked like. I expect that Jacob couldn't either. It was more money than could be saved in twenty lifetimes of farm labor.

Jacob reached out his hand and Henry took it. A bargain was sealed.

"I'll have to leave with you," Jacob said. "If I stay here and they're even suspicious, they'll hang me. Here's the situation. Those new wagons brought more money, thirty-five thousand dollars in specie it's said. It's buried in the same stable as the other money. There's only a little pony in the stable. The money is part of the Confederate treasury. President Davis is traveling this way from Virginia with three hundred thousand in specie and eight hundred thousand in Confederate paper money. After burning the paper money, Davis has been splitting up the coin and paying off some people. He has also put some in various places. Everyone thinks he's in Georgia now. Him and Mrs. Davis might come here and try to escape by boat. Or they might go to Alabama and try to get down to Texas or Mexico from there. They're still fighting in Alabama and Texas, just like in Florida."

All three of us sat there staring at him until Henry said, "It's part of the Confederate treasury. I hold warrants against it for horses and guns. I've also got over twenty-five thousand in Confederate paper money they printed. They aren't about to pay up. They're just going to steal it and leave the country."

We sat there, stunned, looking at each other. The truth of it was clear.

"When do they plan to move it?" Henry asked.

"It seems like they're waiting for something else to happen, maybe for someone else to arrive. It might be for the president himself to get here," Jacob said. "It could be a week, or two, or it might be a couple of days."

"What time are you going back tonight?" Henry asked.

"I'm not going back until tomorrow morning when everyone's getting out to work. No one's going to pay any attention to one black face more or less. I'll slip in before daylight when there's lots of folks stirring around. Only Ma will miss me tonight and she knows where I am."

"Are we going to take all of it?" Coon asked.

"We can't," Henry said. "First, I figure the most they owe us is thirty thousand. Second, it probably weighs too much. Sixty thousand dollars in silver would weigh over three thousand pounds. That much in gold would weigh two hundred and thirty-five pounds. We don't know what part is gold and what's silver. If it's packed so we can, we'll mostly take gold coin. As near as we can, I figure we'll take what's owed us, and what I'm going to pay Jacob to help get it."

"They'll come hunting us for sure," I said.

"They might not," Henry said. "They're running scared and maybe only a couple of jumps ahead of the Union cavalry. There's obviously no written record of this money. Even if there were written records, where would they report it? The captain said the war was falling apart. I think they'll take what we leave and try to escape being captured by the Union cavalry. It's not for sure that the real story will ever get out. Hopefully we can take what's ours by carrying only two hundred pounds."

"Do you think we can actually get it?" I asked.

"We can try," Henry said.

"How?" I asked.

"I'm still working on that," he said.

Each of us lost in his own thoughts, we sat without speaking for some time.

Then Henry said, "No one's going to pay any attention to one black face more or less."

We stared at him. Jacob had just said that.

"We're going in as black people tomorrow at first dark," Henry said. "It'll be dark as pitch by seven. The moon doesn't come up until two A.M. We'll cover our hands and faces with smut, leave the horses two hundred yards from the stable, and walk in on foot acting like slaves going about their business. Jacob, how many guards are watching the money?"

"There's no regular guard until they go to bed. Everyone looks after things until then. After they go to bed, there are two guards at the stable all night. Also, there are a couple of other guards who walk around."

"That gives us from dark until about nine P.M. without a guard at the stable, a good two hours." Henry said. "We shouldn't need more than an hour if it works. We might not even be seen. It's easy to see from the darkness to a lighted area but impossible to see into a dark area from a lighted area. I don't think they're too worried about someone carrying away what has to be well over a thousand pounds of money. We'll carry what we can, mostly in gold. If we move quickly and quietly, we can probably get it done. All we need to do is slip in and get what we want ready to travel. Seeing an opportunity, we'll walk off with it."

"The dogs could raise a fuss, even at that distance and them in the pen," Jacob said.

"You'll have to earn your money. You're going to have to chloroform them," Henry said. "I'll show you how. Can you arrange to be the one who feeds the dogs tomorrow, and do it late?"

"Sure. I do it lots of times. I'm more involved in hunting with them than anyone else. If someone else feeds them earlier, I can go out after it's dark to pet and talk to them. I do that all the time."

"As soon as it gets dark you'll chloroform them and lay them out in their boxes like they're asleep. Can you get us some clothes that will make us look like slaves, dark clothes that won't show up in the dark?"

"Sure I can. I'll meet you with the clothes as soon as I get the dogs quiet."

"What if they spot us, or the guards start patrolling before we get in and out?" Coon asked.

"If we can, we'll put the guards out of action with chloroform or a gun barrel. If we can't, we'll shoot our way out. Once away from the buildings we'll be okay if we don't shoot and give them flashes to shoot back at. We'll all have to carry handguns under our clothes," Henry said. "What about the pony? Is it shy?"

"As gentle as can be," Jacob replied.

As I thought about it, it didn't sound like much of a plan. But then I remembered the time north of Chattanooga. Riding off on those Union cavalry horses, we had inquired as to where the most forward position was and had been saluted and called sir before riding over to the Confederate side. This might work. We talked it over and over until we had everything clear in our minds.

Henry asked Jacob, "If you ask your people to ignore any strange black faces they see tomorrow night, how many would avoid seeing us?"

After thinking for awhile, Jacob answered, "All those that'll be around the stable. I'll be careful about who I tell to ignore us."

"That could be a big help," I said.

"You have to quiet the dogs by a few minutes after dark," Henry said. "We'll all carry a small bottle of chloroform in case it's needed with a guard."

We tried to go to sleep early but it didn't work for me. I tossed and turned until after midnight. When I woke up the next morning I thought I hadn't been to sleep at all, but I must have, it was daylight and Jacob was already gone.

Alternating turns, we watched the white people at the plantation house all that day. Other than for gathering wood and food, they stayed close to the house. A hog was killed and cooked whole. Though the gathering of people was almost like a celebration, we knew they were not celebrating anything. There being lots of them, they just had to cook lots of food. I could almost smell that hog from the woods. We were eating cornbread, beans, and salt pork. Keeping a small fire going to cook, we also took half-burned sticks out of the fire so we would have charcoal in abundance for our faces and hands that night.

It was one of the longest days of my life. I was relieved when it finally became time to put smut on all our exposed skin. Thinking the clothes Jacob would bring might not fit very well, we smutted our arms, lower legs, and feet.

Standing in the edge of the woods, we waited until five minutes before seven to start walking. All of us were buck naked so we wouldn't have extra clothes to contend with after we put on those that Jacob brought. We sure looked funny but none of us were laughing. We were leading two packhorses. Saddled and ready, our other horses were left tethered in the trees.

Jacob met us two hundred yards from the stables with stakes to push in the ground to tether the packhorses to. Whispering, he told us the dogs were sound asleep from the chloroform and that there had been no problems to this point. We were all hoping we didn't meet some romantic young couple out for a walk. That didn't seem likely since we were in a fresh plowed field. We were in the best place we could be.

Him knowing the place best, Jacob took me and walked ahead. Henry, who was also familiar with the place, was to follow with Coon in two minutes. We walked right past an old black man at the edge of the stables. Neither he nor Jacob spoke. I almost couldn't believe it when we entered the pony's stall, located the place where the money was buried, and started digging with our hands. It was almost like I was in a dream.

Two minutes later I almost died when the voice of a man,

who was obviously white, said, "What're you boys doing there?" I almost didn't recognize Coon's voice outside the stable when he answered, "We's gwine ta see ta dat mule's so' foot."

It was as good an imitation as I've ever heard.

The voice answered, "Well, get on with it."

"Yas suh," Coon answered, as they walked on past our stall.

Within minutes they were back. We were not sure it was their footsteps, so we stood with our revolvers ready.

Once all of us were in the stall, three of us started digging. We soon unearthed some heavy leather bags that were wrapped in oilcloth. Holding the pony's muzzle and acting as lookout, Jacob stood at the door. I could hear him whispering to the pony. Two times he stopped us from our task as someone walked by outside. Once it was two young lovers. They stood together for a full three minutes before moving on. I was sweating so profusely that I was afraid all my smut would wash off—not that it would have mattered, we were in it too deep to stop then.

Henry selected the bags. Because gold bags were smaller, and more valuable for the weight, he selected mostly gold. Even in the dark the selection process wasn't too hard. There was some faint light from the stars and campfires that allowed him to see the color. Some could also be chosen because of the size and weight of the coins. We brought some bags to the door to see well enough to be sure what we had.

After we had been there an eternity, actually only forty-five minutes, we had our bags selected. We were almost ready to leave when Jacob cautioned us that someone was coming. Two men paused outside and started urinating. My mind was racing. I was thinking about how I could get my fifty-pound bag to the horses even if we had a shootout. After killing those two, we would have only a few seconds to get into the total darkness. Since we wouldn't return fire from the darkness, thus giving them no flash for a target, it would be only bad luck if one of us got shot. It was impossible to see anyone beyond fifteen yards, unless they were between you and one of the fires or lanterns. In the field, there would be no one further from a light than us. As I waited for the men to finish urinating, I mentally practicing walking quietly so as not to give my position away from noise after we got in the plowed dirt.

Once they were gone, I said, "Let's go."

"One minute," Henry said. "I'm going to put this Confederate paper money and the warrants with their other money. We also need to fix the area like it was. We'll need as much time as possible before they find out we've been here."

As we walked away, carrying a fifty-pound bag each, we walked right by that elderly black man again. He spoke that time but only one word, "Luck," and we were gone in the darkness.

Though there was no immediate alarm sounded, my fears were not calmed until we arrived at our horses and were not ambushed there. No one but us heard our horses' hooves on the soft plowed dirt as we walked them away.

We neither heard nor saw an alarm as we left the plantation.

May 17, 1865

Before daylight, ten hours later and forty miles north of the plantation, we arrived at Aunt May's house. She was in the process of cooking breakfast.

After one look at us in the light cast by a lamp through the kitchen door, she said to Henry, "My Lord, child, I was expecting anybody but you. You all put those horses up and come in to breakfast. And you sure better wash up. Is there any more than the four of you? John," She shouted. "Henry's here. Come help him with the horses."

Henry's Uncle John, having been wounded, captured, and paroled, was home.

As soon as we were washed up, seated at the table, and had been introduced, Aunt May said, "You go right on and tell us about everyone."

Henry talked for twenty minutes. He had talked about almost everyone when Aunt May asked, "How long since you boys last slept?"

"It's been quite a while," Henry replied. "We would like to rest for seven hours. I'm afraid we're on the run again. They're forty miles behind us if they're coming. They might not be coming, but we can't chance it. I would like for you to tell them the truth if they come here, except for who we are. As far as you know we were just four men on six horses who stopped by and paid for a meal and shelter."

"Can you tell me the story, child?" she asked.

"Yes ma'am," Henry said. "And there are two things I would like you to do for us. First, they might or might not come. Whether they do or not, I'd like you to send me a letter to Atlanta and St. Louis. In case one doesn't get through, send one every two weeks until you hear from me that I got one. I want to know if we were pursued. Second, I want a horse or mule. If one of ours comes up lame, we could be in trouble if they are after us. Also, the war's falling apart fast and you're going to need something other than paper money. We'll leave five hundred in specie to see you through. We'll leave another two thousand in specie that belongs to Jacob. After the war ends I'd like for you to help him buy a farm and the animals I've promised, and give him the balance of the money. I'm also going to leave a large sum buried beneath your holly tree. We were going to buy up property in the forks of Black Creek, close to Grandpa's old place, but I guess we'll have to wait for another trip. Uncle John could look into that for us if he can find the time."

"The war's pretty close to over," she said. "John heard at the station yesterday that the Union cavalry captured President Davis on May tenth, near Irwinville, Georgia. That's only a hundred miles north of here."

"You could have been right," I said to Jacob. "President Davis could have been headed for Archer. I guess we were fortunate to miss the trouble at Irwinville. We were not far from there on May tenth. If we hadn't swung west when we did, we would have been right there."

Sending the children away, Henry told May and John the story. The rest of us found a soft bed and got six hours sleep.

With a pack mule to spread the load, and to serve as insurance against a lame animal, we were in the saddle again by mid-afternoon.

As we were leaving, in jest, I said to Henry, "Hopefully we're not going to dig up the other things."

Laughing, he said, "We can wait a year or two until it's safe to travel with it. I think we've carrying more now than we ought to travel with."

Two days later Coon spotted a group of men on horses who were following us. We changed directions slightly to be sure. Because they stayed a mile behind us, we only got an occasional glimpse of them.

Henry said, "They apparently don't know we've spotted them. They might be waiting for us to camp so that they can slip up in the dark and attack us. Let's pretend we don't see them for now."

Coon said, "We can't hope to outrun them. How about if I pull out behind some bushes and wait. With my Spencer, I can do some damage and give you three some running room."

Henry said, "No. Let's swing a little more toward the east and hold that line until dark. It's only two hours from now. When it's dark, we'll build a campfire in a wooded area so we can't be seen except from close up. We'll leave immediately after we start the fire, and then ride straight west for two hours, rest the horses for four hours, and then resume our course toward Atlanta until daylight. We'll then set up in a good ambush site and rest for the day, or until they overtake us. We don't know who they are. If it's not someone that knows about the money, they might even give up following us. Not knowing about the money, they might only be after our horses and things. Since our campfire will be in a wooded area, they can't know we've gone until they surround us and sneak up on our fire. They might not even do that until early morning. Even if the fire goes out, they might think we've gone to bed. We'll have a good start by the time they discover we're gone. They can't track us at night."

It worked. Two hours after riding away through the woods from our campfire, we made a cold camp for four hours. Then we rode directly toward Irwinville. It had been a long time since President Davis was captured so there was no reason for any Union cavalry to be encamped near Irwinville, but some were. During the wee hours of the morning a voice spoke to us out of the dark, "Halt. Who's there?"

"Four honest men on a public road who are afraid to give the wrong answer and get shot," Henry said. "What army is this?"

"This is the United States Cavalry," the voice said.

"Good," Henry replied "I'm a physician. We're traveling under a pass from General Grant."

About that time a couple of fires came to life and we were admitted to a small encampment of Federal cavalry where we rested for much of the day. Those who were following us caught up later that day. They left the area at a gallop when challenged by a picket.

Later, near Macon, we swung east and stopped at the Riley farm. Surprised to see us, but overjoyed that we were there, they fed us well and watched over us while we slept. Though they had heard of two men who had been hanged with a note stuck to their shirts, they had not connected that event to themselves or us. Coon called the women and girls together and told them the story. I had to add to his story. Being modest, he didn't give himself much credit.

Arriving in Atlanta we found the telegraph was working to the north. Henry sent a wire from there. "Dearest Lilly—Everyone is well—Have traded all Confederate paper money—Will arrive St. Louis in eight or ten days."

We split up in Atlanta and proceeded to the Whipmore place by different routes. Our trail would be lost in the streets of Atlanta. No group of seven horses' tracks would be found leaving there.

May 25, 1866

Yes, I can tell what happened to everyone over the next year. Though their oldest son didn't return from the war, Aunt May and Uncle John's family is otherwise well. They sent Henry letters as requested. No one ever arrived at their farm in pursuit of us. We still don't know who was following us. John also located a farm for Jacob as Henry had asked him to. Jacob and his family are now living there. Henry gave May and John the place Doctor Isaac bought next door to their place.

A month after the word was spread that Florida had surrendered Tallahassee on May 20, Nathaniel's sister, Sarah, went back to Florida with Jacob. They are happy together. The old man who watched us trade the money was Jacob's grandpa. He made sure the other slaves didn't stray into the stable area while we were there. He's living with Jacob, as are the rest of Jacob's family.

Nathaniel and his family are still on the farm in Louisville. They're expecting a baby soon. We made Nathaniel a partner in the horse farm. He'll be there forever.

We bought a farm in Florida near where Henry's grandpa settled back in 1821 on the forks of Black Creek. Coon lives on that farm when he's not with Henry. Naomi, the girl we rescued from the garment factory, lives there too. She and Coon are constant companions. In addition to working around the farm when he gets the urge, Coon raises and trains bluetick coonhounds and deputies a little. He also goes off with Henry when there's an interesting adventure to be had. Naomi loves adventure and sometimes goes with them. In fact, they're with Henry now.

Lilly's in Scotland. It turned out that she and Henry both have relatives there. She wanted to meet them and see the place. Lilly and Henry have a daughter. They named her Julia after a grandmother. Henry's ma and Miss Daisy are with Lilly, taking care of the baby.

Jolene and Tyler are still running the farm in Atlanta, at least our part of it. They'll probably be there forever, too.

Ma is still in St. Louis, and single. Since Pa didn't return from the war, Ma keeps looking for another man the equal of Henry. Lilly says they're all taken. Ma says there just aren't any more like him. The hotel is a good place to meet lots of men so Ma still works there. Working there keeps her busy and in circulation. She doesn't need the money because we set her up good. She says she's going back to Florida because that's where Lilly and Henry are mostly going to be.

Doctor Isaac is still here in St. Louis. He soon became well known here. Miss Daisy and Henry's ma are also here when they aren't traveling. Doctor Isaac often talks about retiring and traveling with the women, and moving to Florida. He will, too, in fifteen or twenty years.

Alice is still in St. Louis managing our property. Her husband returned from the war. His family's property was lost, so he works at various things around St. Louis.

We haven't heard from Ella Mae, Coon and Mary's ma, or their pa. It's just as well because Mary and I plan to marry someday. Mary and I both still live in St. Louis. We talk lots about moving to Jacksonville, Florida. That's close to Black Creek. We probably will after we marry. I've got a good practice here, but only work at it three days a week. When Henry's here he goes in for a few days to help, and to stay current on things. He isn't here much. He likes Florida an awful lot. We all will probably end up back down there sooner or later.

I've heard lots of stories about the Confederate treasury money that went to Archer. There's one story of a wagon train arriving there on May 10, 1865, and another of a wagon train arriving on May 15. The first story is that there was $25,000 in specie. According to the second story there was $35,000. I also heard one story about a group arriving there with money on May 20. Being almost back to Atlanta then, none of us know anything for sure about that story. Nothing is ever said about $60,000, or a larger sum. People either tell about there being $25,000 or $35,000, or a phantom sum that's supposed to have arrived on May 20. There seems to be some confusion about the correct amount. The people who have what we left aren't saying much of anything. I don't think they even know for sure what happened. Some people say the money we left in the stable was divided among some high-ranking people after they heard that President Davis was captured. Mrs. Davis was to get one-fourth, but I'm sure she never got any.

There's also those who tell of the treasury being transported from Virginia to Archer on the railroad, but that's impossible. No other rail lines ever connected to the Florida line during the war. The closest they came to connecting was thirty miles.

Some Union soldiers, who showed up at the plantation on

May 22, took some of President Davis' personal bags from there to Jacksonville, Florida. They found $20,000 in Confederate paper money in one bag. That's over $5,000 less than Henry left. Maybe someone held out some as a souvenir, or maybe it wasn't the same money. They could have burned ours when they got it from the pony's stall. Since there were some of President Davis' personal bags with clothes and tobacco in them at the plantation, he might have been going to Archer after all.

We got $35,000 in specie from the stable. Henry only figured $30,000 was his. When I say his, I mean ours. Coon, Henry, and I are full partners. Henry just does the heavy thinking and planning. He likes it. Anyway, he decided we got $3,000 more than we had coming after he made arrangements for Jacob. Cutting Aunt May and Jacob in for a share, we split that $3,000 five ways. Since there wasn't anyone we knew who we could turn it over to, and Henry didn't want what he didn't feel he had rightfully earned in one way or another, Lilly spent Henry's, Coon's, and my shares on resettling some of those women and children that General Sherman sent north.

Lee Greystone is back east negotiating some sort of cotton deal for Henry. Henry's in north Florida working on that end of the cotton deal. He financed the planting of several crops there for this year. Most folks in the South don't have much money right now.

We talked some awhile back about moving cattle from Florida and Texas to the northeast, and about moving the things from Aunt May's house to New York City. We're going to try to set up a deal on Florida cattle when we move those things from Aunt May's in a couple of months. I'll have to go and help, of course. Henry's going to Texas next winter to see about moving Texas cattle to Kansas. I'll bet some interesting things happen before all those trips are over. Maybe I'll get a chance to pass the stories along.

Henry's always working on some kind of deal. At least he won't have to bother with any more Confederate money.

If you enjoyed reading this book, here are some other books from Pineapple Press on related topics. For a complete catalog, write to Pineapple Press, P.O. Box 3889, Sarasota, FL 34230 or call 1-800-PINEAPL (746-3275). Or visit our website at www.pineapplepress.com.

Discovering the Civil War in Florida by Paul Taylor. The Civil War in Florida may not have been the scene for decisive battles everyone remembers, but Florida played her part. From Marianna and Tallahassee in northwest Florida to Fort Myers and Key West in the south, this book covers the land and sea skirmishes that made Florida a bloody battleground for four sad years. ISBN 1-56164- 234-7 (hb); ISBN 1-56164- 235-5 (pb)

At the Edge of Honor, the nationally acclaimed naval Civil War novel by Robert Macomber, takes the reader into the steamy world of Key West and the Caribbean in 1863. Peter Wake, a reluctant New England volunteer officer, finds himself battling the enemy on the coasts of Florida, sinister intrigue in Spanish Havana and the British Bahamas, and social taboos in Key West when he falls in love with the daughter of a Confederate zealot. ISBN 1-56164- 252-5 (hb); ISBN 1-56164-272-X (pb)

Point of Honor by Robert Macomber. In this sequel to *At the Edge of Honor,* Peter Wake is in command of a larger ship and beginning offensive operations on the Florida coast during the tumultuous year of 1864. Along the way he hunts down army deserters on uninhabited islands, risks international confrontation on a sea chase to French waters, and makes the most momentous decision of his personal life. ISBN 1-56164- 270-3 (hb)

A Yankee in a Confederate Town by Calvin L. Robinson. Edited by Anne Robinson Clancy, the author's great-granddaughter, this personal journal follows a loyal Unionist who loses his business and home, his money, and nearly his life in Civil War–era Jacksonville, Florida, when he refuses to join the Secessionist movement. A fascinating, true account of a pivotal time in U.S. history. ISBN 1-56164-267-3 (hb)

200 Quick Looks at Florida History by James Clark. Florida has a long and complex history, but few of us have time to read it in depth. So here are 200 quick looks at Florida's 10,000 years of history from the arrival of the first natives to the present, packed with unusual and little-known facts and stories. ISBN 1-56164- 200-2 (pb)

Florida Portrait by Jerrell Shofner. Packed with hundreds of photos, this word-and-picture album traces the history of Florida from the Paleo-Indians to the rampant growth of the late twentieth century. ISBN 1-56164-121-9 (pb)

The Florida Keys by John Viele. The trials and successes of the Keys pioneers are brought to life in this series, which recounts tales of early pioneer life and life at sea. **Volume 1**: *A History of the Pioneers* ISBN 1-56164-101-4 (hb); **Volume 2**: *True Stories of the Perilous Straits* ISBN 1-56164-179-0 (hb); **Volume 3**: The Wreckers ISBN 1-56164-219-3 (hb)

Florida's Past Volumes 1, 2, and 3 by Gene Burnett. Collected essays from Burnett's "Florida's Past" columns in *Florida Trend* magazine, plus some original writings not found elsewhere. Burnett's easygoing style and his sometimes surprising choice of topics make history good reading. **Volume 1** ISBN 1-56164-115-4 (pb); **Volume 2** ISBN 1-56164-139-1 (pb); **Volume 3** ISBN 1-56164-117-0 (pb)

The Florida Chronicles by Stuart B. McIver. A series offering true-life sagas of the notable and notorious characters throughout history who have given Florida its distinctive flavor. **Volume 1**: *Dreamers, Schemers and Scalawags* ISBN 1-56164-155-3 (pb); **Volume 2**: *Murder in the Tropics* ISBN 1-56164-079-4 (hb); **Volume 3**: *Touched by the Sun* ISBN 1-56164-206-1 (hb)

Southeast Florida Pioneers by William McGoun. Meet the pioneers of the Palm Beach area, the Treasure Coast, and Lake Okeechobee in this collection of well-told, fact-filled stories from the 1690s to the 1990s. ISBN 1-56164-157-X (hb)